OTHER LEOPARDS

ALSO BY DENIS WILLIAMS

The Third Temptation (1968)
Giglioli in Guyana 1922–1972 (1972)
Image and Idea in the Arts of Guyana (1970)
Icon and Image: A Study of Sacred and Secular Forms of African Classical Art (1974)
Contemporary Art in Guyana (1976)
Guyana, Colonial Art to Revolutionary Art (1966-1976)
Ancient Guyana (1985)
Pages in Guyanese Prehistory (1995)
Prehistoric Guiana (2004)

OTHER LEOPARDS

DENIS WILLIAMS

INTRODUCTION BY VICTOR J. RAMRAJ

PEEPAL TREE

First published in Great Britain in 1963
by New Authors Limited
This new edition published in 2009
Peepal Tree Press Ltd
17 King's Avenue
Leeds LS6 1QS
England

ISBN13: 978 1 84523 067 8

Peepal Tree gratefully acknowledges Arts Council support

FOR KATIE ALICE

Some things happen to mankind through more general circumstances and not as a result of an individual's natural propensities. For example, when men perish in multitudes by conflagration or pestilence or cataclysm, through monstrous or inescapable changes in the ambient. For the lesser cause always yields to the greater and stronger.

PTOLEMY 'Tetrabiblos' 1.3

INTRODUCTION

VICTOR J. RAMRAJ

In 1958, the Jamaican author V.S. Reid published his novel *The Leopard*, set in Kenya. It reflected his angry response to the defaming of a legitimate anti-colonial movement, the Mau-Mau, by the British and colonial press. In 1962, a year before the publication of Denis Williams's *Other Leopards*, Derek Walcott published "A Far Cry from Africa", a poem that evokes a conflicted response to those same Kenyan events and, through the powerful metaphor of being "divided to the vein" (Walcott's grandmothers were blacks and his grandfathers Europeans), expresses his particular ambivalence as a colonial individual towards the two worlds in which he finds himself, the local and the imperial.[1] In the year following the publication of *Other Leopards*, O.R. Dathorne's *The Scholar Man* (1964) also explored the symbolic figure of a Caribbean man returning to Africa. In 1968, and without the ambivalences of Walcott, Williams and Dathorne, Edward Kamau Brathwaite published *Masks*, the second and African-set volume of his *Arrivants* trilogy. It was a period when in addition to Dathorne and Brathwaite, other writers such as Lindsay Barrett and Neville Dawes went to live and work in Africa. It was a period when in Jamaica the demand of Rastafarian groups to "go home" to Ethiopia began to penetrate public discourse when the UWI's Institute of Social and Economic Research published the 1960 Report on The Rastafari Movement. In Guyana, in 1961 Eusi Kwayana had founded the African Society for Racial Equality (ASRE) and in 1964 set up ASCRIA, the African Society for Cultural Relations with Independent Africa. Denis Williams himself had spent ten years in Africa between 1958 and 1968: five years lecturing at the Khartoum School of Fine Arts and five years at the University of Ife in Nigeria.

This was the context in which *Other Leopards* appeared in 1963. What sets this landmark novel apart from the other works set in

Africa at this time is its unremitting focus on its intensely ambivalent protagonist, Lionel Froad. Froad, like Walcott's speaker, finds it difficult to choose between the African and the English worlds, plaintively asking "where shall I turn", and Williams depicts his predicament in an impressive, arresting way. In the first part of the novel, Williams sets out the dichotomized life that underlies the crisis; in the second part he dramatizes the search for a consistent, stable identity. Both parts paint an insightful, psychological, socio-political portrait of a tormented and conflicted colonial, but it is in the second part in particular that Williams's novelistic talent is most evident when he shows Lionel Froad trying to avoid falling into the interstices between apparently antithetical cultures and trying to find a resolution to his dilemma.

Froad's disturbed consciousness of his duality is evident from the start. Like the author, he is an Afro-Guyanese educated in Britain. He has come to Johkara, a fictional version of Sudan, ostensibly to work as an archaeological draftsman for an English researcher, Hughie King, but essentially in the hope of finding in Africa his true roots and identity, which he thinks his colonial education has denied him. Intelligent and contemplative, often poetic in articulating his feelings, he informs an unidentified listener/reader what his problem is: "I am a man, you see, plagued by [my] two names, and this is their history: Lionel the who I was, dealing with Lobo, the who I continually felt I ought to become... All along, ever since I'd grown up, I'd been Lionel looking for Lobo. I'd felt I ought to become this chap, this alter ego of ancestral times that I was sure quietly slumbered behind the cultivated mask" (pp. 23-24).

Such metafictional commentary in the opening paragraph of the novel signals us to read the work as a colonial allegory of in-betweenity, and many other elements in the novel – some transparent, some less so – support this direction. The opening locale shows Froad contemplating his divided psyche while stalled on a bus on Kutam Bridge, in a town linking the two physical environments of Johkara; it is "not quite sub-Sahara, but then not quite desert; not equatorial black, not Mediterranean white. Mulatto. Sudanic mulatto, you could call it. Ochre. Semi-scrub. Not desert, not sown" (p. 23). The dividedness of the setting (described in human terms) reinforces the dividedness of the protagonist. In addition to Froad's being caught between the imperial lion and the native wolf ("lobo" is Spanish and Portuguese for "wolf"), as his first names point up, he sees his current identity as "*froad*ulent". Other names are allegorical in a more sophisticated way. Halfway through the novel, distinguishing between individuals who are absolutely sure of themselves and their causes and those who are burdened with uncertainties and doubts, Froad uses the image of the novel's title: "Some leopards think they have no spots simply because they have no mirrors. Others manage to know, somehow" (p. 87). So among lobos and leopards he identifies two kinds: those with and those without self-awareness. Froad clearly is "an other leopard", aware of his spots, aware of his vacillation and ambivalence, and in this duality there is perhaps a comment on V.S. Reid's slightly earlier novel, *The Leopard*, where the eponymous beast is an altogether less complex metaphor. Froad pays a price for this self-knowledge – he who yearns "to be committed, happy. Like everybody else" (p. 24). But given his compulsion to know himself he is unlikely to succumb to the self-deception such response entails.

Hughie King, Froad's nemesis, is evidently an allegorical reflection of imperial power – though more fleshed out than the Old Dowager, George Lamming's imperial allegorical counterpart in *Water with Berries* (1971). But King has an additional allegorical function in *Other Leopards*. If Williams portrays Lobo as Lionel's alter ego, his id, representing the intuitive, the passionate, "the swamp and forests and vaguely felt darkness" (p.24), King is the cerebral, the disciplined, the ordered, the enquiring – the super ego qualities Froad both admires and resents. Despite King's condescending criticism of his inability to be more even-tempered and methodical, Froad is "fond of him", admitting that he envies his "cold intelligence; clear apart mind" (p. 114). Williams recurringly points to their duality through images of marriage and love (the literalness of which the text plays down). On one occasion, Froad states: "I sometimes felt Hughie could read my thoughts… In some things it was like we were married" (p. 129). And at the end of the novel, when Lionel tries to shed this burdensome component of his psyche by killing King,

Hughie appears to be an understanding participant. "So fast it was as though he was greedy for the screwdriver; he came hungrily into it, like we were lovers understanding this inevitable moment" (p. 204). Whether or not we are meant to read a homoerotic sub-text here, it nevertheless reinforces the figurative significance of Froad's assault on his British alter ego.

Williams draws a parallel with another work that has frequently been read as an allegory of the colonial-imperial relationship. Just before Froad plunges the screwdriver into King's neck, he attempts to hum Ariel's song "Where the Bee Sucks" from Shakespeare's *The Tempest*, but he finds he "couldn't sing" (p. 203). Ariel is Prospero's smart, temporizing, diplomatic servant and Froad cannot sing Ariel's song because at the point when he makes his murderous assault, he is not Ariel but Prospero's confrontational other servant Caliban(-Lobo), who uses the language his master has taught him to curse him. Williams suggests Froad's potential is to appear to King/Prospero as either Ariel or Caliban, unlike Lamming (in *Water with Berries*) or Aimé Césaire (in *Une Tempête* [1969]) who both appear to suggest that West Indian colonials are essentially Calibans (without acknowledging their Arielesque possibilities).[2]

Froad, as a self-aware leopard, is ambivalent in his response to the intuitive world of Lobo, his African-native alter ego. He is disillusioned, for instance, when he discovers the true nature of Amanishakete, the Queen of Meroë in BCE 1. In earlier discussions with Froad, King has relegated Amanishakete's culture to the status of the marginal with no influence on what followed. For Froad, Amanishakete was to prove King wrong; she was to counter his dismissive comments, show once and for all that Froad had a noble African ancestry. But when Froad visits the archaeological site where figures of Amanishakete have been unearthed, he finds statues of her flogging slaves. He cannot help seeing her as "cruel, gross, ugly… She knew hate and law. No trace of love and care. She was a spreading desert" (p. 182). With this disillusioning discovery, the Lionel-King part of his psyche wins through, repressing his Lobo identity.

Williams further portrays Froad's divisions in his relationships with the two women he becomes intimate with in Johkara:

Eve, the daughter of "the Chief", a domineering black Christian missionary, who, like Froad, is from Guyana; and Catherine, King's secretary, who is from Wales. Together they constitute another binary opposition tugging at Froad. With patent allegorical intent, Williams has Froad recognize a sketch of Amanishakete in an archaeological volume to be "the image, pure and simple and shatteringly original, of Eve" (p. 102). Eve has married a Muslim against her Christian father's wishes, and, when the novel opens, has fled her husband's home with their baby. Froad, in his Lobo frame of mind, sees her initially as a kindred spirit and becomes her lover. Williams describes Eve, who always addresses Froad as Lobo, never as Lionel, in terms of images associated with the wolf. He compares her to the gloom of forest floors and dark, silent rivers, and (before his disillusion) Froad perceives her as a true descendant of Amanishakete: "Raw, earthy, nearer to the natural state" (p. 90). Froad, in his Loboesque moments, admires her commitment to Africa, her participation in the spirit-invoking women's *zaar* ceremonies and her dancing at local weddings. As Lionel he is less appreciative of her. King has dismissively told Froad that the Amanishakete culture is a "faecal culture", and it is in faecal contexts that Froad, as Lionel, comes to see Eve. On one occasion, furious at her for lying to him about being pregnant, he searches for her in an area filled with scavengers emptying latrine buckets in their carts, and later gains entrance to the place she is visiting through a latrine at the rear of the building.

Catherine, who is presented in almost every instance as a foil to Eve, also becomes Froad's lover. Concerned for his welfare, she acts as a buffer between Froad and King, interpreting King's apparently imperial attitudes in less offensive ways to Froad. She tries to draw Froad out of what she sees as his beloved "Burden", his obsessive preoccupation with self, trying to persuade him that King is not always his nemesis. She perceives Lionel as an Anglophile, matter-of-factly asking him, "You ever wished you were white…?" (p. 42) – a question that angers yet preoccupies him. He shares with Catherine his most analytical, reflective thoughts, which he seldom lets Eve hear. He tells Catherine about his meeting with the Muslim leader who wants him to write for their political organ, impressing on her his role as a reluctant Africanist. While Lobo apprehends Eve in relation to dark tropical imagery, Lionel sees Catherine in terms of romantic Welsh images (an aspect of the novel that draws intertextually on the contrast set up by Joseph Conrad in *Heart of Darkness* between Kurtz's Intended and his African mistress). She is "like those distilled, shadowless twilights you get at times in the Welsh valleys, illumined from the clouds" (p. 78). These elements in the novel point clearly ahead to, for instance, the postcolonial fiction of David Dabydeen. Besides the parallel Conradian echo of *The Intended* (1991), Dabydeen's *Disappearance* (1993) takes his Guyanese engineer from Guyana to England rather than Africa (though colonial Africa is present in Mrs Rutherford's Kentish cottage), but the two novels have much in common in their allegorical structures and fondness for intertextual reference.[3]

Further illuminating Froad's state of in-betweenity, Williams portrays him as caught between opposing political causes in Johkara. On the one side are the secessionist Christian blacks of the South; on the other the ruling Muslim Arabs of the North. Eve's Christian father and Mohammed, an Arab spokesman, both try to persuade him to write in support of their respective causes, one appealing to Froad's Christian upbringing, the other to his Pan-African sentiments. Williams – again underlining Froad's duality – has both sides appeal to him in exactly the same words: they trust he will do the right thing because he is "a Christian Negro interested in the future of Africans in Africa" (p. 60, p. 66). Froad does not see any true devotion to Africa on either side. He vacillates and procrastinates, and though he does write a piece in support of the Northern status quo, he does so impulsively – as Lobo – and from no strong belief. Whilst he envies others who can make unambiguous commitments, he never manages this himself.

In the latter part of the novel, Williams shows Froad obsessed with the ancient Greek myth of Zagreus. Zagreus, the product of an illicit union between Persephone and Zeus (in the form of a serpent), is pursued by the Titans, set on him by the jealous Hera. To survive, Zagreus has to assume many disguises, but in the end is torn apart by the Titans. The novel offers – metafictionally – multiple ways of interpreting this myth as it applies to Froad's plight. Froad perceives himself to be similarly the product of an illicit union and to be in need of protection against forces – more emotional than physical in his case – that seek to overwhelm him. Almost himself torn apart by Muslim women at the *zaar*, Froad empathetically feels that Zagreus need not have perished. Catherine, on the other hand, sees no parallel between Zagreus and Froad; she argues that Zagreus accepted his fate as the hunted while Froad wallows in self-pity, in love with his "Burden". The Chief, by contrast, feels that Zagreus had to die because, as a bastard, he lacked the moral force to fight evil (the Titans) and because he broke with his people. Hughie King feels the myth has significance only insofar as it is read historically or seen as underlining the truth that "opposition is the fundamental attitude of being for *homo sapiens*" (p. 167). To his increasing frustration, Froad is left to wonder which of these interpretations is pertinent.

Other Leopards provides no solution to Froad's predicament. The ending of the novel leaves Froad, like the proverbial possum, literally "up a gum tree" (an apt phase given its ambiguous signification of being in a state of contentment or in a state of great difficulty). After stabbing King, he flees to a belt of Johkara jungle, strips himself of his clothing, daubs himself with mud, and perches on a tree. The last paragraph depicts him in this position watching a brightening horizon and wondering if it is King coming after him – having survived Froad's assault – or if it is really the dawning of a new day. And if it is King, will he be cruel or kind? If it is a new day, will it still be burdened with debilitating ambivalence? The allegorical implication of all this is that, unable to accept that he is one thing or another (unlike Eve in her categorical immersion in Africa, or Catherine in her easy decision to return to her life in Wales, or the Chief in his readiness to be deported back to Guyana), Froad appears to be experiencing a reverse evolution back to a primordial state from which he will eventually evolve organically, naturally, in "his own" time. The tree in which he awaits the approaching dawn is one indigenous to the Sudan region – a *hashab* tree. From this variety of semi-desert tree comes almost all of the world's gum Arabic. As such it is essential to the economy of the region. It provides, too, much-needed fuel and building materials and its strong roots prevent erosion and hold off the encroaching desert. This and the meaning of its Hebraic name – "planning and thinking" – makes it an appropriate tree for Froad to ascend as he awaits, naked, for a possible rebirth or, in his primordial state, for evolution. He does not know what he will become – his own man? – or even what that entails; whether he will discover and accept his African roots, or come to embrace his Ariel-Caliban, Lionel-Lobo conflicted existence. The ending, though ambiguous, is not pessimistic. On the contrary, the images and phrasing suggest a fresh start. What form it will take is not, however, clear.

Williams's own life and subsequent writing offers support for a positive reading of the ending of the novel. In an interview with me, he said that, feeling uncomfortable with Europe and Africa, he decided in the 1960s to return to his own "primordial world", the interior of Guyana. He lived from 1968 to 1974 in the Mazaruni area of the Guyana hinterland, writing and painting and researching Amerindian tribal art, particularly their petroglyphs. He described this as a "tremendous" period of his life, one free of "twentieth-century anxieties". He recalls with pride building his own house, acting as midwife when his wife gave birth, and having no library, no books other than – oddly – a regular subscription to *The New Statesman*, through which he "kept up with language".[4] Was this Williams's own ascent of the *hashab* tree?

In his 1970 Edgar Mittelholzer lectures, *Image and Idea in the Arts of Guyana*, Williams addresses very explicitly the "mongrel" condition, the cultural heterogeneity of the Caribbean and the Guyanas. (Williams's daughter, Charlotte, adopts the expression "mongrel" approvingly for her own mixed heritage – Guyanese-Welsh – in her memoir *Sugar and Slate* [2002].[5]) In an argument that presages the ideology of créolité, of the creative potential of a mestizo consciousness, Williams argues strongly against the tendency of seeing Caribbean history "in the light of biases adopted from one thoroughbred culture or another, of the Old World" (the references in Guyana in 1970 being to African, Indian and European cultural contexts). In particular, Williams argues against the perpetuation of "filiastic dependence on the cultures of our several racial origins" because this inhibits Guyanese and Caribbean people from "facing up to the facts of what we uniquely are".[6] It is an argument, albeit expressed in a more materialist vein, that points us to see *Other Leopards*, in spite of Froad's patently ambivalent and conflicted state of mind, attuned to the same context as two of Wilson Harris's early novels, *The Far Journey of Oudin* (1961) and *The Secret Ladder* (1963), where respectively the old world heritages of East Indian and African (and by inference the European as well) are seen as beset by the tendency to be locked in "ghetto and arbitrary reservations of self-interest", a "self-sufficiency" that, in Ken Ramchand's words, denies the reality of the Caribbean's "complicated and incestuous family tree".[7]

Though the ending of *Other Leopards* points to Williams's later more explicitly positive thinking about mongrelization, it is its ambiguity that attracted critical attention from the moment the novel was published. Gerald Moore sees Froad as regressing towards infantilism; as such he sums up the novel as a record of failure "but it is a failure of the kind necessary to understanding".[8] For Michael Gilkes, "climbing the tree is a symbolic act, for the tree...represents a hollow pillar of light by which the shaman climbs up to heaven or down to the underworld".[9] For Louis James the "pressures of finding an identity have driven Froad...into 'the castle of his skin,' rejecting possession of either Africa or Europe. However agonizing this position, it is the true point of discovery".[10] Edward Baugh believes that what Froad comes to accept is that he is a split individual, adding that it "may seem a let-down to the reader that Froad has taken as many pages to recognize what the reader might have been able to tell him from the outset; but what is important is that Froad now does recognize it" (xi).[11] Mark Kinkead-Weekes sees the ending as "a mordant exposure of what it means to be 'uncommitted' and without 'identity'",[12] whilst Wilfred Cartey reads the novel as being in "search of a freedom in which all times fuse...".[13] As these different if contiguous readings demonstrate, Williams has not written a simplistic novel – whether allegorical or literal – in which he provides easy answers. His concern is with dramatizing Froad's debilitating colonial in-betweenity. Later writers and theorists would offer ways of coping with this colonial-postcolonial predicament. There would be V.S. Naipaul's argument that even though the English tradition is not his, the English language certainly is, or Derek Walcott's view that his "divided self" allowed him a more encompassing, cosmopolitan vision; or Christopher Koch, in *The Doubleman* (1985), simi-larly seeing his protagonist as not disadvantaged when he describes him in that eponymous state;[14] or Salman Rushdie considering it an advantage to be a "translated man" and Homi Bhabha talking positively of a "third space" between the imperial and colonial spheres that allows the colonial the advantage of camouflaged mimicry.[15] All this was to come, but in 1963, Williams is willing to leave Froad up the *hashab* tree, thinking about and anticipating what comes next.

Perhaps there are times in the novel when the allegoric overwhelms the literal, flesh-and-blood creation and develop-ment of character. Williams is preoccupied with the generic problems of racial and national identities, less with the psycho-logical truths of personal problems and relationships. As the first part of his epigraph to the novel from Ptolemy indicates – "Some things happen to mankind through more general circumstances and not as a result of the individual's natural propensities" – he is exploring the effects of the larger, historical-political factors rather than the individual's "hill of beans". There are times, in the first part more than in the second, when the players are not so much individuals as representative figures. They talk about politics, race, and culture – the dominant elements that define their relationships. King and Froad discuss African antiquity in documentary rather than personal fashion; Catherine and Lionel debate about whether he yearns to be white; and Lionel and Eve talk about cultural differences in analytical rather than personal terms. If Eve does briefly reveal her jealousy of Catherine when she accuses Lionel of being "white inside and you can't man me because the whiteskin woman's on y'mind" (p. 171), it is done in a way that leaves the women representative rather than individual figures. In the second part of the novel, which illuminates the last sentence of the epigraph from Ptolemy –"For the lesser cause always yields to [the] greater and stronger" – Williams makes a stronger attempt to impart more flesh-and-blood dynamic to his characters when they explore their experiences with lovers and parents. But however much one may regret the price Williams pays for privileging the allegorical over the individual and the psychological, there can be no doubt, on the evidence of his epigraph, that this was precisely his intention. Like Wilson Harris, Denis Williams was committed to an aesthetic that bypassed the novel of character; as an allegorical work *Other Leopards* is unquestionably one of the most sustained and artistically realized in West Indian literature.

Footnotes

1. Derek Walcott, "A Far Cry from Africa", *In a Green Night* (London: Jonathan Cape, 1962), p. 18.
2. Aimé Césaire, *Une Tempête* (Paris: Seuil, 1969); *A Tempest*, trans. by Richard Miller (New York: UBU Repertory, 1985). George Lamming, *Water with Berries* (London: Longman Caribbean, 1971).
3. David Dabydeen, *The Intended* (1991; Leeds: Peepal Tree, 2005); *Disappearance* (1993; Leeds: Peepal Tree, 2005).
4. Cited in Victor J. Ramraj, "Denis Williams", *Fifty Caribbean Writers*, ed. by Daryl Cumber Dance (New York: Greenwood, 1986), p. 484.
5. Charlotte Williams, *Sugar and Slate* (London: Planet, 2002).
6. Denis Williams, *Image and Idea in the Arts of Guyana* (Georgetown: National History and Arts Council, 1970), p. 7.
7. Kenneth Ramchand, Introduction to Wilson Harris, *Palace of the Peacock* (London: Faber, 1968), p. 7. See, too, Wilson Harris, "Denis Williams", *Kaie* 4 (July 1967): 21-22. It is clear that Harris sees in Williams a kindred spirit.
8. Gerald Moore, *The Chosen Tongue* (London: Longman, 1969), p. 125.
9. Michael Gilkes, *The West Indian Novel* (Boston: Twayne, 1981), pp. 143-44.
10. Louis James, *The Islands In Between* (London: Oxford UP, 1968), p. 10.
11. Edward Baugh, Introduction to *Other Leopards* (London: Heinemann, 1983), p.xi.
12. Mark Kinkead-Weekes, "Africa – Two Caribbean Fictions", *Twentieth-Century Studies* 10 (1973): 37-59 (p. 57).
13. Wilfred Cartey, "The Rhythm of Society and Landscape", *New World* (1966) (Guyana Independence issue), p. 102.
14. Christopher Koch, *The Doubleman* (London: Chatto and Windus, 1985).
15. Salman Rusdie, *Shame* (London: J. Cape, 1983), p. 29. Homi Bhabha, *The Location of Culture* (New York: Routledge, 1994).

PART ONE

Every creature knowth its prayer and its praise.

THE KORAN

Lionel. What sort of name is that! That's what my little sister thought way back smallboy in the Guianas twenty, thirty, a hundred thousand years ago; don't blame me I have no memory worth the name and it isn't important. Lionel! That's no proper kind of name for a man-child of three, so she thought, she a woman-child of one. So too, without much effort and a lot of help, she soon had everybody believing, myself and all. She called me Lobo, and Lobo I became, except that Lionel remained on my birth certificate and is set to plague me like a festering conscience for the rest of my days, look of it. I became Lobo and that's the whole trouble; I am a man, you see, plagued by these two names, and this is their history: Lionel, the who I was, dealing with Lobo, the who I continually felt I ought to become. And there you have it in a nutshell.

Now I'd better say where I was: Lionel embracing Lobo. On a bus, Kutam Bridge, Johkara, Africa. Sudanic belt of Africa. Not quite sub-Sahara, but then not quite desert; not Equatorial black, not Mediterranean white. Mulatto. Sudanic mulatto, you could call it. Ochre. Semi-scrub. Not desert, not sown. Different colour in the atlas (look it up, you'll see); different from the empty blowing spaces of the true Sahara. To the north, though, a few hundred miles outside the cities – outside Kutam, for instance – you do get the blowing spaces: bellied sand, violent hills, volcanic plains, black chasms like the tired creations of a god gone crazy. Here, by the way, a lot of my work continually took me. I am an archaeological draughtsman, you see, or rather at the time I was.

Standing on this bridge, then, or rather sitting in the broken-down Commer truck enclosed with expanded metal, covered with zinc sheeting, painted about nine different colours all primary, and called Public Transport. A Wednesday afternoon, latish. Though the hour was still early – only about twenty to five or so – in a little while the sun would plunge the river, suddenly, as always in Africa, and shatter the day to splinters, into a shower of singing stars.

That's where I was, and when; though the story doesn't begin anywhere near there. It began, way back, with those two names: the one on my birth certificate, on my black-Frank-Sinatra face; and the one I carried like a pregnant load waiting to be freed and to take itself with every despatch back to the swamps and forests and vaguely felt darknesses of my South American home. But I start with the incident on Kutam Bridge because it was then that for the first time I came to realize that I was really on some basic level uncommitted to either name!

All along, ever since I'd grown up, I'd been Lionel looking for Lobo. I'd felt I ought to become this chap, this alter ego of ancestral times that I was sure quietly slumbered behind the cultivated mask. Now on that afternoon I came consciously to sense the thing that has made this story: that not enviable state of being, the attitude of involuntary paralysis, that made them know me in Africa – the more intelligent, that is – as the Uncommitted African.

From the moment of realizing it, of course, I struggled against this thing; desperately. I didn't wish to be uncommitted; I wished to be committed, happy. Like everybody else. For why shouldn't a man, equipped as he is, be happy? That's what I wanted to know. It's why I had come out. But, then, that's the story…

★★★

Everywhere I looked, people; more people than you could think about. All the way down to right down beneath the trees; then behind all the way back to back where the bridge curved round to Kutam North. And everyone standing. Up front I knew they were turning off, but near the bus, down towards the middle, they all stood still, nobody making much noise. Johkresi are quiet people, restrained; but they were waiting till they got up there, up to the top, to the main gate. It was when they got up there that the real bawling would begin.

Some kept tiptoeing and reaching up as though that could get them anywhere; kept trying to see over the heads or between them, between the snowy turbans; trying to be up the top all the way from where they stood. Somebody said, '*W'Allahi*, O brother, if this bus would only go!' Somebody else, 'If you stand, O my brothers, you can see the policemen, the jeeps…' Many said: 'I can see the banners; I can see… Long live Noba! Colours, O brothers, like mirages over everybody's heads. I can see from here…'

I peered beyond the crowd and into the garden.

Maybe I won't get there in time; maybe I don't even wish to. At the last moment, though, I'll know.

Inside the garden the farrashene looked like snowmen melting in the desert sun; mute, detached like snowmen, like cheap toys: Turkish pantaloons of crimson satin, tomato-coloured blouses, silky tarbooshes: the real thing. And the askari: askari white with white turbans, ceremonial; ordinary days camel-coloured khaki against Kutam ochre. Then the ladies: European ladies with breasts aggressively exposed. (Why only the European woman and the savage? Every other kind of man conceals his woman.) Muslim ladies none, never.

'*Zaghareet!*' somebody shouted, which was a kind of yodelling ululation, hysterical sounding.

On the podium the flags of Noba and of Johkara floated side by side. The *zaghareet* gathered force. The crowd began to shuffle forward slowly. The occasion of a visit of the state of Noba to the state of Johkara, Arab and African once more face to face. The *zaghareet* soared like a Comet working up scream. The river looked as though there'd been a giant car smash with all the glass left splintered in the sun over to the ochre of Kutam West. Above it a pillar of cloud hung like the conclusion of a quarrel over everybody's heads. The lorries had raised that earlier, bringing people into town since before the dawn. I leaped off the bus.

But gained nothing by it, for I found I could hardly move. The heart of the crowd, white everywhere – a grey mass of white, for the sun was already leaving, and it was, anyway, now among the trees – stood still. Behind the standing heads the sun turned the pillar of cloud into a pillar of fire where, splintered to a million glittering fragments, the river bent past Kutam West.

The bus heaved alongside me as though borne on by the pressure of the crowd. Petrol-fumes, warm sweat, close stench; no escape. Tiptoeing, I could see the spot where the head of the crowd should have been turning off. But it wasn't; it was being forced back from the turning, made to go straight along the main road. Word came back: 'We're going straight on down the main road, they not letting us into the river walk.' Affronted, shoved from mouth to ear. 'They're turning us back, O brothers, keeping us off the river walk.' Which ran past the main gates; where stood the parked motor cars of the officials and the guests. 'So we won't be in the way of the motor cars when the show's over.'

'I like that: in the way of the motor cars! And who th'hell are the motor cars, eh?'

Those who'd been waiting longest began being easily offended, aggressive, mustard-tempered. You could pick them out: different look from the others, from those who'd come later: possessive, strained to a pitch, ready to start crying or ripping somebody up least excuse. At the negative news some of these spilled off, cascaded down the embankment like water suddenly breaking a dam, and piled against the fence beyond reach of the policemen on horseback, in jeeps, on motorcycles.

Up front unbroken mechanical howling, ragged cheering. After a while word came back:

'He's arrived, ai, they're coming. Two palace cars and the red Rolls-Royce. He's very black, O brothers, laughing, see? There! There under the leaves…on the river walk, they're here…'

'Welcome, Noba, welcome, welcome!'

The band played in a less desultory fashion, even kicking up its hind legs now and then. Suddenly no one could see clearly enough, everyone trying to grow instantly taller; each feeling the next was getting more, getting in his way. Here and there a few sharp sudden rows, but no time, no time – men frantically trying to climb one another – they were here…

'Six, seven, nine official cars, oh, lots of them; they're driving in, see, that's why they turned us off; they turned us off because they're driving in. They're letting those cars through now, you couldn't have a crowd up there; they had to turn us off the river walk because, look, they driving right in through the gates beneath the trees, see? There, isn't he *black*!'

'He's not wearing clothes, robes!'

A roar went up. The newly arrived guests fanned hurriedly across the lawn.

Now the procession moved – a mass of white gone grey at its limits – beneath the trees. The shrubs on the embankment came up sloping downwards. The *zaghareet* came faster, hotter, singed everybody's senses, and died echoing across the river. At the great tables the Prime Ministers, Arab and African, took their ease. The distinguished of Kutam, the leaders of the Moslem sects, the Roman Catholic, the Protestant, the Coptic bishops, all took their ease. The Mayor of Kutam mounted the podium for the welcome speech. The photographers followed, the interpreters, journalists, all easy. People craned for the real-life view that for years to come would lend authority to their patter.

The Mayor's felicitations went unheard, the crowd wanted the Noba Prime Minister. So badly that when he at last mounted the podium they wouldn't let him speak, merely topped up their delirium with ever-wilder shouting. It began to seem doubtful whether they'd allow him to speak at all, but, as I heard him placidly claim a few days later on the occasion of the Chief's garden party, he was far from worried.

'Far from worried man,' he boomed. 'You should see some of our crowds on the coast; got to mind your phrases I can tell you.' Mopping his forehead with powerful ripping movements. 'This crowd was bounded by the road and the river; it was nothing, nothing.' And he swept round, pinning me a moment with a suspicious bulldog glare. This part of the story, then, I put together from the fringes of the honoured little group that hung round the P.M. that afternoon at the Chief's party.

From the podium the P.M. faced the crowd. He faced, that is, from behind the microphones, the guests, but his attention was really on the crowd; on the cheers building up with uninter-rupted mechanical unity. He held the mass with eyes waiting for his moment. Never resist at first; let it come up, let it flood to capacity, wave upon wave. Merely a question of timing. Let them expect something next; keep them that way. There is a moment of pause before the giant roller breaks; that saturated moment will bear you to the beach. You move in on the surge.

Ten, fifteen minutes the howling, darkness threatening. You look at a you crowd, see yourself multiplied a million times. A crowd is not it, or even they, it is I! The P.M. found his moment. He raised his arms above his head. First he took in the audience, then turned his face slowly right, left, let his glance pass over every man of them – each man must feel he's been observed, that I am no better than he; each woman must feel arresting, flattered.

Somebody said, '*W'Allahi*, O brother, just like one of us!'

Arms outstretched, he faced the crowd. He couldn't see their faces, but remember, he told himself, they do have faces. Speak as though you believe this.

The chants broke into a howl of delight embroidered with a pattern of clapping. Men are turning to their neighbours, the P.M. thought, nudging one another in the ribs. At this moment I am a Magnificent Idea; I am the Answer to a Million Frustrations; I am in the Flesh a Force! Each one waiting to make me his private possession, each standing assured behind an 'I told you so', a 'did you know', bewitched by the publicity photograph that went out like John the Baptist to herald the One Absolutely New. Now for the beach.

He watched the breakers. He lowered his arms, slowly. Beyond the fence a gradual hush fell with his falling arms, soft, like the retreating echo of a shattering explosion; a wash of falling sound.

'What a man, by Allah; a man!'

'You could call that magnetism, you know; that's what you call magnetism. This man knows his Africa.'

'People…' he boomed. Unforgettable voice, unforgettable resonance, coming from unexploited African places.

Call them people; not friends, Africans, nor countrymen; keep it abstract. Make no assumptions save only one: I am the Face of a Force. Bundle their emotions into that, let them take it home, take it down the years, outliving the kings of old Nile, the kings of old Axum, Candace, Queen of Sheba, what have you…

He folded his arms. Impressive the silence; impressive his calm, his control.

'*W'Allahi*, O brother, a real thinker you can tell.'

'People of Africa, we have met today…' The voice rose, struck poise, hung for a moment waiting for the farthest echoes to return. This man didn't need a painted mask, as his father would have done, to achieve heroic size; didn't need medicine men and miracles and mirrors to dazzle and subdue; he had his microphones, his unique mind. The man surveyed the heaving breakers. 'We have met today…' briefest pause, 'in Freedom!'

The photographers rushed forward to preserve the image of an historic moment.

'Here the man talk, O brothers!'

The P.M.'s voice floated, 'In this land of ancient bondage, this land of our inheritance…' like wind over muted waves. But facts now, no more emotion, they're not fools; they'll forget the facts, the emotion they'll talk about for ever. It will cause them to invent their own facts, their own reading of the issue according to their needs, more credible than any. This is the way of history. Do not treat them like fools or children; emotion is all well and good, but hang it on to something, appeal to the snob in them. Even savages wish to be appealed to intellectually. Choose your beads. Facts, keep them sober.

Hearing him talk this way at the Chief's garden party I realized the fellow knew his stuff all right; you can't beat these politicians when they know their stuff. I was pleased though, now, to see that the thing wasn't developing into a tedious political affair. This P.M. knew better than that. 'The time, a new time, our time, has come…' Not much gesture, no flourish, cool. '…emergence of this African person carries with it responsibilities unique in the history of mankind…'

'Hear; oh, hear!'

'…being at the same time fraught with possibilities for a fuller definition of the species. People, this living moment can create the world!'

The interpreter was meticulous, pacing the voice like shadow after a flying car. 'Returning therefore from the realms of idealism, we sponsor among the races a situation in which Equality,

Non-Aggression, Non-Interference, and Solidarity are inherent…'

Across the river, in Kutam West, a minaret pointed the sky like a malignant witness. The voice of the muezzin floated across the water; hot Lybian wind lifted the Johkara sand.

'…the last of Empire, the dawn of responsibility; a balance in human affairs now for the first time possible. Not of course in a spirit of revenge, but possessing the future by being truly worthy of the present…!' And so on.

'We would be ill-advised, nevertheless, to put aside the great book of the past, however bitter its pages may sometimes read to us. We seek not grievance, but justice. Your neighbours in the Sudan, for instance, can they wisely forget the memories of Kitchener, of the Mahdi? Indeed the question remains with us all: Kitchener or the Mahdi, as for centuries the West has struggled with that other, Pilate or Christ.'

Justice or Truth! Not bad. Quick vision through my mind of Kitchener 'digging up the lands of the blacks' as some Pharaoh, according to Hughie, had boasted in the inscriptions. What a man this P.M.! Did he perhaps recognize this parting of our mothers' legs by Crescent, by Cross?

The reference was, however, unfortunate. The interpreter fumbled, embarrassed, over it. Kitchener or the Mahdi, Pilate or Christ! What did it mean? He wasn't sure, he dropped it. But the crowd (Kitchener, the Mahdi) they could easily see the challenge to humour, the appeal of the last laugh so dear to Arabs. The cheers were a long time dying down.

'Oh, hear!'

I began picking my way to the main gate. I heard, 'People of Africa, Africa will be free!'

Bit of a come-down that, I thought, but, still, a P.M. can't afford to take chances. Emotion, that's the real prince's garment of the illiterate. The rollers crashed and broke silence once more. The pillar of fire burned itself to ashes. The *zaghareet* ascended, hovered, and spiralled as though plotting a new course in the darkness. I pressed on to the main gate trying hard to feel – how shall I say? – this mystic union, this ineffable what's-it, this identity. I can never be reproached, God knows, for not trying.

2

Ramadhan coming…

Not for a few weeks yet, but it was Friday, the Holy Day, and I was easy; taking it easy, dreaming.

Sun coming down, sand lying down, *el hamdilela!* Air clear.

I watched Harka go over the sand floor. She walked to the place behind the door where she kept the brooms. She found there that the men had gone. Made in Japan: she stooped and picked that up. She saw the men outside the door walk to the place inside the gate where the donkeys stood. The new broom felt in her hand light. Back over the sand floor to the cigarette ends swept up against the beer bottles. Those were marked 'Made in England', these 'Made in Holland'. And Becks beer, too, drunk where they had sat in a circle. Then she saw the donkeys outside the gate walk away under the men to where the window ended.

Round the room the road led off. She pushed the chairs beside the walls. She broke the circle one by one. She pushed Abdalla up beside the wall. She took his footprints from against the table to beside the wall. She brushed them, quickly watered them, and brought Mohammed down beside them. Then Mukhtar stood between the windows where the footprints hardly spread. Back in the centre she broke the circle once again, backed through the backs of circled men sitting from the wall closed. She brought Ahmed back, took Farouk back – they had been sitting closest, speaking softly – and watered them.

Then the room was split: half against the wall, half half circled.

She gathered the glasses, broke the circle one by one. Then the bottles: sherry made in Cyprus, put that down. She pulled Kheiralla up beside the wall; Ali came up then against the wall, next Hassan, and then Zeyn.

Then the room was square.

She circled the table dry and backed it out. She watered the lines the chairs had figured across the sand, up to their legs against the walls. Beneath the chairs it was already dry. A smell came up where fresh water went down drying. The lines lay down. Over to the window she pulled up new footprints, backing the shutters in. Those lay down too. She went over the wet sand floor. She walked to the place inside the door where the old brooms lay and saw the glasses gathered, the light gathered where the bottles stood, and the cigarette ends in the darkness. She gathered the cigarette ends and the bottles and the glasses. In the darkness she walked dry footsteps to the place inside the gate where the donkeys outside had stood.

Twisted slowly, a gradual wrench of the tin-head broke the vacuum. I broke the circle of rubber bedded in beneath the lid. Four-square; sweet-smelling. Tobacco came out, moist between the palms.

Quickly she raised the dustbin-lid and let it fall. I leaned back, looking up. Over sand-colour, clear Kutam sky.

She tracked broad footsteps back over the overswept earth. I took up a thought. To the left she disappeared into the women's *hosh*. The thought went up blue, maundering against the sky. March, April, soon the *haboob*. Unchanging sun, change imperceptible. Could smell it coming up. Over the horizontal year change comes in exact points. First the *haboob*.

Harka returned; water for laying down the outside sand. 'Soon *haboob* time,' she said.

Against the blue my thinking maundered. After forty days the rains; with that the frogs. Quickly after that the flies. August flies stick round the mouth. September sticking to the skin; nothing to be hoped for from September.

'After that the rain?' I asked.

'Start with Ramadhan,' she said. 'The Fast.'

Against translucent blue my thinking stirred in smoke. Nothing to hope for from September. Follows though, the locusts. Locusts bring the winter. That's how you mark the seasons; not by the unsheathed sun that for ever never moves. Change comes always from the outside in, in meticulous sequence, spectacle upon spectacle…

'And after the Fast the Feast?'

Water for laying down the outside sand: the sand, that is, inside the yard; keep that still. If everyone laid down his sand, no haze then. If the Government laid down the sand…

She said: 'What does the Government do? Men gone with the donkeys to the souk. The Holy Day…they talk of strikes…what does our Government mean to do?'

Well, if Hassan doesn't tell her how can I? Keep far from politics in a land not yours. Keep far from politics anyway.

Change not spectacular mostly; something nevertheless to witness always. Nothing springs unseen from this circled sand floor. Breeding towards November, the myriad swarming minutiae of river-fleas come down in clouds to choke the air, fret the eyes, final misery of the burning year. Before the cold sets in. Always, though, the hostile onslaught, the brittle, crackling air.

Rising, she tipped the water round the root of the lemon tree. 'After the Feast,' she beamed, 'the Festivals!' And broke her scars in smiles.

A bitter smell came up where fresh water went down drying. Eyes half shut against the glare, I sprawled in the old canvas chair on the veranda. 'Hassan, he does not tell you these things, Harka?'

'At all, Mr Lobo.' And her scars settled into lines of gravity, pulled down to earth. She moved her mass with energy; finely plaited strings of hair lashed her shoulders, divided over the enormous breasts, fell straight along the ox-like neck.

'He does not speak about these, then, these men come visiting?'

'At all!'

Turning and fetching and swilling. She stooped, dragged the lavatory bucket free of its aperture in the mud wall, grumbled, 'These scavengers never put the thing back right.' She splashed the concrete floor of the lavatory, washed footmarks off the lavatory seat.

'A mother's got a right, y'know,' I prompted. 'Time's changing; a modern man like Hassan…'

'Hassan's a military man, Mr Lobo; is best he doesn't change too much. People upsetting themselves so much we don't know where we going. Hassan says the honour of the country is with the Army and people got to learn to look up to the Army. The

33

Army can't change; Hassan can't change; I don't ask for him to tell me things, Mr Lobo.'

Sun striking backwards with a three o'clock slant drove silver shafts through the crown of the lemon tree. Leaves danced, burnt black at the edges. The tree a mass of black and silver, danced aflame. Harka on the lavatory floor, flesh industriously a-quiver, remarked incuriously, 'P.M. going tomorrow, not so?'

I could see two hefty calves, the skirt raised above the knees, the knees like wood-knots braced by tight tendons that flexed, unflexed, as her weight gave backward, forward; part of the generous backside. A flash danced suddenly round my rim of vision as from a mirror in the sun. A cloudy tangle of shadows, a bird flew out of the lemon tree. 'Who you?' it asked.

Harka's voice came out of the darkness. 'You for the party tomorrow night, Mr Lobo?' sounding near, but nowhere. She rose, turned, stood with the dripping rag beside the mud wall. Above her head the trash roofs vanished to the far blue rim of sky. My eyes came back to where the shadows played over the sand floor, now caked and dry from Harka's dampening. No, but this peace is large and gentle, O Africa!

'Not a party, Harka, he's leaving Sunday morning. It's a press conference tomorrow night, so he can tell the people of this country what he thinks. Y'can't have a party if y'don't have women.'

'Is our customs, Mr Lobo, as you know; is the customs of the Muslims!' With rude pride, wringing out the rag.

'These meetings he has with these men…'

'Is not for a woman to say, Mr Lobo. As you see, I don't go near.'

'What I came for, really, Hassan won't discuss; twice now, y'know.'

'Is so?' grinning; taunting.

'You know!' I said. 'You know quite well.'

'Is all done and finish now, Mr Lobo, he can't discuss.'

'But the girl's in a terrible way, Harka, y'can't see that? She's got no home, nobody.'

'Mr Lobo, is Eve that left this house herself, don't forget. *W'Allahi*, was not Hassan's fault, what can Hassan do!' And she crouched slowly down beside the wall prepared for talk: sweet talk, sweet wrangling ramifications and confusions to pass the time. As always; skirt spanned tight across the haunches, elbows on knees.

'Look, Harka, we're all the same, aren't we? I mean one blood, all African, we can settle things? Forget Eve's a Christian, forget her father's a Reverend. There's the child…your own grand-child…'

'The child's a Muslim; Hassan's child can be no Christian, he's told you.'

'Everybody knows that, Harka; it's his child not hers, we all know that. It's just what I mean though; if she won't come back he can divorce her; the child's still his by law, at seven. Y'can't see I'm thinking about Eve?' Ploughing up old and exhausted soil, I knew. I could see her watching, almost playfully, wondering. 'Why won't he divorce her, why don't you speak to him, Harka?' For the thousandth time. 'The girl's young, pretty; she wants to be free. A woman in this country can't divorce a man, don't y'see how she's fixed? She's only young, after all… I mean, he can marry right now, any time he likes, and keep her for ever like this. Y'think it's right, Harka? Where is his honour making the girl suffer needlessly?'

'Hassan is an officer, Mr Lobo. Is not the customs of the Arabs for a woman to go from a man into a hotel room. Eve brought shame to our house and to our village. My day, my father would have killed me doing a thing like that. Hassan, he has no father, he must think for himself; he's got his pride…'

'Oh, but was different in your day, Harka, y'can't compare. Was only your legal father to begin with, not your real father; you belonged to him. That was different.'

She rose. She dropped her vigorous animal voice to a tired whisper. 'Ai, Mr Lobo, and I'm not ashamed. I belonged to him, that was different. Ai, I was his slave. I didn't have things easy; but I tell you he was a better father than your Christian Reverend!' And she spat into the stiff sand. 'Your Christian Reverend! Your wonderful Chief! Was easy him putting his daughter off like that when she ran away with Hassan; was easy, Mr Lobo, wasn't it! He cut his daughter off for marrying a Muslim. Well, my father would've killed me, straight! Would been better. Would been better for Eve if the Christian gentleman'd killed her straight because, like you just said, no woman lives alone in this country, and the Chief knows that. He knows it, and he let her, your Christian father!'

Silence. Sound of the neighbour's wireless; donkeys braying; sheep, goats, making a grey thickness far away. I watched her pick the rag up from the place in the sand where it had fallen in her anger; she took the bucket by its rim, but remained standing. I watched her expression slowly change. She asked in a puzzled manner, 'Mr Lobo?'

'Harka?'

'Is someone else she wants to marry?' Watching me closely; suspicious.

'No, Harka, I'm sure of that.'

'How you so sure, Mr Lobo?'

'Look, Harka,' I said, 'the Reverend's been good to you; not, for the Reverend you would've been sold again into slavery when your old master died; I got to say the truth.'

'Is the truth, I don't deny; the Reverend's been good to me.'

'Also when your husband died he was good to you.'

'I don't deny.'

'Hassan played round the Reverend's house since a boy. He was a Moslem child, but they played together, he and Eve; grew up together; the Reverend didn't mind.'

'Is so!' she admitted blandly. 'But those times is past, Mr Lobo; they was children.'

'So now, because Hassan went to the university, because he's an army officer, it's different now?'

'Is different, Mr Lobo, because you know why?' She clamped her arms akimbo and said forcefully, 'Gratitude for the past, it don't command the future.' She paused, thinking heavily; perspiration trickled from the frizzy hair above her temples and settled into the folds of her neck. 'Who was to say the girl would do that!'

'They ran off *together*,' I pleaded. 'What's the use blaming only one? They were young and stupid, both of them; why should Hassan ruin her young life, she's not yet twenty?…' But she'd begun to look so stubborn it was pointless to go on. I said in a quieter tone: 'Would you come with me to see the Reverend, Harka? It's what I want to ask you. He wouldn't let anyone discuss Eve, not even me. I daren't speak to him, but if we went together…would you come?…for him to take her back…you'd come?'

'Never, Mr Lobo! The Christian Reverend cut me off too when she did what she did. Was not my fault, but he cut me off too. I hate the girl besides, y'might as well know.' Silence again, briefly, then in a more reasonable voice: 'He's your friend, like the whiteskin people mean by friend. Is up to you. He's old, you young; not for him to say. Go to him. Don't try for Hassan to take her back; y'can't change what's happened because y' can't!' And her face went very coarse and angry. The lower lip trembled slightly, the chin made a spasmodic twitch or two. Then she shrieked so that I started, 'Eve will never shadow these eyes again!' With which she forked her fingers and pulled the lower eyelids down her cheeks to leave me in no doubt at all. 'Even if she was no Christian!'

3

Next morning, Saturday, and late for work. Worried. To make which worse the old Singer Roadster – tired, already finished when I bought it second-hand because of sand in its vitals, tons of it, not to mention the heat – wouldn't go. Something wrong this time with the petrol pump. Easily located, but the devil to fix. Nothing for it but foot it across to the Institute. Not far, but a bother: extended U around three roads, one sand, when I could almost see the rotting old-wood building through the trees from my veranda window.

I unscrewed the pump, put it in the pocket of my bush-jacket, and walked down the grand ex-British Administration gravel path to the main road. Two white butterflies looped into the sunlight from the foliage of an old banyan tree, flitted erratically round each other, separated, circled again like bits of paper in the wind, then lost themselves in a blossoming tamarhindi hedge. I stopped at a nearby tree to rub some of the grease off my palms, but the layer of dust on the bark merely confirmed the mess.

Better waste no more time. I glanced briefly over my shoulder. No taxi in sight, nothing; the whole world seemed already at work. Peculiar sourceless anxiety that morning or rather, what-ever the source, it was well beyond my restless prodding and groping. Seemed part of everything: came off the surface of the river, which, surely, never looked like that (gaunt, reluctant); from the dôm palms on the far bank (vomit-coloured ochre); from the damp, pungent gir-gir plantations along the water. I realized I was almost trotting.

Calm yourself, man, be late again – so what!

I slowed down. I've been called the hysterical type. Thin, hungry, hurried; fingers shake easily (especially to do with Hughie). Lightning temper; violence my friend.

Maybe he's pacing the balcony, just to show me I'm late again; hell with him.

I stopped, fumbled for a cigarette, realized I'd left my case on the veranda, cursed Faraed for a thief in anticipation, and walked on. I hadn't even remembered to comb my hair; disorganized. Found I was hurrying again.

Take your ease, man, take your ease; not afraid of him, are you?

Who the hell's Hughie to be afraid of? If I'm late I'm late; tell him straight. If he says ' 'Morning, Froad', with the faintest rebuke in his eye…

Stopped again to calm myself. Useless. Only Fridays; only sitting with Harka. Wait another week.

I took the pump from my pocket, withdrew the diaphragm, thinking. It was frayed at the edges, flabby, suction gone; finished. A pinhole was worn through one of the rubber discs. I flapped the other back and squinted through the hole, upwards. Leaves against silver; time passing. Why hadn't I changed it before! I'd known all along it'd gone.

Why the hell am I like that? Why can't I be conscious of particular things, like this! Like Hughie is. Like keeping the India ink from drying out on my pens. Was Hughie had to show me that trick with wet cotton wool. Why couldn't I have thought of that myself! Or of making reflectors for the Tilley lamp on site; or devising the light-trap to keep insects off while I work. Simple things! A petrol pump should be inspected periodically, no use waiting till it breaks. All those other things that should be inspected periodically; wonder the damn' jalopy goes at all. Now if I was Hughie, if I was a man like that…

If I gave the contact-breakers lots of screw so they barely open and close, maybe it'll get me down to the Chief's party and the press conference. After work Catherine could give me a lift home. Or Hughie.

If he isn't too angry. (Never seen Hughie angry; not so it shows, the old stick.)

You're afraid of him!

Shite, don't be such a fool.

Then why you crave his approval so?

The man's my boss, I respect his opinion, that's all.

That all?

If Hughie should see me now…when I get in sight of the Institute no doubt he'll stop on the veranda outside the library door and say, 'There comes Froad; observe his elaborate and wasteful gait' – something like that – to Catherine, she smiling, understanding, not raising her curls from the typewriter.

I tried then to get some spring and purpose into my walking, not to jitterbug along in the usual vague manner (hop on the toes, small play with the knees, hop on the other toes: look at a West Indian on the Charing Cross Road, or 125th Street, or anywhere along Frederick Street, Port of Spain, you'll know). I tried to propel myself like a man late for work and concerned.

O.K., you're not afraid of Hughie, you're afraid of his opinion, that's worse!

Well, any man should care for the opinion of his boss.

But you suck up to him; why? You're clever; you're an expert in your trade; you can draw the modelling on a grain of sand 1:3 scale if he wants you to. You're the best archaeological draughts-man in the business, nobody can stop you with hand and eye; yet you can't well finish the last little chip on some silly stone celt and you're off running to drop the thing casually before him, asking some damn-fool question about reproduction; just to see the man marvel, so that he looks up from his notes and says: 'Why, Froad, this really is a stunner. These things…we ought to make a collection of them in their own right, don't you think? As works of art, I mean. So objective, so clinical; like the very best Stubbs. It's the part of you that most puzzles me, I don't mind saying…'

Always like that with Hughie; always after some ought or other; and it gets worse and worse. Squeezing everybody's backsides to fit his oughts. We ought to this, ought to that, ought to produce the most terrific learned journal in Sudanic Africa; ought to be an example; ought to prove Karatite iron-working native; ought to establish the distinguishing aesthetic in Meroitic Art…ought to, by so and so, by God!

Became too much for a man's nerve in the end. Which is why I had to shove the screwdriver into his neck.

I had come to a stop, not knowing. I hadn't heard the car pull up; in fact it was still slowly moving beside me when she exclaimed, 'Lionel!'

I jumped. I said, 'Hi!' Then I said, 'What did you say?'

'Think of the devil…' she said. 'Where's your car, broken again?'

'You falling into local habits yourself, Catherine, with less excuse.'

'It's only just turned seven-thirty: decent start to the week, don't worry.'

'There, smell closely; first of the neem, last of the mimosa; the whole earth's ripening. Wish I had a wife pregnant now or something…'

She smiled. Usual fragment of a smile, driving with delicate electric concentration, as though she'd never relaxed since her first lesson; sitting upright, clear of the seat-back, rather gripping the wheel. A pale lilac handkerchief fluttered from her clenched fist; very feminine.

'Well, can't you smell the neem blossoms? Say something!'

Smile again lightening the lower face, but no answer. Chapel goodness; just right for absorbing my humours. Village in the Ogwen Valley, deserted purple quarries, steady purple mountains. Chapel three times Sunday, Thursday Bible class. Silence like Cambrian granite all over her; in her eyes.

'It's hardly there yet,' she said. 'It's the time of the year I like best, though; when you begin to perspire again. Winters – something slightly unnatural about those bright dry days.'

'Most Europeans out here like the winter.'

'I know; but not this one.' And she slips back into her habitual otherness; can't stay with anyone for long; hearing rather than listening.

'I remember it was an April,' I said, 'when I first came to this country; this kind of perfume all over the place, specially nights. I used to walk miles looking for it; weeks before I found out it was the neem.'

'Gives a lot of people hayfever.'

Playing that down. Naturally in the circumstances; can't blame the girl; it's me who's the swine.

41

She changed tack abruptly; businesslike. 'You ever wish you were white, Lionel? I mean, have you ever thought what a different person you'd be? It's what I was thinking of coming along.'

'White!'

'Oh dear,' she said; and we both laughed.

Do you ever wish you were a polar bear, a sea-cow, a scarecrow? Have you ever thought of it? What the hell was the girl at? 'You mean, do I ever wish for the advantages of being white, don't you?' Quiet; real civilized.

She went into third behind a giant Diesel spewing black smoke to the treetops; down to second to overtake, but the oncoming traffic was too close. She coughed lightly. 'This happened to me last night; behind the scavengers.'

'Camels or tractors?'

'Would that have made a difference, do you think, to my discomfort?'

We laughed again. Always laughed easy with Catherine; that was just the trouble. She made an impulsive dash on to the crown of the road, drove a monstrous American on to its knees, and was clear, triumphant. 'Where were we?'

'Straightening me out.'

She paused, half serious, cocked her head sideways in a manner always made me bite hard on my tongue, and raised her eyelashes. 'I don't really know what I mean, but it's silly enough, isn't it? A person like yourself, I mean, buried in this absurd job moving, dead bones from one graveyard to another, getting nowhere. It's what Hughie always says, this part of the world people expect something of fellows like you.'

Coming sharp. Typical. But not new. Dangerous besides. Could lose my temper, pull up her bloody handbrake, sulk for days. She knows that too, knows her power. I remain civilized. 'Well, like I always maintain, Chicken, it's a question of choice, isn't it? Any kind of choice is positive, way I see it, so long's it's choice; nothing wrong with that, is there?'

And she looked distressed. Even though she merely shrugged and said, 'Maybe!' I knew she was distressed. I like seeing Catherine distressed. Born for it; born to take the rotten end of the rod from some lousy sod. Real woman. Sufferer. Sacrificer.

'I was thinking about what you said the other day in Dr King's office about not feeling particularly responsible to your people, or whatever it was you said. It's why I thought of that coming along…maybe you've been too long among Europeans.'

Absorbed profile, high forehead, hair combed back, a way with the wayward curl escaping over her temple (another provoking motif that), air filling out the blouse, pink sunburn fading to pale ivory where the brassière cupped her breasts. Better not be angry. 'Look, Chicken, let's leave all that alone now, eh?' Firmly.

Outside the university she overtook two other cars, raced up the slight incline on the stretch that led to the Institute. But I couldn't leave it alone, not me. I added provocatively, 'What's lost, anyway!' Hoping she'd answer; wringing the last drop of sadistic joy out of the grave, appealing profile. Could do that for hours too: make her most the thing I want then steel myself. Like pretending not to be the least bit thirsty because a real well materializes in the mirage. Sort of man prefers to see a woman cry before taking her to bed, not after.

'Oh, nothing's lost!' She was straining after indifference; pitiable. 'I mean if it's necessary for you to feel that something's lost, that's different. You're not satisfied, you're not happy, so I just don't see the point.'

Me feeling pampered. Who else would look that close at old Froad? Worth provoking now and then. Mamma's well-loved, well-licked lickle puppy. Dear old devoted, devouring, dead bitch of a mamma!

She swung into the semicircular driveway of the Institute, past the pair of faceless, time-eaten Karatite figures gracing the entrance. Hughie was not pacing the veranda, but involuntarily I looked around for the Land Rover. It was there.

'Don't worry,' she said, reversing. 'Only a few minutes late today; why don't you stop worrying so much about Dr King? He doesn't pass his life thinking only of you.' Head through the window, freckles on the wide sunburned shoulders, knees slanted away; full calves exposed up to the pale lilac fringe of lace; remote, controlled, private body.

I wanted to say, 'Y'know, Catherine, lipstick's not sinful any more these days,' but there wasn't any little flicker of levity in the grey eyes. I remembered Hughie, mumbled automatically, 'Hell with him!' She opened the door and made the alluring exit – knees together – of a woman trying to leave a car honestly.

Womb-woman; worry-woman; puppy-licker. Same damn' thing all over. What the hell y'doing out yey, Froad! We began walking up the stairs. 'What y'doing for leave this year, Catherine?'

'Old Colwyn, the usual.'

'Oh yes, of course, your old man. Well, see you later.' Then I remembered. 'Say!...that thing you said about me being white...'

She paused.

'Yes, Lionel?'

4

I paused, looking at her; turning the docile 'Yes, Lionel?' over. I changed my mind. And began to tell her instead about Mohammed. Bravado? Itch to tell a good story? Or just wanting to hurt and frighten the wondering bitch?

Bit of each.

We'd come to the head of the stairway – she fingering the library door, me ready to fork left along the veranda for my study.

This Mohammed had appeared in my life about three weeks back with a proposition that'd fallen deadweight into the depths of my unconscious, and had taken all the intervening time surfacing to the shallows of reason. Not surprising this, as I'd just returned from the desert to find Kutam ablaze with elaborate preparations for the Noba visit.

It was about twenty past ten on a Sunday night. I clearly remember the time because I'd walked back from the Chief's after his grandfather clock had struck the hour, and that's about what it took – twenty minutes. While I could never actually bring myself to go to church, I often met the Chief outside the cathedral beneath the silvery spires of old eucalyptus trees and walked back with him to the Mission House for a chat – the sermon, the sermon of whoever else had preached, strange faces in the congregation, church affairs, and finance – till sometimes quite late, though not usually, the Chief being often too tired.

A gross American car was parked in the drive near the flight of three concrete steps that led on to my veranda. I thought that Jawlenski, my neighbour, must have a guest; but I could hear him practising 'Count me among the Dead' on the violin. Well, I thought no more of it. But just as I was manoeuvring the inconsiderate two inches of space left between the car and the veranda wall, someone whispered out of the darkness, 'Mr Froad!' And moved.

Naturally I jumped, and, being a nervous type, let out a nasty word. It was no voice I recognized. The man came down a step or two into the glow reflected from the light of the windows above. I rushed past him and found the veranda switch. Where the hell was Faraed! (It was Sunday, of course, his day off.) 'Who th'hell are you?' I pretty well shouted.

'Hoped you wouldn't mind my waylaying you like this; I wasn't too keen to put the light on while I waited, you'll understand.' In much purer English, I noted, than I myself possessed. Upper Johkresi; society intelligentzia; Friends of Thought Society; polish. 'Name's Mohammed.'

'Mohammed you said, mister?' Hot, disturbed. (Pretty, girlish; semi-Negro, semi-Arab; much more Negro.) 'Mohammed, like a million other Johkresi! Where's the rest? Or is it Mohammed Mohammed!' Jumpy, pumping in the temples and throat. He noticed that. He grinned.

'You'd be no better for that. Mohammed Mohammed's also a very common name, like, say, Evan Evans among some of your Welsh. May I come in?'

'Do!' And I led the way through the kitchen door. Catherine had never seen my flat. I described it. 'P.W.D. effort,' I told her, with what I considered manly detachment. 'You come to the kitchen before the comforts; real English.'

She was writhing a bit, but managed to put up a fair show. We weren't, after all, hanging around the lawns or verandas; we'd actually arrived at work, in case Hughie should start coming funny.

'I collected a couple beers and two glasses as we passed through the kitchen, while this Mohammed chappie went on ahead and switched on the living-room light uninvited. When I got in I found the man nosing around among my props: you know, bits of painted pottery sherds lying about on the table, the sandstone fragment we'd just brought back from Old Karo, the cast of Augustus sent us by the Khartoum people from the head they found at Meroë (I'm supposed to be making a drawing of this, by the way, minus chips, for reproduction); then there was the mathematical analysis of the human skeleton I've held on to since my diploma days; you know, root five rectangles, golden section, the lot. Impressive. Means the same to me as other people's television masts and baggage tags.'

'You live very simply, I see,' Mohammed purred unctuously, almost sniffing.

So I shot him a hard, good look and said, 'Siddown!'

'I hear you're just back from the desert.' Seating himself in his own time, just as though I hadn't spoken. 'I've been hunting you a fortnight now, nearly.'

'Oh? What for?' Weak, I know, but I couldn't manage anything more acid or ugly. The words, in fact, rushed out with a nervous heat that annoyed me. I poured him a beer. He fished out an impressively vulgar-looking cigarette case, helped himself, then made a rude little shove with it in my direction. Arab – self-assured generosity, the gesture – Pharasaic.

'Thanks, no; don't smoke,' I said.

'Oh, I felt I'd seen you somewhere with a pipe? I remember someone remarking at the time only foreigners seem to find pipe-smoking cool business out here.'

'I smoke a pipe because I'm a foreigner; mere pose! Poor profile, you see.'

(Not commanding in presence; indifferently built, rather slight, too short. Kind of face looks like a dried-out coconut; no impressive shock of hair to carry it off. My head's covered, in fact, with a kind of coarse, emery-clothlike substance that clings to the three sullen-looking carbuncles occupying the space above the occipital bone.)

'You're out of town a great deal, I hear.'

'I've a living to make, you know.' And taking an elaborate draught of beer I went over to the armchair by the reading lamp. I regretted this at once as it left the fellow the benefit of the shrouding darkness of the rest of the room. Just what he'd wish for, too, with his mysteries.

'Well, and are you finding it pleasant?'

'Oh, pleasant enough, you know, I like your country.'

'Sure! Sure!' Rudely, cowboy style. 'Matter of fact we know you are a great lover of our country: the hardships you meet in your profession,' With a glimmer of a smile that was hastily drowned in a short noisy gullop of beera, as they call it. 'Which we consider a very important thing at the moment. A man like yourself, you see?'

'Don't see; no, I don't, I'm sure I don't see.' And I took another restless draught. 'Y'better make it fast, eh, mister? I'm tired.' But the man was easy, not for hustling. He watched me calmly, his girlish good looks toughened faintly by the cold glow of the daylight lamp.

He said reflectively: 'Of course, being out of town as much as you are there're things, important things, you'd lose sight of about our country, or unhappily miss altogether. I'll tell you in a minute what things I mean, just let me finish.' Raising a palm to fend off some imaginary interruption, looking at me as though I was about to start barking or something. Really, I was so far from grasping what it was all about the man could just as well have been talking about Icelandic literature, or the Book of Kells, or…

Suddenly I wondered whether it wasn't some kind of Friends of Thought overture with full programme to follow. Was the fellow, with his disgusting self-gratulatory urbanity, working up to some outlandish proposal for a lecture or something? I resolutely set myself to be out of town if he became obstreperous.

(Obstreperous: any type of overwhelmingly disconcerting behaviour irrespective of nature or source. Origin: small boy, way back, witnessing a policeman arrest a woman for looking on in an 'obstreperous manner' while her son, a full-grown man, was hustled in for urinating on the sidewalk.)

Well, if this chap should become obstreperous, especially at the time of night when I liked to strip my mental clothes and let my thoughts walk around naked, I wondered what I should do.

'What I mean actually is in the political line, you see?'

I said, 'Oh,' so relieved that he seemed briefly taken aback.

He made a guttering yellow smile like a brave birthday candle holding its own against the last resolute child, and continued singeing my indifference to Johkresi or any other kind of politics with, '…problem, you see, every good Johkresi is interested in, and, I may add, many foreigners too; not always wisely, unfortunately…purrrh…purrrh…purrrh…' Something about the southern situation, more purring. '…gradual evolution of these Negroes…' Lengthy gap, then, 'except for the present

48

absurd [that's the word that struck home] crisis in Africa today: impasse, dead end.'

I uncrossed my legs and listened.

'Minds poisoned by the British, of course, who never leave a country without having made sure of its capacity to split itself to pieces in the shortest possible space of time: part of the technique, you see, of denigrating us in the eyes of the world.'

I gave a considered grunt, and this brought him to an uncertain pause. He measured me like a coiling snake. I hated the man.

'But you now, as a Western Negro, well, of course there must be judgements you could make in a situation like this; unique light you could possibly throw…'

I began to worry that it might after all be some veiled obstreperous manoeuvre: Schools Broadcasts (Good Morning to you all. In the part of the world where I come from…). Political pep-talks (Today as an African bred in a Western Democratic environment and inheriting the finest traditions of…of…). No, the man was no fool. It was my turn now to measure the force of this *afreet*, corkscrewing in a determined path across the wide, wide plains of my indifference.

'Well, come now, Mohammed,' I protested. 'The British didn't do it all single-handed, you know. The race riots you had here couple years back – Negro against Arab – the British were as good as gone by then. I mean, if you people hate these Southerners so much, then surely you must expect…'

But no, that got me no nearer the centre of his aim. He was a man pointing a weapon from behind a cloak. Ages he continued, spinning with the suavity of the practised politician, swinging forward in his chair, swinging back, crossing his legs, uncrossing, hitching minutely at his trouser-creases, all with the smooth, shallow elegance of the civilized Arab. He was in no hurry.

Catherine, obviously waiting for a suitable pause, now said politely, 'I'll just give Dr King his diary,' and made to go.

But I grabbed her arm. 'No, no, I'll make the rest of it short, I've got work to do too.' So she took a quick nervous peep into the library, through half an inch of door, and turned back to me with an empty smile. I said to her:

'Well, skipping all that middle part – I was yawning boldly by now, accompanied with elaborate drawn-out sleepy noises – he came at last to: "I said a while ago you see, Mr Froad, these are the things you miss by being away so frequently. What's been happening here the past few months has been not merely disgraceful, but downright dangerous and alarming. I speak to you as a foreigner, of course, and a man of colour…'"

Man of colour! That did it again. Western Negro, man of colour! You just don't use words like that in Johkara. No, not like that. There must be some stress, some pressure. Negro! The word simply means slave! (Arabic, *abid*: the worst curse in the world.) The black Northerners, to save confusion, call themselves green! *Akhdar*! The Southerners, same colour, are called by them *assuad*, black!

I measured Mohammed once more, wide awake; but, far from being rude, the man was actually trying to be ingratiatingly modern: dispassionate: Western. Why?

He said: 'You'll understand, of course, that an opinion like yours would be invaluable to us at the present moment. Unfortunately nothing we can say at this point would meet with anything but scorn from these Negroes.' And he paused contemptuously, making an obvious effort at self-control. 'Put it blankly, Mr Froad, our politics is divided racially, as you very well know. Now they've picked up these names: pan-Africanism, Arab Nationalism, it's a situation we Arabs just must control, especially with the Noba Prime Minister coming. We fear the effect of this visit on these people – you know the primitive mind as well as I do. He couldn't have chosen a worse moment, in fact, for this tour of African states, but we couldn't very well refuse, could we? We're on the brink of an important general election; the South is inflamed; Secession, Federation, Partition – words they don't know the meaning of. Now comes a black Prime Minister from a successful independent country. Do you see how we're fixed?'

'Well, yes,' I conceded, fairly well battered by now. 'I can see it's likely to have some kind of effect.' This could hardly be the kind of opinion, though, that Mohammed was keeping me up for at this time of night. I went to the kitchen for another beer; introduce relief. After topping up his glass I remained standing nearer him, braced against the edge of my desk, ankles crossed, neutral. Not indifferent, not too much interest. If the beer had poisoned him stone dead straight away I should have wondered what it'd all been about, but certainly I would've lost no sleep doing it.

'To make which worse,' he continued, 'our boys have been campaigning very unwisely in the South. I don't mean my party particularly, I mean both the Northern parties. Even people like merchants and Government officials…they've made a proper mess of the situation, destroyed a lot of the underground work we'd carefully built up; for instance, we had many of the chiefs pressuring the constituents, even some of the candidates – you know the power these chiefs still have. Now we face nothing but hatred, solid hatred, and nobody can think what to do about it.'

'Worse than it's ever been?' I coaxed.

'Look!' He put on a thinking frown. 'Something basic you must understand about our situation out here. Out here power is power over people's emotions, no matter who wields it. Africans are swayed by people, not by ideas. Get that? The personality is the only way through to the primitive mind. I know these people; my father freed many of them on his death-bed; I know what I'm talking about. When you get the parties accusing each other to the blacks about meaning to bring back the slave trade, suppress their Christianity, expel the missionaries, take their land and cattle, they don't know how inflammable all that is. Yes, Mr Froad, it's worse now than it's ever been, since you ask me; worse even than after the massacres, because then at least we had Southern Members in the House; they voted with the parties in the Transition Government. Now these same people have swung to a bloc: one party, one bloc. The South for the Southerners. You can see it's bound to play hell with whatever Government goes in, destroy any idea of democracy. It would never work; there'll be chaos. Apart from the domestic issue, we just can't afford this state of affairs in the eyes of the world; not with Africa as it is at the moment. There, are people just waiting, I know, for something like this to take place; working for it even, I dare say. I've reason to suspect so, at any rate. Now, Mr Froad, do you see how you can help us?'

A messenger came to say I was wanted on the telephone. Hughie opened the library door and nearly knocked Catherine over. He said, 'Oh dear!'

Catherine said, ' 'Morning, Dr King!'

Defensively I said to Catherine, 'Come to breakfast, will you?'

On the line was the Chief. He said, 'That you, son? He said, 'Where's the thing?'

'What thing, Chief?'

'What y'mean what thing? You said Friday, didn't you? Where were you yesterday?'

Friday! Something important. Must be, to have the Chief so early on my neck. I said, 'I said Friday, Chief?' Remembered well enough saying something about Friday, but what? What?

'Look, son, no playing around; *y'haven't done it?*' Beginning to thunder.

'Done what, Chief?'

Terrible pause. What? What? What?

'Look, come over here. I want to talk to you; right away. I've got someone coming.'

'The car's broken, Chief.'

'Talk nonsense, son, I'm waiting. Take a cab, I'll pay.' And hung up.

What? What? What?

I was still biting my lips raw with fright, and searching desperately for a cigarette, when Hughie came into my room.

Fresh, sunburnt, discreet smell of Imperial Leather. White bush-clothes in town, khaki on trek. Nifty suede boots. (Well, with all these visiting experts and foreigners, you know, chap's got to toe the line; show the flag too and all that, things not being what they used ter be. All right for you, old chap, isn't it? No harm meant, of course.)

Now the great hairy paw will come down on my shoulder.

'*Salaam Aliek!*' breezily.

Hughie hearty. Hughie covering up. Something on little Hughie's busy mind. Damn' sight more tolerable, though, than Hughie reflective, Hughie responsible, the real Khaki Hughie. O.K., what's it you're hiding, Hughie? Let's have it, White Drill Hughie. '*W'Aliekum salaam*, Hughie.'

'Terribly sorry to barge in like this, old man, so early; ha, ha! [Because of my hanging around with Catherine, that.] Just hunting the Karo sketch-plan actually, the one with the room numbers.'

Pause. That's not it, Hughie; come again. However, I look interested, even make a gesture among the pile-up on the old settee.

'Was it with you or with the surveyor?' he beams.

You know damn' well who's got it; we both do.

'It's with the surveyor I think, Hughie; he stayed back with you on site, remember, after I left.'

'Oh, bother, of course! I'll get him on the phone.'

'I can do that for you, Hughie,' and reached across my desk towards the instrument; calling his bluff.

'Not to worry, old chap, I must see him anyway.' Not removing the unlit pipe from between brown, manly teeth.

'Sit a minute, Hughie?'

'Don't mind if I do; what about all these papers, what shall I do with them?'

'Sorry; just shove them on to the floor beside you; room's in an awful mess…'

'No one to blame but your dear self, is there?'

'Oh, not complaining, you know. Something to drink? Tea? Coffee?'

'No, thank you, not before breakfast,' rising restlessly. 'I'm not all that Johkrified…Johkricized, what would you say?' And sits again. Hughie facetious even; hmm!

'Johkrified! Sounds like petrified to me: one thing these people just aren't, however you look at it.'

'No, I must say I'm with you there.'

Quick sudden frown. Glimpse of Khaki Hughie. Petrified! He's chewing on that. I've hit! Immediately, though, his light spreads again, expands. 'No, it's like we've always agreed, there's that to be said for them, whatever it may amount to. By the way…'

'Formlessness, after all, is neither good nor bad; simply a condition nature doesn't tolerate for long.'

There I go; lost it with my early-morning philosophizing. But I try. 'By the way what, Hughie?'

Which wouldn't do, of course. He deflects. 'Something of the ultimate shape should be present, though, in the formlessness when you're thinking about people – I mean inherent, wouldn't you say? You know, matter and will, that kind of contention.' Starting, for something to do, to fill his pipe.

I try again; try to shrug that off. 'Who's to say!' Immense indifference.

He stretches his long legs out. 'I mean, you've heard that about if the Greeks'd hit on a place value for the cipher we'd've had our atomic age over and done with by now, in all probability? Even before Meroë?' A thin, dry smile, not the one I like, a watching smile. 'You see, in the Greeks y'had the European thing there from the very start; the germ – if you get me – of the European idea. Take Meroë now, where's the germ? Ethiopic, Kushite, Meroitic, whatever you like to call it, you can't point to the beginnings of anything like a germ in the Sudanic civilization. What d'y'see around you after such a start…see what I mean?' Lighting up. Puffing big blue smoke into the air. Large, leaning back on the spine, ice-eyes tolerantly smiling. City Hughie; White Man Hughie. Marble Face. Why y'don't come straight! 'See what I'm driving at, don't you?' he presses. 'I mean, to get back on to the old thing for a minute, a chap like yourself –'

'All right, all right!' I wasn't having any of that on top of Catherine.

'All right then, nothing to huff off about, is there, old chap? Why, I've not even mentioned the word this time; you get worse and worse.'

'Hell with the jokes, Hughie, let's not start, eh?'

'Right, we'll keep it abstract. Work it out this way: Meroë – fringe culture of Egypt. Old Karo – faecal culture of Meroë. My word, that's damned all right now, isn't it? Must make a note of that! Come on, Froad, say it's good. Faecal! Faeces of Monophysite Christianity from the sixth century onwards: no connection with the parent. Fifteenth century, Islam; nineteenth century, us; you've got to accept it. After us, what? Where's it all going to if somebody doesn't have the guts to get the whole thing straight! I really don't see why you choose to blow off each time we come near the point, it's got to be faced sooner or later. If we can establish some purely original aspect of African culture at Old Karo – something germinal I mean – forgetting personalities for the moment, I would say –'

'Doesn't mean a damn to me, Hughie, and as for seeing the beginnings of any pattern, germ or whatever...' But what's the bloody use! How many times! The man's a maniac.

He firms his jaws, though, on the pipe. 'Well?' Expectant.

So I let him have it; laziest emphasis on the 'other chap'. 'As for that, Hughie, how would you like to be on the bottom rung of a ladder with some other chap up the top trying to kick the whole bloody show down because he's got no further to go?'

Three in a row, but as usual nobody wins; same thing, same damn' thing each time. What, though, did I care! I hadn't even said what I felt; sure hadn't felt what I said.

'Scorning the base degrees, eh?' Rising abruptly to go.

'That's right, Hughie old chap; provoke a peaceful man then just bugger off; typical!'

'Look, I'm sure there's something in that, Froad, but I absolutely must dash; I'm on my way to see the minister. Wouldn't do to keep him waiting, would it, while we unravel these pressing puzzles? See you later.'

Then, putting his head round the door the very next moment, casually: 'By the way, nearly forgot; don't on any account leave the office this morning, will you? I may be quite some time; you'll be holding the old fort, eh? Good old Froad, so long.'

Smiling, door closing. White Drill Hughie. Clever Imperial Leather Hughie. Something cooking, all right; I'm no bloody secretary, why hold me here when there's Catherine to put his business to rights! No, you got to come again, Hughie, whatever it is. I promised, 'O.K., Hughie, it'll hold.'

But he'd gone.

5

Straight away I went in to Catherine to borrow her car. 'Got to see the Chief,' I said. 'Urgent.'

'I think Dr King wants you to be around.'

'I can't help that; you're here, anyway, aren't you?'

'Besides, we're supposed to be having breakfast together.'

'Forgot!'

'Nice thing to say; then shall I forget it too?'

'Oh, come on, don't be so jumpy, Chicken, let's go. Let's go to my room.' I raised her up by an elbow, attentively, to make up. We stood, the typewriter between us, staring at each other. One of Catherine's eyes doesn't point dead straight. Funny thing that, you know it even though it's too fine a measure to perceive; you feel one part of her glance going past your left ear. Myself I liked that; made the face itself seem more present, more physical. Illusion of being able to sneak past at least part of her gaze, past the buffer of personality. Attractive down also on the upper lip, as with some Coptic women.

We went back down the corridor to my room. 'What's the mystery, then?'

She didn't know. Hiding something too! She sat on the few inches of settee Hughie had left clear – between the rolls of old drawings, drawing paper, blue-film – and pulled her hem down. 'Where d'you eat?' she asked, looking round for some plausible spot.

'Never mind, anywhere; lap or anywhere.' And I went to the phone.

The phone said, '*Aiwa, aiwa, aiwa!*' which means, 'Yes, yes, yes!' and then said nothing. I looked over my shoulder at her. She was examining the map of Johkara on the wall – a shape like the gap in a broken window-pane lying across the face of the great Sudanic savannah. There was her back, the close fit of the dress round the lumbar region, full skirt falling to well below the knees. The phone roared in another voice, a hefty bull-bass, *Nam!'* which means a different kind of yes, firmer. The bull seemed after that to roll over on its back and kick up its legs before I could get another word in, and kept making the same sort of noise until it could again bring itself to say, '*Nam, ya sayed!'*

Hamed, head *farrash*, *soi-disant* terror of the canteen: Bugger Hamed. '*Ya Hamed!'*

And at once someone else shrieked close by, '*Yameenak ya Mohammed, hinaak!'*

But over that the bull-man continued, '*Aus haja, ya sayed?'*

I said, '*Futur Inglezi, nimra khamsa, itnen.'* (Two breakfasts in number five).

'*Da geega, ya sayed.'*

Hamed's minute, Eastern time: a long, more or less silent, gap in which the bull seemed to be tucking itself in between cushions somewhere. Soft, rubbing noises. I turned again towards Catherine, found her looking straight at me with her familiar strained attentiveness – taut, always taut, the wind lifting a few strands of hair across her forehead like grass fluttering on bleak Welsh hillsides. I turned back to the telephoning with vigour.

More soft dumb sounds, so I shouted, 'Allo, Allo!' The sounds ceased, as though frightened, but no answer. After a while the bull roared, so suddenly that I started, '*Futur Inglezi, nimra khamsa, itnen!'* A great belch, a sound suggesting that the receiver was being effortlessly swallowed; silence.

Please, Lord Jesus, tear his eyes out.

' 'll be hot for you out at Old Karo,' Catherine was saying. 'Y'know, we ought to get you one of those plastic ice-boxes, those water-bags aren't much good, are they? The boxes keep ice three days or more, they say.'

'And after that what, eh, little woman?' Dropping close beside her on to the settee; she eased away imperceptibly. 'The water-bags are all right, specially the goatskin ones; nature-cooled; no complaints, don't you worry.'

'And you shouldn't work nights by lamplight; can't you fix up a proper light from the Land Rover?'

'What's it now, Chicken; more than two years in the trade!'

'You come back so exhausted each time though, don't you?'

The door ground open, seemingly of its own accord, pushed over the edge-curl of the dusty blue carpet, and let in a bare black left foot. A tinkle of dishes, and the *farrash* followed his foot into the room under a huge, vividly coloured, enamelled tray. *Futur Inglezi*, the usual: eggs, bacon (rather wooden-looking), toast, jam, pot of tea; *itnen*! The *farrash* looked around with a wondering smile for some place to lay his load, even down his baggy cotton drawers and behind them. He decided on what remained vacant of the long wooden settee, and began making for it. Catherine had, however, started managing movements among the rolls of blue-film and drawing paper. She took the tray from the man and laid it on a small stool.

In the middle of the room the man suddenly stopped and began to boast profusely, presumably because it concerned us both, of the rapid growth of a lab-lab vine he was training into a form of garage for the staff. 'Three inches a day, and flowers!' grinning.

Catherine was suitably astonished. '*Ma maghoul!*' (Impossible) she protested; but the man was the picture of untainted truth. He curled backwards, contracted with pleasure, right hand lightly touching his heart in the name of Allah. '*W'Allahi ya sitt, W'Allahi!*' The same whose donkey was a menace to Hughie's immaculate lawns.

'Strange people, aren't they?'

'Why?'

'Like the gardener where I live who's supposed to let in water for the hedges. Y'know, he ties his donkey in the same hedge so it could feed all day; what y'say to that!'

She smiled. 'Perhaps the hedge itself is not his job. The one tending the hedge itself would probably block the water off for *his* donkey to drink!'

We both laughed.

She was busy putting food on to two plates, arranging things. 'Strong or weak?' (Doesn't matter to me.) 'Milk?' (Sure!) 'How many sugars?' I noticed she poured the tea with the leaves in. 'Strained?' she asked.

' 'Course! Isn't that always done?'

'I suppose so, but I like the leaves myself.'

'No milk, no sugar, just pure strong tea with leaves?'

'Lovely!'

'Like lead mixed with saltpetre.'

She handed me the tray.

'Look, this wouldn't do.' I said, 'You'd better have the tray – your dress; I can manage perfectly well on my lap.'

Easy! Why not! We'd forgotten Hughie. But I needed to discredit water in the midst of the mirage. I finished telling her about Mohammed.

Minus Mohammed's pleonasms and satanic overtones, the proposition boiled down to this. Him talking. 'What we need now, you see, is a different type of propaganda altogether; we can't afford to let things rest as they are. If you get any of this federal talk, partitionist talk, secessionist talk, going into Parliament, it's bound to end in breakdown, chaos; and you know what comes after that! No, our situation is crucial, with all this nonsense about pan-Africanism.'

He said: 'I speak to you as a foreigner, naturally, and that's the whole point.' (The man hated me, too, that was clear.) 'You're a model, in a way, of racial adaptation: just what we foresee for the Southerners out here; your people having evolved as minorities in Western civilization. You're a *model of freedom*, Mr Froad, that's what's important to us. You see why no one else but you can help? Africans, as I've said, worship personalities; they need such a model. With your help we plan to sell them the inevitability of environment; you know, like your own people have understood it among Europeans the last three hundred years. It's the only way we can hold them now. Give them an ideal to keep off this African pestilence; give ourselves a breathing space. In time, of course, we'll absorb them, we've got to, you'll understand. It'll be a dreadful day when all these black Christian countries are free. I mean no offence, but you see how we are fixed, don't you? Granted we're only thirty per cent of the population out here, this whole Sudanic savannah's ours; by blood, by history, by destiny!' (And not a blush.) 'The great medieval empires of the Sahara, they were all of them the glorious creations of our Moslem genius. The Africans say to us, Take your genius and go back to your peninsula; leave us our land and our freedom. Terrible word that, these days, don't you think? You see, Mr Froad, what does it mean, between you and me, in the mouths of black savages! All new talk; infra-Saharan talk. We were trading these people for salt not so long ago; what do they know? Where would they've been but for us these past three thousand years!' (Islam: 1,300 years old, but I swear that's what he said. Maybe he was cornering the far horizons of Egypt as well?)

'What we want you to do is to play a kind of subtle directive role – I wouldn't call it propaganda – more in the ideological sense, if you understand. You see, these boys will trust you as a Christian Negro interested in the future of Africans in Africa. I've heard your talks and so on; I know you're the man. Suppose, say, you write us a series of articles, say about six, for the *Southern Cross*. It would mean nothing at all to you, but would make the hell of a difference to us, to the whole situation, can you see that?'

In earnest of which, at this point, he produced a thin cheque-book with the same offensive flourish as he'd employed with the cigarette case, mumbling, while he signed a blank, 'In a way you could say that the whole future of democracy out here, and perhaps elsewhere in Africa, rests on what we do now.'

He said, 'Sure you'll agree with me there,' absently, and handed me over the cheque to fill in my figure, watching me all the while like a bucketload of vomit beneath a sick man's smile.

The look of puzzled consternation, which had all along been deepening Catherine's usual gravity, now froze into one of distress, then plain bewilderment. She said bravely, 'I suppose this kind of thing flatters you no end.'

Which made me only grin. Of course it did. 'There isn't another man could do it; see that, don't you? None of the USOM chaps because of their Embassy, and a fat lot the British would care if I sold a few Christian blacks to a few Arab blacks in a country they've left, anyway.'

She said, 'Whom d'you mean, the British?'

'No true-blue foolishness now, Catherine!'

She put her voice up two-three semitones. 'You haven't *done* anything, I hope?'

Which reminded me with a stab of anxiety of the Chief's rigmarole. 'Look, Chicken, I got to dash; just remembered.' And started pawing her apologetically.

'Sit down, Lionel.'

I half sat beside her. She said: 'I don't know why you seem to find it so funny; what about your contract, you've thought of that? You'll get yourself into the most awful trouble for your vanity. Why get yourself into trouble, don't you ever *think*?'

'This isn't politics, they can't touch me; there's nothing in my contract about selling brother man.'

Cathedral silence; mountain silence; massive silence of the weathered walls of Conway Castle. After that another well-bred turn of the scrooch. 'You mean, then, to do it!'

'No idea, Chicken; he gave me a couple weeks to think it out, but he hasn't turned up yet. Chicken, look, what y'worrying? We could get married or something on the money, go live it up on a West Indian beach; why y'worrying for?'

Which didn't cause her to laugh one bit, or even to look pleasant. So I jumped up, pulled a dust-cover over the drawing-table, and said finally: 'See you later, then, eh? Won't be long.'

'Oh, be as long as you like!'

So I made an amused soundless sound: sort of rapid nervous exhalation. Just a woman: sweet!

Then she said, 'What can I say!'

Well, just a woman! 'Look,' I said, 'I hadn't ought to've told you, f'get it.' But no; trick! Trap! She stood barring my way. Never bloody trust a woman.

'If you're saying that to hurt me, Lionel…' Working herself up.

'I only said –' I began to explain.

'I think you're a poor sort of man.'

'Now, *wait a minute*, Chicken.'

'Mean, destructive thing to say, and I think you're a poor… take your hand off me!' Bosom heaving.

I shrugged. 'All right, then, lemme go, will you?'

'You shouldn't make me pity you…you…I sometimes think you're quite abject.'

'O.K., then, now *lemme go*!'

I wasted no time getting down the stairs. There was the lace-fringed lilac handkerchief on the floor of her car. Sent that flying through the door before I could bring myself to move off.

So flustered after that I could hardly look the Chief in the eye. Which he noticed and started coming strong. 'Here!' and 'Look here!' sort of thing. 'Sensa responsibility…social conscience… your people…shut up!' Hughie stuff.

He kept rising from his desk and sitting down again, and I watched his mouth opening and shutting with – well – plain terror. Between the peals of thunder I ventured a few odd smiles: with teeth, without; with one corner of the mouth; with whole mouth; British upper lip; watery-cowering; quavering that didn't light up at all. Nothing doing. What was the man at? I didn't dare ask!

He said, 'Weaknessa characta,' and 'Mark my word,' and towered up again. He said, 'Never get you anywhere, y'better realize.'

The Chief is a frightening type; ten foot tall; thick. (You should see the bed he sleeps in!) I shut up.

'Now what am I going to tell the Bishop, eh? You tell me!' Blaring all out. But suddenly he finished the sentence so soft and sweet, looking past my shoulder, that I turned round. I saw the Bishop coming in.

A man looking like a withered coconut-palm: thin, grey, waving on top. Jolly type none the less: shirt-sleeves, V-neck, sandals. Not like the Chief: solid, full black in any kind of heat, morning suit and spats if the people in the palace merely opened the doors for an airing; head like a punching bag. He said cheerfully, 'Right on time, Bishop; come in.'

The Bishop said, 'Hullo, hullo, what's new!'

'This is Lionel Froad, Bishop; countryman of mine; with the Institute.'

The Bishop pounced on me – one large lunge across the room – and greeted me clubman style: shoving my shoulder backwards with the left hand, pumping vigorously with the right; hearty smile. Trial-of-strength tactics. Bet he knew all about it, too. You couldn't say he didn't have the common touch, you couldn't! He meant it. Sincere English type.

'Y'better step out here, Bishop,' said the Chief, 'This way. One minute, Froad.' On to the antique-Indian veranda – wood-carved, bat-infested – overlooking the birds and flowers, the garden-party lawn. I let them.

What? What? What?

Sorting the thing out, my eyes picked up 'The Broad and Narrow Way', an ancient print over the Chief's desk. Chief's comforts. Through the gateway called Death and Damnation the Many in Victorian elegance travelled the Way of Perdition to the Firepits. The glass was cracked over the Firepits. Bustles and stovepipes and pale hands I loved beside the Shalimar clustered around the ballroom called Worldliness opposite the Theatre Royal. In the background laboured a Monstrous Evil called Sunday Train. How simple not too long ago damnation was! The Rich Man in his castle, the Poor Man at his gate; God in his Heaven, all well with the whole bloody business; every man a place. Along the Narrow Way the Poor, as Morland would have painted them, laboured righteously on to a brown, spreading stain.

Couldn't've been easy for the Chief these thirty-odd years out here. Bowed by the weight of centuries he leans upon his Faith and gazes at the Cross.

Outside I could hear the Bishop say, They don't understand power, they've got to be guided…strong Christian bloc in the South…their last chance now with the British gone…' And the Chief's Demerara profile bent across the window towards him, looking like her. Like his daughter Eve.

Eve! Her mammal smell all over the hotel room, sweat making cold lights on her warm, creek-water flesh.

'So what if I do nothing about you, too, Eve, so what then? Pure chance meeting you again like this; doesn't mean I mean to be involved. You could've been anybody I know, it doesn't mean…'

She, sighing, 'Just now, when we met –'

'Oh, I know.'

'…You were so kind…'

'Chrissake, y'don't have to call it kind. Woman and child in a heat like this; cost me nothing to give you a lift.'

'You were kind, Lobo, please don't explain; I don't want anything of you. What you mean I don't know; I only said it's good knowing you're here.'

'Well, what's the matter now! God's sake don't start crying.'

'What do you care?'

'If you won't go back, Eve, what will you do? Two months now, nearly, the little money you've got. Does he send you anything? *He* doesn't, I know. Who I mean is the Chief, the Christian Reverend, your father. He can't have left you like this. It's what I want to know.'

'Lobo.'

'Yes?'

'Lobo, look, this trouble's all nothing to do with you; I'm not asking you to help; you're Papa's friend, there's nothing you can do.'

'Your father, you know, won't let anybody mention your name, but you can't stay here even so; no woman lives alone in this country. You got to go back to your parents whatever it costs, Eve; try again. When your papa refused to have you, few months back, he may've been trying to force you back to Hassan. You got to try again. I got nothing to offer…'

'Like what?'

'What d'you mean, like what? Look, I'm going now, I got to go.'

And she looks away then, not answering, to the baby asleep, the image of Hassan, in the cot.

'I mean the Reverend being my good friend and all that, that's what I mean, Eve, see?'

Us two then staring, silently staring each other down. Me going…

Small bird strutted across my view on the garden-party lawn like a fragment of something else I thought might be haphazardly moving – twig, leaf, paper, anything else. No, but it was a bird, and I was content. He too, look of it. I laughed when he asked, 'Who you?'

They called me on to the veranda; the Chief did. Bishop said, 'Now the Reverend tells me you're having second thoughts, Mr Froad?'

'I haven't done it, Bishop.' (Their evidence, not mine.)

'Yes, yes, of course, as you see fit; no question of pressure, naturally. You understand? No point in that, is there?'

I tackled the Chief with a questioning glance, but he merely cleared his throat and said, 'You must know your own mind, like the Bishop says,' and looked poison at me behind the Bishop's back. The Bishop hitched his khaki trousers and leaned forward in the wheezy wicker-chair.

'Put it abstractly, Mr Froad, nobody can be indifferent nowadays to the problem of power in Africa.'

Boss-man; sincere: couldn't help it: his generation. I said, 'Power for what, Bishop; power for getting things done?'

And the Chief bellowed, 'Mind y'tone, son, y'being out of place.'

Well, all right, then, I shut up. So did they. The silence spread backwards and told us a car had just started down the luscious gravel path next door that concealed these gardens from the main road; that the larks were happy; that Mrs Chief had banged a door upstairs. The noise of the car merged with the neutral sound of distant traffic. I let them squirm in their exalted certainties.

After a while the Bishop changed tack. 'The Arabs are fighting with religious conviction; the Mosque and the State are one, you see; they've a sense of mission.'

'And we've professional missionaries.'

'We've got to fight them with the same fervour.'

'Who, Bishop?'

'Why, the Arabs!'

'I mean, who to fight the Arabs?'

'Y'don't understand?' (Chief). Why go over all this again?'

And simultaneously, 'We're talking, let's get this straight, Mr Froad, of the Southern situation.' (Bishop, acidly.) 'You understand, don't you, there's no question of politics involved, no call for misplaced caution…purely religious matter. You'd be doing yourself no harm writing the articles for us.'

Articles!

I fumbled involuntarily in my back pocket for Mohammed's cheque. Not mine yet; I hadn't filled it in, but it was there, would remain there till I could get the whole thing straight. Selling

Christians to Arabs, Arabs to Christians: needed time to think out the difference. The Bishop was smiling. The Chief was talking. 'I've told him, Bishop; I've explained he is the only uncommitted person; that any message we have must get to the boys through a strong respected figure; that the Church can't play a hand in the heat of the general elections, and in any case Africans love personalities, real people. We've discussed it, Bishop, and he promised to let me have the thing yesterday. That's why I asked you to call this morning to see it. Now the young man from the *Southern Cross* will be here any minute; I don't know what we'll say.' And he glared at me again.

The Bishop cooed: 'And it's all in your line, too, your publications at the Institute: the thousand years of Christianity in the eastern Sahara, for instance, before the Moslem conquests. It could almost be semi-official.' Then in a different voice, as though the sermon over, now came the greetings and confidences at the church door. 'You're the only person we could turn to, as the Reverend says, they'd trust your word as a Christian Negro interested in the future of Africans in Africa. They need help, I tell you, against what's coming from the Moslems.'

'He knows all that, Bishop; something's happened to make him change his mind, I can see. What's it, son? What's on y'mind, why don't you stop fidgeting?'

Coming hard.

'Nothing, Chief.'

'Then why y'don't understand? What's the difficulty? Y'can't let us down. You'll write the thing now?'

'Don't know, Chief. I've…I must get back to work, I think; we'll talk. I mean I got to do some thinking, Bishop, y'see?'

I stopped in on the way home for a drink, fell asleep sprawled in Mohammed's chair, and woke too late to return Catherine's car.

6

So then…

Next time – second time – I go back, fecklessly threatening my kingdom. The thing is maddening, inconclusive; I want nothing of you: I've nothing to offer, anyway. What the hell! Dishonest fire-play; desire without love; tossing from each to each the responsibility that somebody in the end's bound to accept; daring each other, stalking each other; pushing too far; the guilty retractions, the ultimate elaborate breakings down; the reserve right of blame.

All a question of everybody minding his own future. My future – I cannot see it in your eyes, Eve. How about that, tell her that?

Whistling 'Grey Sand and White Sand' I went leaping – there was a bluebird in the eucalyptus tree; a pile of broken boxes beneath it – leaping up the stairs beside the inner courtyard of the 'Colony'.

Eve, do you know 'Where the Bee Sucks'?…'Thirty Days hath September'?…Do you know, Eve, 'Twinkle, twinkle, little star'?…

When I ask her that she'll look as though it doesn't matter; she'll open the smooth armpits and the delicate mouth and breathe through her suave skin, and draw herself mysteriously inside her flesh like eastern moon behind dark leaves.

If you don't, Eve, I don't know who you are!

And her smell, like humus on a forest floor, will come up from inside the bosom, for surely there it grows; and the dark light of her eyes like forest glooms will suggest without saying: There are things most ancient, man, between us; damp and rich and greener than all your learning. She'll sprout with meanings and break the earth in green spaces and heave, oh, and heave! And you will plunge from your treetop into the warm depths of creek-water, forgetting…

From the narrow veranda of the 'Colony' people have strung washing across the yard. Smell of frying and steam. Because of these people I knock on her door, preferring really to go straight in, find her with head dishevelled, tangled dress, clothes tailing from chair-backs, fecund.

I knock.

But towering above me, martial in khaki and brass, smelling of sun and leather, her husband Hassan!

Oooooh, strange wild sounds of lutes and cymbals! Hassan contained, suspicious; suave gaunt Negro, immaculate Arab poise, Arab gravity, Arab courtesy. Don't worry, Hassan, I am guiltless of her flesh. I plunge like a light into your worried eyes, guiltless. '*Salaam Aliek*, Hassan.'

'*W'Aliekum Salaam*. Welcome.'

And all not well, Hassan, not all well?

'Will you be seated, Mr Froad?'

You will not have her; you will not let her. She will not come back, you will not let her be.

'Won't stay a minute, Hassan, it's nothing; a message from her mother.'

'Eve's out.' And then, suspicious still, 'Her mother has not cut her off?'

'Cigarette, Hassan?'

'Thank you, Mr Froad, no.'

Flawless Muslim, of course! Many a wiser girl than Eve would flee her Christian father for you, Hassan.

'No, her mother did not cut her off; she comes here regularly, in fact; helps with the baby.'

A bough grazes and bangs the roof like someone impatient waiting.

'Eve's never told me that; of course there's no particular call for her to, is there?'

'Naturally, Hassan.'

'Eve's very independent, Mr Froad, isn't she! I speak to you almost as a member of her family. She's stubborn, don't you think?'

'Eve, you know,' I say, 'I do not know very well. Her family, yes; but she was already married when I came out, y'see, so I've seen her, really, only off and on. I certainly know her less well than you do. There was the time I ran you home, the both of you…'

'I know.'

'And afterwards –'

'Of course.'

Listening, us two, to the dusty morning sounds outside: the taxi-men (*Bahari! Bahari!*), the bottle pedlar's chant (*M'ak gizaaze! M'ak gizaaze!*), pieces of voices let free in air; machine-sounds purring, breaking, braking. And the bough against the roof. 'And what do you think of our country now, Mr Froad; the troubles, I mean?'

'The strikes, the demonstrations? Emotions, y'know, people easily swayed. No harm in Foreign Aid, I say. It'll pass; Johkresi are like that, most charming people in all the world. One could be very happy here.'

'One could, I agree; the people though, in spite of what you say, are not happy. Independence, you see, is a bitter lesson.'

Suddenly grave, self-contained, sure; responsible.

'Well, transition, of course! To be expected for a while, won't you say? You've had a long and confused history out here, after all. Will take time settling down; then there's all the various elements before imperialism still in the national character, if y'see what I mean.'

'Yes, I quite see.'

Hassan the graduate; taking the world unto himself. 'I know what you mean, but a great deal of it can be discounted, can't it? Our Islamic culture here in the North is all-embracing, integrating; very old…'

Hassan, first-generation Muslim, defensively extreme, spurning the base degrees. '…things rooted deep in us for building a state. You do not know, Mr Froad, very deep things.'

Self-justification. Never mind, Hassan, you were only young then, both of you, mere children. Nobody can blame either. You are not bad, I suppose, and now responsible.

'…an integrated people, an embracing culture.'

'It's something as a foreigner I always wonder at, actually; Johkresi culture, being so stubbornly itself after all this colonial rule. Something, I feel sure, to be proud of, though I've never understood it.' True too, that; no empty flattery. Only the senior and the shallow-ambitious in Johkara have any truck with the West. 'The Johkresi remain indifferently themselves, not so?'

His whole face a-smile under the velvety skin, but he remains thoughtful. 'You will have noticed the regrettable exceptions, I've no doubt. Unfortunately they are not few and not without influence. Still, as you say, our culture lives stubbornly on, and do you know why that is, Mr Froad? *A Muslim cannot take any man of another religion to be his brother, to be his guardian!* You see, by the way, why we cannot accept this Christian aid?'

'I see,' I say, looking deep into his earnest, soldier's face. First lieutenant; clean-shaved, head-shaved, pips gleaming metal support to the flat, stupid eyes. Go on, Officer Hassan; go on from strength to worse.

'It is our great good fortune, you see, Froad…'

Plain Froad now! Familiarity breeds attempt. Next thing trespass.

'Our great good fortune, you see, has been that we had a different language, a different religion, from the imperialists.' Crossing neatly stockinged legs, leaning back into Potamides's dusty cushions, leaf-eyes slanting arrogant assurance.

'You Americans, you're all called that, I suppose you know.'

I watched him lazily. I was a bit squiffy, by the way, that morning, and couldn't care less for hearing myself called a Magyar or a Croat. I let him rip. Money was on my mind mainly: cost of liquor chiefly. What with rum and whisky running to three and a half pounds a bottle (work it out at five-six bottles a month, the least, not counting entertaining), and you see how I was fixed. Then there was Faraed, eight pounds: electricity another six (all those fans, fridge, hotplate, iron, and radio), the old jalopy drinking another ten on its own for petrol and oil, added to which there was always some little extra shock; a new back axle, a new petrol pump… I started every month down, God's truth, and always ended the last week raising a few coppers from the Chief. I'm no kind of extravagant fellow, but I just couldn't ever say where the money went.

'…you took the Western languages, Western religion, didn't you? And with what result? Little Rock, Notting Hill.'

Impudent Hassan, begging for a whipping.

'…simply because you wished to be integrated, isn't it?'

'Real Arab double-think I call that, Hassan; we're both tenants in somebody else's house, only you're satisfied fooling yourself, we're not! The American Negro at any rate recognizes he's black –'

'He's been made to, you mean, Froad; he's not happy about it. In every way that matters he's white. Yourself, your real religion is integration, isn't it?'

Can nothing shake the little beast! 'You so content with your lodgings, Hassan? You're black, but don't dare face it.'

'We Arabs don't need to; the problem doesn't exist. A man only needs to be a Muslim…'

'The American Negro's broken with father, mother, Africa, all; that's a new kind of man, you'll see. It's why we're so modern.'

And Eve comes in. Stops dead, seeing Hassan, and involuntarily clutches the baby tighter. He moves to greet her but she recoils, frightened; a rain of silver droplets along her upper lip, along the line of forehead beneath the headscarf.

Brother of my blood, wife-whipping Hassan, your eyes fork and dart around this new situation, one down now. Who parted our mothers' legs – us three, all African?

'Sit down, Eve, just rest the baby here.' But she rests it beside her on the pillow, suspicious, a man could snatch his only child. *Son of a Muslim may not be a Christian.*

'And how are you, Eve, how's the boy?'

'The frogs at night…' In a tired beat-down bedroom voice I do not recognize, not looking at him, untying the headscarf. '…he's teething; they keep us awake.'

I say, 'These Johkara frogs, you know, they're the queerest I've ever heard – blowing like bellows, snorting, rattling like marbles in a jar – anything but croak decently.'

'So you do have your prejudices about our country, Froad.'

'No, Hassan, y'couldn't mean that. Way I seem to hear it it's no part of your country at all. They all sound coming up from the guts of mother earth, way beneath everything.'

'Depends on one's attitude, surely, as in everything else.' One down, hunting a whipping-boy.

'Well, if the honour of your blasted country rests with the frogs there's hope yet for you, Officer Hassan.' Hotting up.

But Eve, diplomatically, 'Did you wish to speak to me, Lobo?'

'Oh, your mother says would you like the baby to spend Sundays with her? The Reverend's at church, nothing much doing around the house.' Clean lie, but what was I to say with the man in such a state! What was I doing in the woman's room to begin with, that alone! Still I'd once heard her mother say if only the child could spend a few hours now and then, except that Eve was so stubborn she'd never hear of it.

But Hassan, alarmed, 'The point I'm here to make, Eve' – me understanding little, but enough – 'not a legal arrangement or anything like that, of course, not being divorced. My mother though…have the baby till you're settled; naturally only till you leave this place, till you're settled.' Very martial, Muslim husband Hassan. Treat a woman like bloody dirt. What chance would the girl have, giving you her child? Me pleading silently with eyes, Don't do it, Eve, let me take the baby home.

Unnecessarily.

'Will you come, then, for him Sundays, Lobo?' Ignoring him. 'And bring him back nights?'

Hassan then shouting: 'This is important, Eve, I tell you. While you haven't a proper home for the baby, I tell you…by law…' Towering over her, frightening her.

So I bawled him out, 'Aw shut up!' and levelled up with him. 'What y'really care about the child? Why y'don't support y' child? Where's the money for the child?' (Wrapping myself for the leap from the treetop; what for?) 'What's it matter who deserted who –'

He hit me so fast I'd no idea, the swine. I could hardly see him for stars. Wasn't easy, military man and all that, and Eve on my back howling. I brought him down, searching for something to break to hell. But the man was in form, breathing easy. He wasn't for it much either in front of Eve, Moslem husband and all that. He stood up and shoved my chest back an inch or two, contemptuously. Then turned his back and began brushing his uniform.

He said, 'You're not being very wise, are you?' Picked up his cap and swagger-cane. 'You're not being very honest either,' and went through the door.

Didn't care much for staying alone with Eve after that.

7

In the noble Conference Room of the palace the New Men strove for place, the New Black. From inscrutable portraits round the walls the Old White regarded them, the pressmen pressing expectant – phoenix moment – round the P.M., the P.M. in robes of gold and earth sitting at the table top, people along the veranda and in the great hallway crowding against doors and windows.

Someone said something, someone answered, 'Quiet; the press conference is beginning.'

A young pressman's voice fell on the hum like the last drop on a saturated landscape. Johkresi, tribal scars still looking painful, like dried-up trenches down each cheek, timidly asking, voice awe-struck and broken, about African Solidarity. 'You spoke at the reception, sir, of our essential unity…'

And the P.M.'s voice. 'This thing we have begun, it is inevitable; we cannot rest in the struggle until Africa is entirely free. We are committed; we've got it to do, and do it we must…'

The writing heads, the virgin pages; a few ounces of matter that would move great mass. New fragments of old words, rocks from ancient volcanoes, indifferent pieces fitted together to build new freedoms, new barriers, new securities. The scratching pens skipped along lit-up perspectives of self-liberation, self-conscious power, opening on to a neon future. The P.M.'s deep-sweet voice wrapped answers up in layers of reassurance, served them back round the long, oak table. Arab and African, black the both, borne each along on his particular hope. 'Africa will be free!' The past was ashes; a mystical future sending wave-impulses back to a hopeless past. The future hardening, tick-tackated like an alarm clock to its hour. Everyone saturated, the alarm would work off to the ultimate consummation: the orgasmic flood, the freedom realized, the old-thing butchered, the new-thing born.

Only wait, fit your life to waiting. Time moves backwards too; echoes of explosions yet to come.

Excitement bubbled and tumbled so loud around I hardly heard someone say: 'Got to work itself out; it's got to come right, else faith, love, things like that, is not true. Means God is some kinda whiteskin man.'

I turned to hear him speak. Black from down south. Mojo Kua: Church of England. Tribe: Bungoba. Race: African (pure, unsold). Education: Fourth Grade Elementary. Conjugal status: Married (to a girl of twelve). Profession: Journalist, *Southern Cross*. Culture: *Mare clausam*. This man once said to me: 'I am the true original thing, pure African. I've never been sold, never been a slave. I've got a name, Mr Lionel Froad, and a tribe. Now tell me who you are!' His mother's legs had never been parted by Crescent or by Cross. He was finishing:

'...on this question, sir, of race prejudice?'

But the P.M., oh, so diplomatic, or perverse, missed the point. 'Race prejudice, gentlemen, was the natural corollary of Colonial Exploitation...'

Odd, these words! Does one these days really speak of Exploitation, more dead and gone than, for a pick, Imperialism, Lynch Law, White Man's Burden; rubbed thin underfoot by a decade, two decades, of the mighty tramp back; blackened, lost in sharpness, sunk into minds now moored to new sounds? People these days speak of Tension, Commitment, Deplorable Propaganda, and Peace If – shining words, square at the edges, sharp still. No, Colonialism, already past-tensed, soon would have a second generation. Exploitation too a past-tense word.

'When Colonialism is finally stamped out race prejudice in all its forms will automatically disappear...'

And the question not answered. It will destroy Africa like a creeping plague, Arab and African, but no one dared now face it.

The Negro, anyway, took comfort. I pushed with the crowd into the sand-smothered evening.

8

Late again next morning, Sunday, because I'd followed the crowd out to the airport for the P.M.'s farewell.

Make things worse I stopped on an impulse outside the 'Colony' to warn Eve that I'd be fetching the baby to her mother, and found her dressing to go too to the airport. (Anything's a sight in Africa, any day.) So we went: baby in a wicker cot in the rear seat, she unnecessarily close.

At the airport the crowd was thick, gay for the hour, seventhirty, and waiting loudly. The helicopter, Eve said, was due at eight o'clock. I asked, 'What helicopter?'

'The new one,' she said. 'Y'don't read the papers? Goes now between Kutam and the airport, for passengers.'

'But it's only about a mile,' I said. 'What they want to spend all that money for?'

'That's not the point,' she said, so I asked, 'Wha' choo mean?' and she replied, 'It's not a question of the money, it's a question of we got to project the African Personality, y'don't see?'

When the crowd became impossible I had to hoist her on to my shoulders so she could behold for the last time the One Absolutely New. Don't remember a thing else about that farewell, except the pressure of her thighs against my ears. The skirt was full enough to cover her knees, the rest of it ballooned down my back. I had her by the ankles, and as the sleek Ilyushin swooshed almost vertically into the silver morning I went dizzily with it, dazed somehow. For, steadying myself, I gave her legs such a frantic pull she let out a yelp above the screaming crowd, above the screaming jets, and landed me a clout so fierce only the rabble pressing close kept me standing after that.

Couldn't understand this delirium, whatever it was – hell! I eased her to the ground, frightened silly; looked at her frank, headscarved, full-bodiced, full-skirted morning indifference and felt a monster. A sick sensation lodged itself with electric crepitations in the guts and wouldn't budge.

All the way back to the 'Colony', though, I talked fast, breathless, a great deal, drowning the thing off, throbbing worse than the engine in the old jalopy; but she didn't mind, hand it to her. Just sat there feeding my palpitations like a well-greased dynamo, waving to friends.

I took the baby to the Chief's. Had an excuse, too, pat and ready for Hughie, but he wasn't there. Catherine said he'd rung to explain that he'd gone straight on to the Ministry; would I complete the drawings for his paper on Meroitic Iron – important.

She was pretty in greenish mustard – chartreuse, faintly acid; sleeveless, neckline chaste, a catena of black buttons curving down her spine. I said, 'You know what it's all about, don't you?'

A flock of small yellow birds feeding on the lawn of the Kutam Club next door broke wing. We drifted down the veranda to my study door. 'Come in, sit down, I'm not all that curious really; only if he thinks he'll keep me sitting around... what the hell, makes him feel important or something?'

No usual little smile, as usual. Indirect eyes, indirect answer. 'You know him better than I do.'

'Y'better sit over there, over on the settee; don't bother telling me the place is in an awful mess.'

'Anyway you saw him yesterday at the Mission House party?'

'What's it he's after, Catherine, what's the mystery?'

She sat down, tucked her knees, fists over them. 'Lionel you know...'

'And you keeping his secrets, too, what am I to say to that!'

'*Plus ça change*, Lionel, you've ever heard that?' Putting on a bleakness meant to provoke (wild gorse, wild broom, peat on the plains of Ysbyty Ifan). 'What's it matter, all this?'

There she sat...

She said, 'The reception, the press conference, the airport, Friends of Thought, the Chief's garden party, Fridays with the natives...what's it you're really after, Lionel, how d'you find the time?'

No word about Mohammed, not a word! No, she was incapable of malice, subtle shafts, obliquity. There she sat: wholesome, upright, attentive. Just like the way she drove. 'After!' I exclaimed. 'Well, what y'mean, after! That lil' secretary's mind of yours, Chicken, really!'

'People often don't know, you know.'

'And how 'bout you?' Just like that: truculent. Sitting on the high stool by the drawing-table, leaning forward on my wrists over her, kind of, so she had to keep looking up; so now she was hurt she couldn't hide it a bit. She tried nevertheless keeping down, not answering, inching her hem through thumb and forefinger, but it showed plain so that I was sorry for her. 'All right, then; never mind. Suppose I start on that sketch-portrait right now, eh? Death-grey line, pure, pure, no colour; cold sad mouth; eyes…Dolores the Doleful, let's call it.'

Catherine's loveliest hurt. Then she's like those distilled, shadowless twilights you get at times in the Welsh valleys, illumined from the clouds. I added seriously, 'We've got a few minutes just to get started…' But she rose, arms swinging like bell-tongues clapping out an angelus. 'Oh, don't do that, Kate, don't go away.'

'You're supposed to be busy, and so am I.' And started picking her way through the bellied-out sheets and rolls of old drawings, smiling, you'd think, with them; remote.

'Really, Catherine, I'd soon have it finished; I mean that. Serious.' Wildly, for something to say. Five inches of curve along the nape of Catherine's neck, O my God!

'Not if you mean to put everything into it, as you always say; the memory, particularly, or whatever it is you call it.'

She was inching away like a thief, trailing something profoundly mine. 'Catherine, what's wrong with you now? Come back here!'

'What's wrong with *you*, Lionel?' Not even turning. The line of black buttons ended round the lumbar region. Eyes on them, I daren't move. Daren't.

'Catherine, I say, this can't go on, you know.'

She closed the door softly.

Best thing to do with that, I decided right away, was to marshall my resources for an offensive. Throw a greyish greeny-black sulk two three days, put her in the wrong; send her fishing in her own deeps, so she'd appreciate the shallows when she came wading back; bring her to her senses. She wasn't content with the appearance of a rolling stone seeming to gather some moss. No, she had to come poking and prying and sighing for the incrustations and accretions and obfuscations – the real thing. Puppy-licking. Full battery of silent reproof and all. Hell, I was having none of that – she'd see.

…and Hughie said would I complete the drawings for his paper on Meroitic Iron. So I did; so I worked right through that Sunday after everybody'd gone – no lunch, no siesta, blistering heat – till late evening. Then I took Eve's baby back, and returned to the drawings. Next day and the next the same, tray after tray, the waxed, rusted, decaying atrocities wrapped in cotton wool, indexed for the second burial. Minor domestic utensils mostly: tools, nails, knives, axe-heads, that kind of thing.

The big thing with Hughie was that he wanted to establish whether the iron we'd found at Old Karo was native-smelted or imported. Myself, I didn't give a damn; just did the pieces blind best I could, and that's saying something! Because, what did it matter? Whether they were Meroitic, or Lybico-Berber, or really Karatite? It mattered, he said, because if these people had smelted, then he wanted to know what had stopped them creating a truly powerful and far-reaching culture once they'd mastered the means of revolutionizing their society.

By Wednesday I'd done the work. Real first class! Lots of heavy-bladed spearheads that must have taken giants to wield. Axumite? Meroitic? North African? Or merely the teeth of a martial Karatite people bared on their own home front?

I had no doubt myself that this native iron-smelting had never existed; that Karo itself, in a way, could hardly be considered to have existed, since it was merely a breakaway princedom of the Kingdom of Meroë (faecal, as he himself had called it). I was sure that all our objects had filtered through from the parent culture, strained though relations had always been between them. (Meroë had, after all, been smelting since around the third century B.C., and we were examining a culture that had been founded some four hundred years after that!) I was sure no new society had taken root and flourished at Karo, simply on account of that persistent inertia among African peoples that has repeatedly and fruitlessly gobbled up the most provocative influences only to sink rapidly back into the long silence of exhaustion, broken only occasionally by the squalls of savagism. Not scholarly, but I had no doubt about this. I felt it in my system, in my bones, almost as a necessity.

Old Karo with its crumpled-eiderdown, camel-coloured landscapes, its strangled, pathetic, dead litter of pyramids, its cacographic carvings and reliefs, its beast-worship – all faeces! Africa was one great, stinking, sweltering pile of faeces, and the maggots sprouting in it had grown accustomed to the stench. I was one, sure. But why worry! Why burrow deeper! Why raise the putrid stench higher than one man could bear!

I did the drawings, iceberg eye, content with the petrified surface. I gave them to Hughie. He was enthralled. That was enough for me. I cared neither for the putrescent entrails nor the picked bones. Like a surgeon, indifferent to the question of life or death so long as the operation is perfect, I made my frigid record and was content. I dared any man push me further. Dared Hughie, that is, silently.

Yet he did, shoving his wet pipe-stem into my face and saying things like, 'Jolly good, old Froad, we're well away now, eh?' or 'Once we've disentangled this iron business we can get down to the aesthetics of the thing.'

Around the Saturday he dropped a gaping hint, 'Sometime when we've had a real first-hand look at the Meroitic stuff.'

'Like how?' I wanted to know.

He changed the subject.

I went one better: I discarded it (or tried to). Because I'd begun to guess at what was coming, to understand those mysterious visits to the Ministry; Catherine's silence. (She'd taken me up on my sulks, and wasn't budging.) Now I began to suspect she was in with him arranging some obstreperous visit to Meroë in pursuit of some of his more fanatical ends. The evidence was clear. a, This was something Hughie had always wanted to do.

(He was gone on Meroitic script, absolutely; and the fact that it was still undeciphered merely fed his frenzies.) *b*, The Sudan had just announced the completion of excavations at a Meroitic royal building – Amanishakete's palace, in fact – very similar, by the sound of it, to the one we were just digging at Old Karo. *c*, His determination to keep the subject of my supposed 'research' constantly in the forefront of my mind, by *d*, his yawning hints.

Apart from my total lack of interest in the matter and a determination to have not the least truck with art-scholarship, I loathed the thought of leaving Johkara for two reasons: First, Mohammed. His two weeks had gone by; no word from him. His blank cheque was burning my conscience somewhere; I had to resolve this indecision pretty soon. Second, I had a lot of very boring work to get through before May when we went on leave, the roads out to the desert being then closed for the rainy season, and not reopened until October. The digging season was therefore November to April with, in my time, a gap of a month for the Fast of Ramadhan. Before May, then, we had to complete some measurements and other work on site. The measurements concerned a few Axumite-looking sandstone columns (together with some barely perceptible design work on their capitals) before they were ruined by the rains. They were at present lying around exposed to sun and sand and wind, and couldn't be expected to be of any interest once the rainy season had wreaked its worst on them. They had to be done.

Worst of all, though, I hated having my interest forced – a thing that remained like a constant threatening charge between Hughie and me. I repeat this though I've said it before. Hughie was a person prepared to sacrifice himself and anyone over whom he had any authority, never mind how nebulous or unnecessary. This was his 'fatal flaw' in my way of thinking. I didn't resent him as my boss; in fact I respected him profoundly for qualities I knew to be lacking in myself. At times my feelings overflowed from mere respect into the most un-self-conscious love. Especially while out in the desert for weeks on end, or times we went hunting the gazelle. Something, though, about his ceaseless admonishing and iron example began round about this time to plant the beginnings of a nameless guilt in me. And this, coupled with my own doubts and troubles, I deeply resented. No one, I feel, has that right over another.

It was no part of my contract (or temperament) to engage in philosophic crap about the distribution of the Nile Frog motif, or neo-classical form in the rendering of the Meroitic physiognomy, or Hellenistic elements in Meroitic architecture, and all the rest. But Hughie felt this 'ought' to be done, and that I was the man to do it. For my part my choice has always lain with the simple present. I live in instants, you see; sensationally. That is my nature. As I believe it is with others of my race. Added to this, for personal reasons I also respect the condition of utter nescience; unlike, by the way, many of my race. I felt no responsibility for the past (bugger the past!) and wanted no truck with the future. Choice in the present was what was important to me; I didn't want that choice conditioned by obligations to past or future; I didn't want that right tampered with.

But Hughie chose to press. He was a man of strong will and effortlessly ingratiating influence. Besides, I was, as I have said, fond of him. I could see a climax ahead, and, best as I could, prepared for it.

It was Sunday. I'd waited all the morning for a phone call from Mohammed. Nothing. I was, in a way, relieved. I'd no idea what I could have said had he called, for to tell the truth I was as far as ever from a decision, or any clear idea of what a positive decision would imply. However, I was so agitated after lunch I couldn't have the usual siesta. So around four I went to see the Chief; Eve's baby needed to be taken back later, anyway.

Siesta. The whole country flat on its back. The streets lay down like dead zebras: ochre striped with black; so secret and private you felt you had no right. Goats noiselessly reduced careful hedges to skeletons; the hour your front gate is furtively opened and the animals let in to finish off the lawns; let in by the police, too, who show lethargic indignation in face of protest. (What else, O brother, are they to eat in this desert; why leave it all for the locusts, anyway?) High up, astride his camel, General Craig inspected the distances outside the palace gates from the depths of an imperial shadow; gazed back into the gory old days. Had himself cut to pieces, this man, putting down savagism and slave trade out here; now…but by their fruits…never mind. Somebody had to do it, the Johkresi say, spitting; so what! Competent bit of work; lifeless as the bronze it has wasted.

Past the Post Office, Pugin-style Gothic. Victorian Gothic, Victorian Regency, New Brutalism: Kutam. There was the square in the centre of the town across which the business headquarters fried drearily in their shadows. There were the pavements dotted with rust-coloured rags inside which people slept. There were the usual grease-spots of semi-nude mechanics, performing a languorous and approximate engineering on the guts of ancient souk lorries and decrepit taxicabs. These assaulted the donkeymen with indolent superiority. They were superior: they walked with the century.

There was a loud tumble and commotion from the top of the stairs at the Mission House. Trouble. In the shapes of two very black Southerners rolling and gasping down the stairs, fiercely tangled with each other. I leaped aside. They landed in a heap inside the door, the Chief pressing magisterially behind. 'Here!'…'There!'…the Chief never spoke in whispers. 'Leave him alone!' Tearing them apart. But not before the more agile of the two – a farouche-looking individual with a viperous little face and reddish eyes – had sprung up and landed the other an accurate one in the mouth with plimsolled feet. Blood. I stopped to help the shaking fellow upright while the Chief dealt, in his manner, with the other: much tugging, a great deal of stertorious rebuke, a few sharp clouts.

'…no way to go on…get you nowhere…House of God; dare you!' And so on.

A ferocious interchange of tribal dialect meanwhile threatened a further crisis, viper-face straining with an effect of frenzy against the Chief, spewing ancient curses. The other chap, still quaking under his blue polka-dot headscarf, was frantically transferring an incisor from between his fingers into his gums, taking it out, studying it with outraged disbelief, and shoving it in again. Over and over. Trying to keep his split upper lip free of the lower, which caused the blood and spittle to dribble down his singlet in gayish pink-and-orange ribbons. He looked festive.

The Chief pushed viper-face through the door and bolted it.

The wounded fellow, at last accepting that he'd lost a tooth, began to demonstrate and show off. He offered it around with a kind of perished whimper that had the quality of explaining the utterly incredible.

The Chief made short work of this; and of him. I wasted an hour running the fellow to the hospital, back to the police before he could be admitted, to the hospital once more, to a half-asleep Johkresi doctor and a queue of half a dozen blood-ribboned Southerners in 'Out Patients'.

When I got back the Chief explained, 'These boys, they fight all day Sunday – drink and fight; nothing to do; get restless and take it out on each other; frustration, you know.'

The 'boys': disposal workers, so-called (scavengers, really), had gone to the Chief to announce their intention to start a strike; to get his advice. Viper-eye was for striking forthwith – had in fact done a one-man walk-out on his own. Split-lip was for negotiation: had got his way with the Chief, who had anyway already raised the matter with the City Corporation and was awaiting action.

'It's like this; put yourself in their position. You could call them men and not men; y'can't blame them. Any man likes to know he has a meaning, after all. I've talked them quiet for a bit, but, mind you, it can't last; I can't see it lasting. Only a matter of stalling till I can get the Corporation people to think up something for them. See, these boys just don't believe the meek shall inherit the earth.' Laughing, as usual, at his joke.

I said, 'Really, though, fancy a city like this, no sewerage!'

And still laughing he replied: 'Well, home wasn't built in a day, son; you're in Africa, don't forget. Can't be home for a long time yet to come; no use hiding our heads in all this sand, is there?' I joined with a smile, make him feel good. Feeling good he continued: 'Know what they're striking for? Y'won't believe!'

'What, Chief?' I asked. Make him feel better.

Feeling better, he said, as though it was the most explicable thing in all the world, 'It's not money they're after; they striking for *daylight!*' Cool.

So just as cool, I asked, 'Y'don't mean they want to work *days*, Chief?'

'Just what they said. "We want to see our shadows." Their language is very poetic, son, very expressive. "A man not seeing his shadow, how can he know he's there!"'

'Lovely expressions, Chief, but think what it'd mean!'

'Be terrible, wouldn't it. We got to see this thing as a human problem, though, that's what it is; is what you call a human problem. They striking for more than money is what I'm meaning, and such things usually mean trouble, you take it from me.'

'Funny time to start these antics with the elections coming?'

'More in it than you think. Communists behind all this, I got a mind.' And let the matter drop mysteriously.

So we talked; prised the times apart; chipped and examined bits of it. And thought. He had me on his mind, I could tell, but he wasn't going to come the strong stuff all over again. 'Plantation time,' he said. 'That's the rock-bottom time. Puts things in the bones, son; it puts things deep into the bones.'

I turned that over. The Chief went back to the black rivers of the plantations, the white light. Up from slavery, no crying out loud. If the future was coming to meet you, anyway, better let it meet you coming. Nothing to come could be worse than what had been. Every day from there, therefore, a realization the more, a confirmation the more, an attitude learnt, an inflection assumed. For the slave-march up from the slave state, that was growth; a growth by accretion: an addition without total. Complex attitudes memorized, learned by rote, overlay the simple assumption: from this I can only rise.

From here the Chief looked out on race, from this rock bottom. Impossible to view the thing as before him his father had done, whose father had been a slave. The generations change; one man born into one thing, another into another.

'You, son, you do not know the rock-bottom time, you do not feel the plantations. That D.C. chap saying your face is not African – it's hard, I know, for a man like you – but he maybe could've been, in a way, right.'

Coming slow; the conscience stuff.

We talked the sun down the sky and the wind to whispers. The Chief stroked the corners of his mouth, thumb and forefinger, like I'd seen him do a thousand times; thoughtful. Like they say he did the time they told him Eve had run away with Hassan. 'Now these elections coming. Funny thing, you know, son; there's something the whiteskin people never taught us, y'know, something they mean us to find out for ourselves, y'don't think?'

Coming.

'Got a mind y'maybe right there, Chief.'

'This Africa's kind of…of *bleeding*, son; bleeding away. Y'see my meaning, son?'

Old conscience stuff; papa-pushing (y'gotta duty to the race, m'boy). O.K., Chief, shoot!

'What I'm meaning, I mean the times is decisive, son, if y'see what I mean.'

'I can see that, Chief; I see y'meaning.'

'Anybody standing by time like this, y'know…question of the future of power out here, put it that way.'

Coming.

'…just criminal, if y'ask me, irresponsible. Time's running out.'

Frontal approach. Do something, Froad. Say something you mean and feel.

' 'll all come right, Chief, else faith and love, things like that, mean God is some kinda whiteskin man.'

Yey! Mojo Kua. Sure. So what!

'What about the articles, m'boy, y'make up y'mind?'

Direct.

'Don't rightly know, Chief; can't rightly say. Still got some thinking to do, kind of.'

We talked the sun to death.

He rose for evensong. I took the baby home to Eve.

9

The little contretemps with the Southerners might have had something to do with it, I don't know, but curiously, by the time I arrived at the 'Colony', I knew the matter had been decided, and that I'd play for Mohammed. Bugger the Chief and his certainties. Some leopards think they have no spots simply because they have no mirrors. Others manage to know, somehow.

The matter had been decided because, without my taking any part in the process, the theme, title, even treatment of the first article presented itself formed in my mind.

'A Eunuch in the Desert!' Typewriting itself across the white sheet of headlight as I drove. 'The man was African, way back,' I'd write, 'from the Southlands of Egypt; from the land called "Of the Burnt Faces" by the Greeks; "Of the Blacks" by medieval Arabs; the "Kush" of Holy Writ; the land of Piankhy the Great, and Tarhaqa of the Book of Kings whose armies had fronted the Assyrian might; the land of the Candaces of Meroë, whose eunuch was baptized by Philip "on the way that goeth down from Jerusalem unto Gaza". This man was African, and he was a eunuch. And there you have it; our history in two words!'

And so on.

I should have been borne along on the flow of this rather lurid approach and rushed home to put the thing down while I could, had not Eve come downstairs to fetch the baby.

She'd been waiting more than ordinarily impatiently it seemed, not for me, clearly; from the way she was dressed, which suggested private and feminine involvement in Sunday trivia; no time for guests. But one look at the hair done into shiny black knots skewered by curling-pins, the dark, greasy neck and shoulders, the shapeless, fusty, half-dirty day-before-yesterday's frock with the ripped-down arm-hole, her confident, absorbed management as she hoisted the child on to her shoulders and pulled two-three scraps of this and that out of the cot with the same movement, made me far forget the eunuch and his disabilities. I mounted the stairs behind her, carrying the cot.

'Your mother says to tell you she's got the Farex,' I invented.

'What Farex?' And as I didn't answer she began grumbling absently. 'Been awful here all day without him.' Him, the little black ball, slumbered with the face of Grief on her shoulder. (Some babies, really!) 'He'll keep me awake now all night, you bet.' Which seemed, looking at the little man, most improbable.

I resented her indifference; felt like shouting into her back what the hell she thought I was getting out of it all. But I realized I'd tangled myself, no one but me to blame. I'd leaped from my treetops all right. Now this complicity with her mother to get the baby home, to get the prodigal herself eventually back, well, no one had forced me to it. It'd all started, of course, with that little lie I'd been forced to tell Hassan about Mrs Chief wanting the baby. What, though, was I to do with a suspicious Moslem husband!

At the top of the stairs I put some of my resentment into, 'Y'haven't even asked about your father!' and took a last look round at the world before diving into the scents and presences of her room.

After the sun a lingering, uncertain sediment of heat oozed from the walls of buildings, rose from roofs and pavements, and was trapped beneath the trees. Around the rim of horizon could be seen the silver incandescence where sand-clouds hung, lit up from the city lights. The glittering serpentine hollowness far behind, beyond everything, that was the river. Kutam West, an area of the imagination in the farthest darkness. Beyond it the final unproduced desert spaces; roads north to the Sahara. Way back behind, back beyond advertising neon and the three red lights on the mast of Broadcasting House, roads south to Johkara's Equatorial Province.

Below, white-robed crowds swarmed out of back streets and sand roads, clustered like night pests round street-lamps and shop-windows, loitered, sprawled, left behind the aimless strew of trapped people revengefully enjoying themselves. Trapped, because, in spite of its many foreign amenities, Kutam is physically an oasis town, and there are times in the year when everybody begins to feel it. The next month – April – would be the last you could call normal. After that a kind of repressed hysteria until the release of the rains: moisture and clouds, and puddles in the streets.

Eve's room had grown flesh over the skeleton of it I'd seen in the morning: clothes, underwear, half-open drawers, slippers, litter of various greases and balms on the dressing-table, a half-used lipstick tube, the floral-linen cover on the bed tumbled and insulted. She'd evidently spent the day wandering through the various compartments of herself and turning her few disastrous errors out for an airing.

She laid the baby down in the cot.

'Like how y'mean, ask about him?' she challenged. 'What's it to me, what y'talking about?' like a person stamping something unpleasant into the earth, out of sight.

She toed her slippers off and more or less collapsed on to the bed; released something in her public personality, that is – like a woman shedding a corset with a sigh – and let her spirit free.

I don't know whether there's much point in trying to describe Eve, though I'm aware that I've not yet done so. I don't even know whether I can, because so much of what most profoundly moved me about her was not external, and naturally not everyone would have been as susceptible as I was. The overwhelming quality of her personality was one of imperturbable sullenness. For want of other means I liked to compare her to physical things: to the gloom on forest floors, to dark silent creek-water, to the immense black rivers of my South American home; the virginal strength of our equatorial forests. But Eve should more accurately be compared to certain sombre psychological states: to the nausea of inspiration, say, or to the nameless yearning for origins that besets most of us, or the compulsive, sick, sinking gloom of the spirit in the state of utter desire, or fear, or longing, or guilt. I think, looking back, that she was captive to some obscure state of guilt or fear, whose source she was herself far from knowing, but which pervaded every attitude of hers and stamped her with her characteristic secrecy and defensiveness. She was resonant as a result; contained, unfathomable, indifferent. And no mirth could relieve this.

Her flesh, well, yes…she was exotic. And in the most common sense. From the moment I first set eyes on her I had an image of her freshly drowned in the burgundy-red water of one of our plantation rivers, among the floating, orange-coloured plums and withered leaves fallen from overhanging trees, smothered with poinsettia drifting over her body and through her black hair. She always seemed to me improperly dressed in the fashionable European clothes she wore. Which I know now to be the reason I preferred to see her unkempt and dowdy, raw, earthy, nearer to the natural state.

I sat unbidden in the armchair opposite the bed. 'I mean about the baby, what he felt having the baby; y'not interested?' Dammit the girl ought to be shown at least how good I'm being to her. Y'don't care?' And, as her flat dark stare said she didn't in the least, I blurted out, 'Heaven's sake, be reasonable, girl; it all depends on that!'

Couldn't've said anything more silly. 'All?' she asked, puzzled. She stopped swinging her legs. Then I could see her slowly begin to take the situation in. My little role – solicitous uncle, mother's confidante, whatever it was – amused her. Of course! It was all my own meddling and fiddling. What had she to do with it! But I didn't like it one bit more for realizing this. I didn't like it either when she repeated, provokingly, 'I wonder what you mean, all?'

So I flared up. 'I should never've bloody given you that lift to begin with, that's where it all started – that's what's all. Messing around!' And found I was in a kind of panic.

'Lobo, like I've told you before, I don't know what y'mean.' Small, smooth voice. I searched her face for mischief. Just as well look for the bottom of Lake Titicaca. Nothing in the jungle mammal's eyes, the moonlight voice. She began swirling her legs playfully, teasingly, leaning back into her shoulders, like she was saying, 'Next move's yours, now go on, play!'

'Hell, it's up to you what attitude you take; what do I care! Sooner or later you'll come to realize this can't go on. I mean' – gesturing cruelly round the room – 'I mean, you'll see in the end the old man's all you've got.'

'Y'don't have to shout! I really don't see who this is all for; Papa, or Mamma, or…or who?' The 'who' grated out with the sound of a bolt drawn from a rusty lock, followed rapidly with a screechy, 'Who th'hell asked you to come fetching my baby and meddling, anyway?'

And I heard myself shriek, 'Meddling!' very loudly. 'What y'mean meddle, eh?' And I'd covered the few feet separating us and landed her a clout across the mouth. The ingratitude hurt like a wound. I shouted, 'Mind y'talk!' and belted her another; good hard one this time. 'Mind how y'talking!' She must've been seeing stars by now, because she bent over and made no move to dodge the third blow. 'Don't talk me back that way!'

She screamed and leaped up and started clawing, so I palmed her face and shoved it back downwards. She fell on to the bed. I jumped her with knees in the stomach. 'Shut up, y'lil' fool, y'want everybody up here?' Trembling something silly. 'Shut up, I tell you,' holding a back-hand poised over her eye. 'Y'don't know your friends?'

And she began blubbering more softly, 'Y'hit ma head on the wall, y'brute; I'll show you.'

So I warned her. 'Y'better understand, Eve, right now…it's nothing to me, all this, I tell you. Get that? If y'don't mean to go back to your father…'

But something in her face made me stop. It'd gone like new-fired brick; I could see the flush under the sepia. No feeling. The image of her father had blocked everything. A look had settled round her eyes should have told me I was battering on a spot long beaten numb; but I went on, 'Y'just got to reckon it out for y'self if you don't want to be reasonable; don't count on me.'

I eased off then, and went back to the armchair.

'You mean, bullying swine, y'call y'self a man? Y'think any woman can count on a thing like you? I hate you, y'hear me say? I hate the both of you, y'understand?'

I said, 'Aw, shut up, Chrissake, y'making me angry!'

And she bawled, 'Get outa here, y'dog!'

I let her lick her wounds and smack her broken chops and sulk a bit. Finished a cigarette I wasn't tasting. I realized the last thing I really wanted was for her to go back. Her eyes were dark and hurt with tears. She was lovely; freshly drowned. Chief didn't deserve her. Nothing in me wanted her to go back to her father. Why the hell then was I molesting the woman! She said, 'I'll make you pay, Lobo; I'll mess you for hurting me like this.' And passed her juicy upper arm across her eyes. 'I'll mess you good, you wait!' With real hatred.

'What's the use!'

'Ask y'own self that! Y're the same like him, the same: a mean, nasty bully. Why y'don't go and leave me alone?'

'I'll leave you alone all right, that's just what I mean to do. We'll see what happens when your money runs out. That bride money can't last for ever, we'll see! You made a Moslem child and Hassan won't let you be; we'll see…'

'Why y'bullying me, Lobo, and…and…frightening me so; what y'getting out of it? I tell you I'm not going back home, if it means I end on the streets. Lobo, y'don't know how to treat a woman and talk to a woman.'

'Why y'messing the old man to me for? What's it y'after, tell me say?'

'What th'hell y'think I care about him? What y'think I care about Muslim and Christian and the whole of you? Leave me alone. Y'don't think I want to be free like anybody else? Go sit with Papa and leave me alone.'

'If Hassan hadn't beaten the hell off you, half killed you, if it'd worked out all right, a fat lot you would've cared now making mess about the old man. You leave the old man be, see?'

She folded herself moodily into the kind of night-bag-overall thing she was wearing, and wrapped the shadows round her, moving in her own stillness like a Bacongo carving, like any piece of good sculpture should. She was a fetish figure propped up in the leafy glooms waiting for the sacrifice, waiting for the blood, for somebody's blood. Like hell she was waiting.

'It's you who's like the old man,' I stalled.

'I thought you liked him, that he's your best friend and all that. Really, I never met a deceitful swine like you, Lobo, y'got no feelings? Y'can't feel nothing for nobody?'

'O.K., leave that be, Eve, I'm not having any more of that.'

She drew her legs up under her, and the skirt skinned out backwards over her knees. 'When you stop feeling guilty that you're not African you'd be easier, that's what's the wrong with you.'

Her play. Damn' well done too!

'You'd be more honest too,' she added, coming sharp.

A knock on the door. Two-three lightning movements and she'd hitched herself together, tied the hanging waistband, stepped into her slippers, and opened the door. Sure wanted that to look fast and smooth. Well, this is it!

I heard the wife of the proprietor apologize in a high, hurried voice. Greek accent; richly flavoured flood of protests, slight fat panting and heaving that said urgent, my car was blocking her husband's garage door. Red, with the roof-cloth broken, no? So sweet, the peeping hag.

Eve opened the door so I could speak up for myself. I could see the great blowzy woman blocking the veranda light, cobwebby black hair haloed against the ceiling. I prevaricated long enough to register an uncompromising image, correct the impression of fracas of a few moments ago. All right, the 'Colony's' a respectable place, Mrs Hag, make what you like of me being here.

All the way down the stairs I listened to her grumble between the layers of fat the good life in Kutam had wrapped around her. 'So many times a day chasing people around; it's a big place, all these stairs…' Inverted pride.

'Better than sponge-hunting in Mykonos though, eh, Mrs Potamides?'

No answer; didn't even seem to hear. 'So many things to think of day in day out, everybody wanting something all the same time. Y'know when we had the British here, not a trouble, I remember…'

'The British set you people up all right out here, didn't they? What y'grumbling about?'

Potamides stood placidly by his garage at the 'out' end of the driveway, underneath the sign he'd himself clearly painted in English, Arabic, and Greek: 'Please, No parking here.' To which some local wit had added in Arabic, 'But don't go anywhere else; we want him fat'. And decorated with rude *grafitti*.

Life was fat and easy for Potamides. Uneasy too. The Johkresi didn't like life too fat and too easy for predatory aliens now things were in their hands. Potamides had to look sharp; but he knew how. 'It's always the younger men,' he joked anxiously. 'You

93

Johkresi young men,' mis-identifying me as many people did. 'So happy-go-lucky, eh? The people with the large cars, they think more.'

'Which is why they have the large cars, not so?'

He let out an obsequious bull-roar and landed me a punch in the shoulder with his great butcher's fist. I cleared his doorway and he went in to extract the glittering white mammoth – latest edition – from its cave.

'Genius!' I exclaimed, as the unleashed beast breathed past.

'Life's little pleasures, you know.' He embraced the purring power, and slithered slowly out into the avenue, the car winking maliciously, like a child being rude.

'Living off the fat of the bloody land out here.' Just for something to say as I settled back into Eve's armchair.

But she objected literally. 'Fat of the land nothing. Y'think these Greeks know anything about the land? They trade and pile up their cash and smuggle it out, but the land's ours; they can't touch that!' Fiercely, with pride. Now what the hell does that feel like?

Catherine and her granite hillsides and ruins and legends and history flitted through my mind. Now what the hell does it really feel like? Hughie and his traditions and his burden and his conscientious fanaticism. The Chief and his certainty and his duty and truth and all that. Every man a place! I'm like the bloody scavengers; no shadow.

Eve had done a lightning job on her hair; transformed the lumps into tight shiny curls that now caught the light and gave her face density and mystery. Like a ritual mask smothered in animal fat and buried in dung, and unearthed and polished and set up on a shrine. She fixed me with her sacrificed gazelle's eyes, waiting. Her dress, though, was the same: some crazy synthetic stuff that had shrunk the wrong way in the wash.

'Why y'don't stop worrying so much about Africa? That Greek's not worrying, man. Only foreigners and people like you…people out here just thinking how to eat and live.'

'So then what y'think I'm doing?'

'Y'got a good fat job, I can't understand why y'chewing y'self up for.'

Talking with the voice of the ancestors. Coming right. This is where I rend my cloth and cover my skin with ash and prostrate myself, and sacrifice the white cockerel, and spew the blood all over her. All over her face and everything, and mess her.

She got up and threw open the shutters. 'Hot inside here, y'don't feel it?'

The neon glow from the 'Colony' sign spread a film of crimson across her neck and shoulders. She turned back towards the room; sat again on the bed-edge. A sick silence. A radio monologue which had been providing soporific Arabic background noises somewhere in the hotel now ceased abruptly. I felt pitchforked into the sudden vacuum like a solo singer who hears the orchestra die behind him.

She said, 'Is really no use for anybody to go on chewing himself, is there!'

She said, 'I mean is not as though y'getting anything out of it; y'looking thin, if y'ask me.'

She said: 'Y'don't enjoy y'r work, Lobo, or something? Why y'always fighting and chewing so?'

She said: 'Y'don't want to be happy, man? Y'eating y'self away like a rabies dog.'

Sweating wind. Scent of neem. Bough grazing the roof like the sound coming through deep water. She was measuring. Like a deep-sea creature measuring its distance from a depth-charge. She said, 'Time y'start thinking about getting married or something, y'know.'

'Come over here!' jumped out of me. Stern, abrupt. Made her start. The play went out of her eyes like a light. She sat watching me astonished, unmoving.

'Come here!' And this time I ripped the words out so rough she rose in a kind of fear, took two faltering steps to right beside the armchair, and stood over me agape.

'Switch the light off!'

She dragged herself in slow motion to the door. As they reached for the switch her fingers trembled slightly. She half turned to face me, tried a little smile that seemed sick and silly, then plunged the room into darkness. The glow coming through the window from the neon sign drenched her in crimson from the neck downwards. Below the waist she melted into the gloom. I watched her like wary cat measuring inches of snake. Heard my voice rasp out:

'On!'

The light jammed the four walls of the room into my eyes. There was the captive acquiescence, the tense grey waiting. My solo virtuosity astonished me. I might've been alone in the room for all she mattered.

'Lock the door!'

And swiftly she drew her breath: two continuous gasps like a child ceasing to sob. She turned the key hastily, missed, tried again more slowly, elaborately, anxious to make no mistake, then tested it. Secure, she turned, still grasping the door-handle. Her breasts heaved violently out into the red light, then collapsed into the darkness under a great sigh.

'Switch off!'

And I eased back into the chair, head touching the hard cold wall. Real water at the heart of the mirage. I couldn't believe it, I couldn't! Fumbled, though, in my pockets. An unpaid electricity bill, Mohammed's blank cheque…

Felt her come close; smelled her flesh; felt her weight. 'Look, Chicken, I got to go.'

'Lobo!' Astounded. Coiling tight, rubbing like an anaconda feeling for the bone beneath the skin. 'Lobo, what y'mean?'

'Got to go, Chicken, forgot something,' easing from her clutch.

'Please, Lobo, be a gentleman to me; how can you go, what's it matter now?'

She wasn't budging, so I shoved her and got up. She began blubbering and talking a lot of stuff I couldn't be bothered to understand.

'All right, maybe I'll come back,' I said, and unlocked the door. Then she was on my back; screaming, biting, sucking me in. 'Lobo, y'swine, y'can't go now, y'hear?' Wetting me all over; ears, throat, everything.

Hell, I really had to rough her then. 'Haul off, y'savage, y'hear me say?' and gave her a hardish shove. Trying to come free, that's all, but she went down on to her knees. You never know how much a woman's hurt; lot of pretence, mostly. She was crying like a child, knees and forehead on the floor.

'Bloody selfish if y'ask me,' I said to her. 'I forgot something, I tell you, y'don't believe? Y'can't wait?'

No answer, so I banged the door and pushed off.

Got me into such a state, that, I found myself heading for the houses of the Ethiopian women and their thousand-and-ones. Those women knew how to make a man happy, no nonsense and messing. But on the way I thought I heard a wrong sort of noise in the car engine. Couldn't be sure, so I changed my mind.

10

By mid-week I couldn't stand the strain any longer of waiting on Mohammed. I wrote the 'Eunuch'. Not a bad piece of thinking; the facts! Not simply a matter of making a case, there were facts. Evolution of the Negro within Western Institutions; the break with Africa – a new race. Negro in the New World: his dynamic synthesis. Period of tutelage, period of independent creative growth, period of self-definition. Future of the Negro within Arab-Islamic framework – a creative challenge. The lie of blood: the inevitability of environment. Facts!

After I'd got all that settled I said to the Chief that if Christianity had been an understood idea-force out here all these centuries Africa'd now be giving aid to underdeveloped countries all over the place; we'd been dabbling with the thing long enough and we'd better forget it, where's it getting anybody…

'Don't talk disrespectful!' he said, superstitiously. 'Y'don't fear the Lord, son?'

'Nothing personal, Chief,' I said. 'I'm just thinking about Africa: future of power and all that, and why I don't feel to write that stuff for the Bishop.'

But he shot out: 'Think of my thirty-odd years out here and don't be so selfish. Y'want to destroy everything I done in the twinkling of an eye? What will I tell the Bishop; why y'don't get a grip on something?'

Didn't answer that one. Couldn't have him undermining Mohammed's money with his certainties. A bastard's indifferent to father and mother, both; possesses the naked instant, bare of past or future.

11

Where, though, was Mohammed!

Monday morning, quivering with anxiety, barking easily, fingers trembling when I spoke to Hughie. His time was past by more than a week. Typically, I hadn't the least idea where he was to be found. Felt I'd go to pieces if he didn't call soon. I'd settled everything; I was ready. Where the hell was the man!

I sat before the Lepsius portfolio staring blindly at his raceless Meroitic people. Bags of work, but…Catherine dropped in for a chat. Self-contained, taut. She walked over to the window and watched the flock of yellow birds at their customary cascading from the tamarhindi hedge on to the lawn and back again. It was hot. The ceiling fan groaned and stirred up an oppressive odour of dead air, cobweb, old paint. For lightening the atmosphere I started on the old rib about the sketch. 'Wouldn't be your head so much, y'know; not your wide cheekbones, your delicate nose, those silent lips. Nor your mothering eyes nor the brooding in your shoulders…' Her shoulders did brood, like an ocean. 'No, what I'd go for would be – know what I've always said? – the thing that will never come back however you pine after it, the memory…'

She was looking minutely into the far ochre, as though trying to anchor the mirage with her will. There was the sun furiously dematerializing the landscape, sinking its teeth into the river, flattening the desert beyond the hills. There was the purple distance, the Arabian sky.

'No use telling you you've got it all wrong, is there, since it's what you wish to believe?' She turned away from the window.

'Sit over there,' I said. 'What's it you think I've got so wrong, then?'

'They'll be having a difficult time for Ramadhan this year, it's so very hot. When's Ramadhan, by the way?'

'No idea; you pay more attention to these things than I do.'

'Funny the way it gets hot all of a sudden like this, isn't it?'

Tension easing, *Hamdilela!* 'Means things'll begin to get interesting now.'

'In what way?'

'Y'haven't noticed! I always find people go funny round about April, May; lose their heads, kind of. I mean everybody, not only the local people. Chap in the bank I remember last year, English chap I know, couldn't remember his name when it came to signing his cheque.'

'Lionel!'

'*W'Allahi!* People go funny, y'must've noticed. Why y'think we got to get outa the country for three whole months? Been worked out, scientific.'

'What about all those who have to stay?'

'It's what I'm telling you; they go funny. Look last year, all that fuss over Foreign Aid, all the demonstrations; it was just about this time. You'll see, after the elections.'

'After the elections there'll be Ramadhan; they'll go to sleep then.'

'Worse when they wake up. Y'know the Arab mind, worse when frustrated by idleness; and it's always frustrated.'

'You're in a funny mood, Lionel.'

'Like how?'

'You're…what's worrying you, tell me?'

'Why y'say that? Nothing's worrying me.'

She knew all right.

'Lionel, if you're having anything to do with that Mohammed, you…'

Pause. Sweat trickling down the small of my back; grandfathers' flutters in the guts. 'Y'don't mean to say y'been worrying all this time, Chicken? F'get it, I tell you; I haven't even seen the man.'

'Don't Lionel…'

I wondered, gaping. Where'd the woman get her assurance?

'…or there can never be anything further between us,' she said. 'It's what I wanted to say.'

The Lepsius portfolio – the *Denkmaeler*, whatever that means, I've never asked Hughie – was compiled by an indefatigable traveller of that name and his team of artists, round about the middle of the nineteenth century. It is invaluable, thorough, Teutonic, massive (its cabinet is as large as a large fridge), impressive, inaccurate – nobody knows how inaccurate since many of the sites and buildings are no more: the earliest graphic record of the sites and ruins of the Egyptian, Napatan, and Meroitic civilizations of antiquity, and a pillar, naturally, of the archaeology of the Nile basin.

One flaw: the people he portrayed! At first I took no notice of these; mere diagrams, I told myself, and why not? The details of pyramids and pyramid-chapels, their plans, the location and appearance of vanished sites, the character and content of the art of the various periods – that's what the thing was meant to talk about. And there for me the matter would happily have rested had Hughie not kept prodding me, pestering me, about my responsibility to my people, duty to my people, that sort of thing, and particularly forcing me on to some *tour de force* of art-scholarship in which I'd single out the wheat from the chaff in Meroitic Art and demonstrate once and for all (better than and long before Ifé) the ancient creativity of this Negro kingdom, *ergo*, of my race.

Ha! Nobody even knew what the people looked like, let alone that they were Negro. Added to which, all the bright chaps who'd worked Meroë from the turn of the century onwards (those who'd felt the matter to be worthy of attention) had fallen over backwards proving that the Meroitic was not a Negro culture at all! Negroid, declared one splitter of ethnographical hairs, but not Negro!

Lepsius was no help. Not that I went to him for help. I had no problem. It was an understood, unwritten part of my work to relate it, wherever I could, to the work of contiguous or in any other way related cultures. Design-wise, that is. For instance, a column excavated at Old Karo could have design affinities with one from a Meroitic palace, which in turn could have Axumite, or even Roman, echoes. The horned gods we were unearthing could have religious significance relating to the Amon cult of Egypt, to the sacred ram of Meroë, to the Shango cult of Nigeria, and even farther south to rites in the Congo basin. A *kohl* pot would certainly be of Egyptian origin, a bronze lamp of Roman, an amphora of Hellenistic, and so on. There were even Chinese and Indian correspondences in a few cases, since Axum had certainly traded in antiquity with the Far East. Very interesting, but of course not for me to speculate upon.

It was Hughie who, by profession, belonged to that race of fabulists or pied pipers whose business it is to charm us out into the desert spaces with their desert songs and there leave us footlessly listening to the empty music of their spades down the corridors of time. But this distinction I could never get Hughie to allow.

My work that morning had taken me to the tenth volume of the *Denkmaeler*. The problem was simply to relate a convention of drawing which had appeared on a fragment from one of our pyramid-chapel façades to its design source at what, in this case, I believed to be the Egyptian temple at Philae. Some personage flaying the hell out of a group of other personages hanging like a bunch of grapes from a branch. I suppose I was in a jumpy, light-headed state of mind at the time, for suddenly, out of the page that I had seen a thousand times, leaped the image, pure and simple and shatteringly original, of Eve!

Why hadn't I thought of it before, this thing that so strangely compelled me to the woman! Later I came to ask myself which image had first stirred something in the depths and brought about the confusion that was to follow? Eve herself? Or this timeless African creature?

Now, though, there it was. On one of the hundreds of reliefs I'd worked for the past two years. Amanishakete – I went right away to Hughie's books for this – 12–2 B.C. Gave me the worst turn I've ever had in my life, before or since.

The drawing was as lively as the efforts of the average biology master in a council school, but there was no mistaking the incipient steatopygy, the thick square shoulders, the down-pointing, almond-shaped breasts, the pear-shaped backside. I was trembling. I had to get to the bottom of this. But Hughie came in.

One look, you could tell he'd been through the treacle and tedium of a Johkara Ministry. The way it had rubbed the pink and glow off his after-shave type of freshness; the way it had stencilled grave shadows round the thinking eyes and fixed the mouth in opposition; the way he now sat splitting matchsticks with his fingernails and picking the pieces from where they fell on to the carpet. Khaki Hughie.

'So that's the position, old chap, and no use letting it get you down like this. If it means putting forward your leave a bit, well, that's rather a trifling inconvenience, isn't it? considering…'

'Considering this golden self-created opportunity of a real first-hand Meroitic inquest, eh? All that royal-tombs-of-Kush business, pyramid-pilfering business, temples-rotting-in-the-sun business; and inscriptions, oh, and inscriptions! You'd go without leave altogether for those, wouldn't you! Well, it can all damn' well wait. Me who's to get through the hundreds of bloody drawings before May, not to mention the business out at Old Karo. Why can't it wait till next season? Our work, as you know, can't.'

Not Hughie's kind of talk at all. But though you could usually foresee them, it wasn't easy to find the tactics to forestall his lines of objection. He came in like a tank, whatever you said. Always, to begin with, the same narrow, more or less direct, appeal to sense of duty. (Ignore that.) Then the stuff about the joys, the real lasting value, of original work in the field. (Laugh.) In the end, though, the final grating carry-on (Hughie had a rapid, rattling voice, like the Johkara frogs: marbles in a glass jar), his carry-on about responsibility: a man's particular responsibility to race and region (which was sacred and obligatory in face of everything), as well as his general responsibility (to himself) to take possession of some bit of the future for the sake of the future. Example: 'Seems to me in a matter like this, Froad, it's downright betrayal not to consider oneself the only instrument capable of performing the particular function and to hell with one's feelings!' (At all costs that must be headed off in time. Several times it had meant simply giving in.)

'The point though, you see, Froad, is it just won't keep, either. The whole palace is exposed now; inside it's only sun-dried brick, you know. What d'you suppose it'll be like after leave, after the rains? There isn't a roof on the thing, you know; it's why the

Khartoum people have invited us over just now. They'll be paying off their men in time for Ramadhan, and then that's that; no guides, nothing. Why wait? Short notice and all that, I know, but it's nearly three weeks now I've been after Ministry approval. There's the Karo work of course, as you say, but then there's one's duty to these people, dammit. I wish you were less pushed, naturally, but there it is.'

'Well, as you know, Hughie, I've got myself down for the twenty-fifth of May; you sent in the leave sheets yourself.' From the back of my head. 'I got plans, you see, difficult to change.'

I turned then and caught his calm, firm expression, so I rapidly countered the coming objection (leave's a privilege, old man, not a right) with, ' 'Course, the work comes first and all that, and it's for you to say.' Eyes on the floor.

He rose and with heavy energy, indicating imminent boredom, began walking towards the desk where I'd left the Lepsius opened. 'Glad you see it that way, actually,' putting the unlit pipe between his teeth. 'Besides, since you don't pin much faith in this bag of tricks, now's your chance, isn't it?' He looked up with a smile that made no pretence at levity.

The sibilant whispering coming from the bowl of the empty pipe irritated me. So did his aseptic men's-dept. smell.

'It's all hardly been touched, man, think what it could mean to you!' Rocking on to his toes like an insurance agent displaying an unquestionably attractive policy. Low premiums, painless deductions, and consider what your loved ones stand to gain…

'Taking into account the long view, Froad, surely…' A Brighton-and-Hove smoothness creeping into the voice; the improbable frog-moan of Egyptian music penetrating from somewhere.

This is the moment to let out the big-mouth nigger-laugh, or spit through the window, or something. He's probing, searching; show him now the nothingness he'll find.

'…a whole new field to be opened up in Meroitic studies…I can't think of anyone more capable than yourself…knowledge of Greco-Roman, Egypto-Roman forms…African background into the bargain, you see. This business of establishing a distinctive aesthetic as the life-force in Meroitic Art…debunking old Lepsius…crucial…'

'Shite!'

He fell silent, still looking at the book.

After a moment, 'Have it your way,' fingers reaching with fake indifference into his pockets.

'Why th'hell, then, don't you let me!'

He went slowly over to the drawing-table and absently began rolling the ruling-line across the board. 'Trouble is, old man, you so much enjoy observing these poses you strike.'

'Right, we won't quarrel, eh, Hughie? What's your orders? If only you'd stop preaching and just give the bloody orders…'

'Would that be of the slightest use, d'you think? For the next three weeks we've got to eat, sleep, and work together in the desert. I don't have to tell you what that means, do I?' Sandstone covering metal: Hughie covering Hughie.

'Even if I was interested, Hughie, y'realize it'd take years?'

'My dear man, of course! You couldn't arrive at conclusions in a thing like this in a few weeks. I mean, there're so many things you'd have to get behind before ever you come to studying design motifs: religion, for instance, its effect on the plastic culture; then there's the development of the native script; number, and its effect on trade, all the artistic influences resulting from contact with other cultures through trade. Then you'd come to the social revolution brought on by the use of iron, and the effect of that on the plastic impulse. This palace we're going to study…bound to be a wealth of historical clues in the architectural motifs, the building technique, and all that. I mean it's such a chance for you, don't you see, Froad? By the time you come to the design idea in pottery, the treatment of the human figure in the reliefs, their original conventions in three-dimensional sculpture, well, yes, years…you've got stuff to live on there for years.'

Hughie projecting Hughie; as usual. 'I don't live on stuff, Hughie. I'm not interested in the future; I've no sense of it, y'don't understand?' I hung from the high stool and began dangling one leg, casually, to prevent the thing becoming too intense this time. I had my reasons. I didn't want a row; didn't want to be forced to give way over Meroë. I had to stay in Kutam at all costs because of Mohammed.

He said, flippantly, 'Of course, that's another of your treasured poses, isn't it!' Jab of iron outcropping the sandstone surface. But at once he went on in a conciliatory tone: 'It would mean so much, you see, if this thing were done by a person like yourself.'

'To who?'

'Why, to your people. Some time or other you'll have to take over in the real sense, you know.'

I tried to match his well-bred calm with, 'So, then, Hughie, since you won't give your orders, lemme just tell you what I want, we can maybe strike a bargain...' Then I became conscious of imitating his attitude, stopped, lost my temper, and bellowed: 'Dammit, man, who th'hell y'think I am! Twisting, probing, suggesting. Who give you the right; y'think I don't know my own mind? Since you –'

But the door opened and Catherine came in. I considered hastily whether or not to finish the sentence. She said, 'You've missed your breakfast, Dr King,' in a hurried little voice. 'Shall I send for something?'

(A small stab of maybe jealousy pricked me at that.) Hughie swung round towards her like a giant bird changing course in flight, took a long time focussing her meaning. 'No, no, never mind, Miss Hughes; nice of you. Did the telegram go off, by the way?'

Telegram! Well, there was no question of it now. I finished the sentence in a quick loud rush. 'Y'd better decide between Meroë and your blasted work, Hughie, because I'm going end of May.'

In the silence that followed Catherine glanced uneasily from Hughie to me, then back again to Hughie. Her gaze remained enquiringly on his face. 'Yes,' she ventured. 'As soon as you dictated it.' Timid, wondering, sure she hadn't done wrong.

Hughie put out a satisfied grin; show who was emotionally on top. 'We've just been on to the old ticket again about responsibility. Froad here [oh, that *here*!], as you know, feels no obligation...' And in the grand manner wafted his presence round towards me. But he stopped suddenly, as though I'd interrupted him. He added slowly, 'Oh, well, don't let it get under your skin, old chap, never mind!'

'Oh, bugger that man,' I spewed. 'Don't let it get under your skin; don't take on so; don't for God's sake get nettled; don't get hot under the collar! What th'hell y'think? Don't let your hair down! Well, my hair's not the sort can come down; not like yours. Me, I'm like none of yours – get that? So take your beak from out my clothes, and your heart from off my beak.'

Stepped back to gain distance, to take Catherine in. 'Take your clothes from off my heart!' And the stool fell over. Very nearly, too, did I go with it. Clutching manfully at the thing – what the hell was it? – bulging impossibly from my pants' pocket, confusion for a moment met Catherine's worried gaze. 'You anyone-but-you Sunday-teacher! Chapel-hound…you…you…'

I managed to come free of the clutching stool, bellowed again, 'Look!' Like midnight man grappling with sorely menacing bedclothes. I continued stepping backwards and didn't stop back-backing till the corner of the cupboard sliced me in the back with a sharp metallic presence. Startled, I looked round at the thing, defensively, suspiciously (not wanting to take my eyes off *them*!), as at further unseen threat just about to declare. Then the cupboard insolently swung its door open; slowly, heading like a slow slap towards my face, coloured inks grinning maliciously from the darkness of the shelves. With a furious baying I slammed the door to, heard the catch grip, heard falsetto shriek wildly uncoil like steel rope leaving a winch, heard my sound, 'Hammer and anvil man, hell!'

Clenched my teeth. I saw Catherine look swiftly round the room for trace of, presumably, liquor (she must've thought I was naming a public house). Hughie went pillar-box-on-crowded-railway-platform red, but private and detached. I heard, '…and you can do better than that, I hope, by way of witty nicknames!' Acid, isolated; Hughie clean off the mark as usual. 'Now just pull yourself together.'

He began moving off. I heard him mention 'the proof sheets' to Catherine; heard him grasp the door-handle; heard the marble voice rattle out, 'Because we're leaving Saturday.'

Jesus Lord!

I saw Catherine move towards the settee from the line of fire. I took one stiff, careful step away from the cupboard, feeling like a man who has lashed out with bare hand at a fly and found only a bloody mess on his fingers. I took another. Against painful inner resistance a third. Then my body came round the drawing-table; I could feel it beneath me. Dragged along the edge of the drawing-board my fingers at last fell off, fell down my side, and I was alone.

With all those five paces across the carpet to Hughie.

I heard, '*Wait!*'

And Hughie glanced up. Resigned indifference, fingers lightly touching the door-handle. Gradually, though, fascination, then something like apprehensive respect in his expression, eyes tightened to extremity by the puckering lower lid. Inside me, then, something shouted, '*The cat!*'

And I stopped dead.

Saw again myself crossing, footstep after leaden footstep, the five hollow paces of carpet to where the chain was drawn taut from one arm to the next of the armchair. Leaping wildly, the cat had coiled and tightened the thing about its neck, and hung now twitching, hoarsely croaking: a low, strangled, twisted croaking.

The empty house echoed. The cat hung. Circled shuddering from its gibbet it hung, mouth-hole uselessly gasping. I saw again myself stand like dead stone, gaping; felt again in the guts my own life groping outwards, not breathing; heard again, inside myself, Touch it now it'll die; leave it alone! And the cat, circling on its gibbet, flung out a screaming claw that touched, grasped cushion, scrambled wildly, lost hold.

Cat dying, gurgling. Me, grasping my head, shrieked, '*No!*' in furious fright.

In furious fright cat hearing, leaped; sprang all at once in every direction, teeth skinned clean, claws clean, all bone clean and jerking, flesh strained against the gripping steel. Somewhere, something giving, cat landed free, spat, lay flat, panting, on its side.

In the darkened empty house it grated its life back like old wood against roofs. Then its eyes stood open, unseeing still. Violently trembling I quickly crushed its life.

Hughie stood like stone dead, staring. Circling from my gibbet I closed my words with care.

'*Leave me alone*, Hughie!' Then, pathetically, 'Can't you understand, man?'

Then, in the centre of the carpet, I was sick.

12

Round the whole deep circle of foliage, and from every depth and distance, the persistent melancholy contralto weeping as into the pit of somebody's grave, 'Who you, who you, who you…'

Sometimes, from disquietingly near, 'Oh, who're you, who're you, oh…'

They said it was the turtle-dove, not to worry. Purplish, covered with ash. A mourner.

I lunged at the coarse manly-looking insect that had landed on the pillow and stood now with slow impudence, rubbing hands together within an inch of my eye. The blow stunned the fly. I flicked it swiftly on to the tiled floor of the veranda; with slow satisfaction ground it with my boot-heel. That I hoped was the last of them inside the mesh.

I lay back on the *angarib*, lulled by the sight of other insects searching the mesh for flaws. Watched the cunning beast-play of the spiders and the lizards – the master-minds among the mass. Watched the higgledy-piggledy undifferentiated mass itself: common prey-stuff; with not a thought in their heads, every variety of crawling, wriggling, thriving, unambitious life silhouetted against the afternoon sky. Then the scavenger lot: the coarse, ungainly, anty, carcass-dragging scum, carrying bodies many times their size to distant lairs. The master-minds feed on living prey, the scavengers on dead. The master-minds need shrewdness, vigilance, speed, efficiency; most of all foresight: all virtues to do with some view of time. The scavengers, inevitably posterior to action, merely need brawn. But the master-minds and the scavengers meet on levels unsuspected by the thriving mass.

Mid-March, a fitful untidy wind blowing, it would seem, in accurately vertical blasts; splaying tree-heads open, whirling butterflies like protesting snowflakes everywhere. All over all the gardens the leaves growling protest too, with voice of forests. But if that makes wind at all to shift, it would be only for here and not for long, so in the silence here there will be a growl back yonder, like counterpoint from distant brass waiting to rejoin the swelling theme. In face of which surging hooray for a withering winter, small birds make sturdy piccolo sounds, wildly defiant, regularly drowned by ring of ass-brays sounding distant chorus.

No, but this peace is sweet; wind bending green, stripping flowers, polishing bare the metal sky.

I sipped hot sherry, gulped iced water; sprawled luxuriously, feet sloping against the mesh.

Thing about each meanest creature up there...

Fly nosing enquiringly up to where faint silver threads fanned against the light. With a venomous leap the spider darted. The fly laughed merrily, circling far. Furiously the spider puffed and pumped its frustration out on threadlike legs. I'll get you yet, my man.

Nah, nah, laughed the fly.

Each meanest creature a place...

Light slanting through the new vine-leaves tinted the metal. Wild vine. You could almost watch it pull green from earth, twist and uncoil the young tendrils with blind life. Like a satisfying drawing; like a good dancer.

The wind lifted the tree-heads up by their chins, so you could see the bare, straining necks, the lifted collar-bones.

No, this peace is deep.

Sudden frantic buzzing, vibrating along the mesh. Pouncing furiously upon the caught fly the spider wound and spun – spun fly caught like a capstan inside straining ropes – wound the delicate silk tight, crushed the buzzing power. Bound, strung by arms and legs, that fly must be grossly screaming now; hurting... Uselessly screaming as the spider slowly jerks terribly backwards, back into a darkness, there in poisonous leisure to suck it dry. Must hear loud bells buzzing through the gripping silk; metallic mesh-sound vibrating of distant telephones sounding from world of life, shattering all earth. Poor fly going down a darkness backwards. Not crushed, like under the heel of my boot, but sucked; sucked and spewed empty forth for the scavengers.

Buzzing calling along endless silken threads…

With a start I surfaced; came back to; broke through the film of dream, ran to the telephone. Catherine!

'Something wrong, Catherine?'

'No, I just wondered, are you all right now?'

'You had me in your web. I mean I dreamt you were a crab!'

I saw her face close to mine as the nausea had come pumping up; her shoes on the dusty blue carpet spattered with bits of slime; felt the cool, tender fingers on my forehead. Ages of not caring, sitting on the old settee, Catherine saying: 'Never mind, you'll be all right now; you're tired. It's the desert. You shouldn't work such long stretches without a break; not in your nature.' I saw again the silken hairs of her armpits.

'I mean I was a fly, I think.'

'You sound as though you should be in bed.'

'That's just where I am.'

'With a doctor.'

'One's enough.'

'You shouldn't really be going on this tour, either.'

'What to do! It's not that I feel tired or anything like that; don't feel a bit tired. Other business, actually.'

'Thing is, Lionel, this is so important, isn't it!'

'Oh no, not to me; not for putting off my leave.'

And she fell silent. So I shouted quickly, 'Catherine!'

'Softly; I'm still here.'

'Where's Jill?'

'In her room somewhere, I suppose, asleep or something; why?'

'Just wondered!' Trying all I knew to keep her. 'Don't you ever rest after lunch?'

'I don't sleep, if that's what you mean; can't sleep in the daytime.'

'You should, though, in this climate; tells on you otherwise in the long run, they say.'

'I wake up feeling dreadful; we're not all alike, you know.'

'What do you do, then?'

'Oh, just things, you know; d'you sleep?'

'You bet!'

And she said, in a concluding voice, 'Well, I'm glad you're better, anyway.'

So I hurriedly put in, 'Catherine, hey, I was thinking –'

'Tomorrow would do. Better get back to your rest.'

So I shouted again, 'Hey!'

'Yes?'

'Y'know "Twinkle, twinkle Little Star"?'

'Yes, why?'

'Y'know "Where the Bee Sucks"? "Thirty Days hath September"? Catherine, I bet y'don't know "Tyger, Tyger, Burning Bright", with a Y…tell me…'

'Lionel, go back to bed this minute.'

'What y'wearing now, Catherine, right now?' But I heard the line go dead. So I went back to bed.

Tossed and sweated in the consuming heat, and my mind went back to the time, a year back, not quite…

Hughie sharing the last drop of radiator water to save our dehydrated bodies, and laughing about it too, to give us courage…

That was a time! Hughie saying, 'We can't be here for long; something'll come by sooner or later, give us petrol!'

Hughie the only man white among us and we believing him, of course. Even knowing it was the day the roads closed for the rainy season; that the last trucks were through; that the roads would now be empty for four long months to come; would soon be obliterated in the fury of the desert rains; that the law meant it, meant to save lives. But Hughie, talking, 'If they say the roads close on May the tenth, there's bound to be somebody going through on May the twelfth; Johkresi are like that.' Smiling, in his manner, lower lip only.

May the twelfth nobody going through; last trucks gone. Yet who was the man to worry! Not much water, and who was to know that eating makes you thirsty? Who was to care!

Us all drinking the water, drinking free. Five men not setting up for a siege or anything, we drank it. It didn't go far. Even so, something was bound to come along.

'Because it is a heavy road!'

'A main road!'

'Someone's sure to come along.'

'Sure they'll send to find us.'

'If the rains don't come.'

Our first trek together, Hughie just come out. Me believing in his work, in us working together. Liking him. Us happy on trek. Two, and three to do the cooking and the baggage; good chaps; except for that fellow leading us so close the river we got stuck in the clay three o'clock of the morning, me driving.

We would've had it then, wasn't for the sand-planks. Wasn't for Hughie's eyes intelligently seeing.

'See, the wheels spin on the offside only, where the slush is; the nearside wheels don't move. Means the earth is solid there.'

Hughie's boots stamping the surface clay, firm and deceptive, knowing. Me, wondering into his intelligent eyes. His car on its belly and new; no panic. 'Means if we get down to the slush and force the sand-planks under…'

Hughie cool.

Land Rovers are notorious in slushy mud, four-drive or else; not much good. Nothing's much good in slushy mud except for using up the juice. It's the low-gear ratios use up the juice; and the four-drive. Four-drive's much too strong for slush and mud: digs too deep, sinks you down. Four-drive's good for traction, good for using up the drink, water boiling, power going. You need the transfer drive at times like that. And the sand-planks shoved like iron skis beneath the wheels.

Hughie after hours, cool. Scraping the slush with tyre-levers. Methodical. No panic. Hughie on his belly, going down and down to the slush until the wheels came free in a grave long as two men, deep like two men, where they had been buried.

'Clean the wheels and let them dry. Clay caked on will give them grip.'

Daybreak opening back the desert. Chill on the river, but Hughie sweating like a water-bag. 'Fill the trench with trash; dry it out. Lay pebbles down!'

'No pebbles, Hughie, here.'

'Then dry earth; break earth and lay it smooth; shove sand-planks under!'

The hours it took; Hughie cool, covered with clinging slush drying out and caking on his arm. You could see it bite the pink and make it white. Covered in clay like a mourning savage. A man like Hughie! Me, eyes clinging to him, thinking white men made to master matter, see the point in things. No panic; no feeling.

Me, though, liking Hughie's cold intelligence; clear apart mind. Even striving for a kind of stony expression like his, bawling, 'Two nearside wheels straining to the nearside pull!' Which was so stupid I could feel the shame-hairs raise up on the seven little bones at the back of my neck, he not even bothering to answer; of course, since it was he doing it and he could feel the thing rocking in his seat and along the bottom of his legs. The car standing on the sand-planks in the slush, straining like a plough-horse to the low-gear pull, growling spent power through the exhaust. Magnificent things, these cars…

When Hughie got her out.

And that's where – nobody's fault – the petrol went.

And three days later, three hundred miles from water, radiator rationed cup by cup, we sat there hating Hughie, him sitting brown and stern across the bumper, shotgun in his lap. Me therefore thinking: This kind of thing becomes the white men. Natural masters; moral imperative, that sort of thing. Each man his drop of rusty water! White man answering to the future; that's the difference. If it means somebody's blood for the present you answer for the future. That's the big difference. No feeling, man; Jesus!

But wasn't for Hughie's mind, what would've happened then!

Us all crouching that second day round the front of the car, hating him. Me, eyes clinging to his intelligent eyes, clear, keen as a lion's, loving him.

The sweat stood on our skins the third day. Losing water. Bad! Hughie would not leave the radiator; the men would not leave the car; the car would not leave where it stood, petrol gone. So by the time the sun went the men were howling, sweat on their skins, fire in their throats. Like beasts!

He had to drain the radiator then, me thinking perhaps just as well, they would sure have killed him. And I should've had to fight over his body for a drink, he having kept all the cartridges.

Fourth day, water gone. Men crying out four days. Crying to Hughie like he should've known. The last trucks surely gone. Food dry, bread like stone. No will to eat; mouth dry. Only water, drink water, O God water!…water!

Retching in the guts.

Drying in the eyes.

Lightning in the head.

Hughie!

That same night Hughie chopping up the cartridges, us all watching. Hughie silent. He chopped them up. He put the gun behind the seat inside the cab. He sat with us under a tree. No shade much, thorns; branches withered. Acacia scrub; life irreducible. Us all looking at him, looking to him. He quiet; us all quiet.

That was the day we stopped moving, no one deciding or thinking about it. Stopped being separate; stopped blaming or talking, us all one now, seeing into one another, breath coming, going, solid; rasping. Coming into one another like one thing withering slowly, windless. Drained, dry, dying.

Fifth day Hughie said: 'Wrap close in your blankets. Don't move; don't do anything at all.'

And I wanted to cry how his voice was: soundless, scraping. And his tongue taking ages lifting like boiling lead over the ridges of his teeth. His head went down like he was crying too. But nobody could cry, there being no water. Then his head came up. As long as you can see a man's eyes, believe me…

His lips began to move, and the scraping came out different from the movement, like Hassan's *haboba* talking about when she was a child, time General Craig's guns broke the skies apart. His lips moved slowly open…slowly only, because along the fibres he was forcing them to obey, you could tell. You could see Hughie's will shove his lips down, they trembling and white. But he could not make them sound. Because life's breath's not for a man to force. No man may force that.

Hughie, mouth down soundless, waiting.

Like one who stammers.

Sound then scraped its own path along the windpipe, and

flaked off when it met the tongue; flaked or fell off whole, so he said much more than we heard. In chunks.

'...don't speak!...'

His eyes closed like he was going to die, me watching, feeling nothing, watching them take ages opening.

'...don't even speak!...'

And we knew the rest was, If you speak you die!

And time went. And every trace of feeling.

And shadows began to search the sand of vultures against the sun.

Then Hughie began to talk. Urgently; like one mad. Made warped noises that seemed to turn inward and seek the guts, and strangle him in the insides.

No man answered. Him speaking like that frightened a man. A man making sounds like that; faced striped like that. A man like Hughie! I stretched over and whacked him one across the ear, him whimpering a bit, no one even moving, not looking even. Me trembling all over from the effort.

Could be heard all that day and after...

magnified crystal tinkling of sand colliding and falling; faraway buzzing.

Could be seen...

crystal streaks and flashes; bodiless explosions without centre; flies crawling all over faces; shadows searching of vultures against the sun.

Could be felt...nothing at all!

Huddled in sand beneath thorn-bushes, scared. Waiting to scream, but fearing that would never stop. Scared and numb, whispering with eyes desperately into one another.

Until the sixth day.

An aeroplane went by the sixth day; going to Shaggerat. Sixth day tongues sticking to roofs of mouths. Silence. Now only out of one another's eyes life lifting. You couldn't hear the silence any more. Not for the thunder in your ears. Us all crawling into the shadow of the car, close together away from the trees because of things at night.

Sixth day me saying to them all, 'Don't sleep!' Not knowing why but knowing surely, If you sleep you die!

116

No one answering, but after that they all looking to me in silence they could no longer hear. Us all looking into one another, fear connecting. Fever burning. May, but the shivering under the sun; the retching in the guts; the drying in the skin! You couldn't feel when it tore on the face, only on the lips. The lips you couldn't touch, tongue sticking.

Us all perspiring no more, gathering with eyes to see one pass water.

Drops!

After that no one moving at all, us all hoping against sleep. Don't sleep!

Remembering only this in the shimmering darkness, If you sleep you die!

Watching through the night. Watching next morning a savage with a spear come along the track. Watching with no interest a naked man walk along the road; hearing with no interest what he said:

'The lights went slowly round the bend beneath the trees. The lights went round the bend looking for something; looking for you. I saw them in the sky last night.'

The waiting without interest.

Seventh day effort to move the eyes, no one looking to anyone. Effort to keep the eyes open, us all, each on his own, dying on his own, past thinking that they'd sent to search for us; that savage had been right.

Three trucks came in the seventh day along three separate roads. Us being long past where the three roads met, three separate trucks came down from Shaggerat to find us.

'Soak down the *kisra*; soak it down and dry it out! Don't give them water.'

'Don't give a man water?'

'Not a man water; water's too strong, burst their vitals. *Kisra* mashed to a baby's pulp trickling down the throat, give them that.'

'Water too strong for a dying man?'

'Water, I tell you, too strong. Squeeze *kisra* dry.'

'And a cigarette? This one needs a cigarette.'

'Let him have a cigarette. After a bit, mind you; after a bit.'

Me having one too soon and it knocking me down like an express train. Me going out…

Me next to Hughie, Hughie next to another, each next to each in the hospital at Shaggerat. One, they say, gone to drink from golden streams beyond the sunset. One endlessly weeping.

Hughie's lips like fallen leaves; his fingernails rotted and fallen. Hughie's skin like carbon, broken and falling.

After you have died with a chap you should forget the trifles.

13

That phone call led to my first big mistake with Catherine, and to all the rest; because next day when she asked, 'What was it you were trying to say?' I answered, tongue in cheek, 'Just wanted to take you for a swim.'

I know she thought I meant the Club Pool – from the casual way she said, 'Well, that'd be nice, but I've got Garden Circle today, important.'

'What could be important,' I wanted to know, 'about a lot of females sitting around on somebody's lawn talking about "them" or "these people", and grumbling about prices? Come on!' I said.

'Tomorrow?' she suggested, and unrolled some sheets from the typewriter in a final manner.

So I promised to pick her up about four, and went round to Eve's to work off the disappointment. Lot of bother and fumbling; hot and cold. And the chain round her neck with the crucifix thing: ripped that and sent it flying. She threatened again to mess me. I said, 'Hell with you,' towering over her, naked.

She said: 'I know now I could kill you, Lobo, easy! I hate you, just you wait.' Threatening, as usual, in her manner.

Next afternoon at four o'clock we went to the river. Catherine was alarmed, I knew, though she didn't show it. No European in Johkara swam in the river; in fact no one but fishermen did: purely utilitarian. Besides, there were crocodiles. I didn't tell her that. I said, 'Perfect place this for a rape, eh?'

'It's lovely,' she said, to show she wasn't alarmed.

There was the stretch of virgin sand scored like a white wound between cold blue water and the dense vegetation. There were the rusty, cast-iron hills, the steely sky. There was a *felucca* inching timelessly down the flow; there was the small silver sound of birds, the nervous fluttering shadows, the hard, exploring sun.

There was the carpet of yellow leaves blown before the blossoms. There was a dried-out clay-pit, a disused earth-kiln, a roofless watch-hut.

'You know,' she said, 'I think we've made a mistake coming here, don't you?'

We had, though I didn't know that yet. I tossed her floppy straw hat aside. She watched it fall, then looked at me in a sensible manner. (Modern, intelligent, responsible. Ha!) 'I've not much of a thing for beaches, as you'll see.' Behind her sunglasses. I took those off.

'Never mind, you've come a long way from your Gothic perch; you'll do.'

Then stripped and left her. Ran down the steep incline from the trees into the open sun, across the burning sand – a good five hundred yards – and into the water, and didn't stop running till I fell headlong. Surfaced, took a delicious breath of air I could almost taste, and haloo-ed back to where she sat among the trees. Couldn't see her; I struck out for the opposite bank.

I breast-stroked the play of the wavelets, silver drops flashing and dancing in directionless motion above my head. Interminable instants. I thrust against the womb-pull of the river, threshing unconsciously. What time it took – twenty minutes, three times that – I couldn't tell. Not a bit tired, I clambered up the far bank, utterly released, no self, no consciousness, inhaling solid draughts of air; drunk. The current had dragged me far to the north. Now I could see the tiny mustard-coloured speck of her swimsuit against the luminous sand; felt I shouldn't have left her alone in such a deserted spot. Felt, too, self returning, so I ran half a mile or so up-current – much less than that would have done – to allow for the river-pull back to her, and plunged in once more.

Blue concentric rings kept working inwards towards my eyeballs, exploding in tiny flashes as I collapsed, grunting like a sea-cow, where she sat in the shallows. She said, 'I'd have been impressed with half that, you silly man.'

Couldn't answer; feeling suddenly terribly sick.

'Here; come and rest your head on me.'

In the pit of her damp thighs. Could as well have been damp stone for all I was conscious just then. She pressed her thumbs into my temples and worked them firmly round in circles. Worked wonders, brushing the river-fleas away, not saying much, sitting calm. Like a dove in the shade at noon that lets out an occasional satisfied coo-coo.

Slowly the pounding in my chest, in my ears and neck, the spasmodic tremors along the legs, subsided; the trembling in the fingers. I began to notice the colour of the sky, to sense again the wild freshness in the air, to be conscious of where I lay, a speck in the exhilarating spaces of Africa, cheek against the comforting moisture of her belly, cushioned in her splayed-out thighs.

She was looking down. I saw her face against the sky, peeping out of the egg-shape of the white bathing-cap: two opposed ovals, like a classical O. Very sweet. Puppy-licking.

'Now you're feeling small and vulnerable and afraid you could be gobbled up, eh?' I didn't like that; didn't answer. She put two fingers over my eyes. 'Now if I had to do a portrait of you' – put another finger over my mouth – 'I'd…I know you'd like one of those terribly *tachiste* things – all manner of coloured lines tangling each other, called "*Me Judice*" or something like that. But no, I'd simply draw a rather thick, perfectly round, circle – one colour – with a tiny gap left in the circumference to bring time into the thing; internal time, external time.'

'Clever!' I mumbled, acidly.

'Because time's your cross, you see, little man.'

I kissed the palm of her left hand and snuggled my face into the damp swimsuit round her belly. Then wondered why I was feeling so flat.

'Think I need a cigarette,' I said, and sat up abruptly.

'They sent your plane tickets, by the way, today. This time tomorrow you'll be in the Sudan.'

'F'get the bloody office, Chicken, God's sake!' Irritably; something far from right somewhere.

'Then let's go get the cigarettes, eh? They're in the car, I think.'

Extravagant desert sunset; extravagant colour settling mistily through layers of atmospheric sand. Freckles on her shoulders. Something in the way she moved: controlled, full of memory, ancient: the bones of the suggestion always present inside her clothes. 'You look damn' all right on a beach, you know. Take the cap off, let's see your crowning glory against the sun.'

Day-to-day public colour on the limbs, private indoor colour on the body; secret cupboard-colour in the armpits, up the thighs. What a difference, these two women! She was stooping, sifting particles of gold-dust from the river silt, letting it fall in handfuls into the water, wondering at the slow play of the spangles glittering; absorbed, like a very small child. 'Really incredible, isn't it?'

I unbuttoned her swimming-cap and peeled it off. 'Look for the explosion that follows the sinking of the sun – what's it called – something to remember.'

She gazed dutifully. 'I didn't know it had a name; I've never seen it.' Huddled, earnest, honest.

'Best of all on the West Indian beaches,' I boasted. 'Hits you smack in the eye.'

After ages: 'I didn't see it, did you? You were talking…'

'You must've blinked. That wouldn't do.'

'I…now I can't see you; where are you, oh!'

I helped her to her feet. We began walking back to the trees, arms round waists. Dusk smell, river smell, smell of damp bathing clothes, damp skin. Delicious presence, but why was I feeling so flat!

She leaned heavily against me, scuffing up the sand as she went, like a tired child, trailing the bathing-cap. Her hair in the wind licked softly at my shoulders and neck. Circle of grey: Whistler grey. Pale blue lights of Kutam Bridge shafting the river in the distance; the last incandescent glow of sand-particles in the sky. Early stars. Whistler evening.

'This time tomorrow you'll be in the Sudan.'

I didn't answer.

'Lionel!'

'Umm-hmm?'

'Do you love me?'

Well, I wanted to say, now don't spoil it, Chicken, but I didn't want to say that. She skipped around and pressed me to a stop, gently holding me by the shoulders, blocking the way. 'I mean, are you content with me? that's all I want to know.' Simply, no emphasis, her fairness outlawing the darkness around her, as though she had secretly retained some of the afterglow of the sun.

I said cautiously, 'It was a mistake coming here, y'agree?'

She said nothing; didn't move: merely stood lighting me up so I couldn't stand there any longer doing nothing. I put both arms round her waist, noted the sensation of her size (rather ample by modern standards, but I liked that), and kissed her. Well, I don't know how I felt, sick or elated or what. The flatness was still there, but coloured now by a confusion I couldn't understand. I kissed her; but not unconsciously, not deliriously. Myself, I could never get what people mean by that sort of thing. I don't think she was unconscious or delirious either. She hardly even seemed satisfied when I let her go. Certainly not serene or any of the things you would've expected, given the circumstances and the setting. Me, I felt a kind of gratitude, and that's all I can say there was to it.

Except for the anxiety.

We came to the steep incline and entered once more among the vegetation. There was the mud-walled watch-hut where she had concealed our clothes. There was a patch of white *gellabiya* against a lantern moving away into the plantations. There was an enormous breakdown in one wall of the mud hut. There was a thorn tree growing in the centre of the earth floor. There was the Pole Star and the Plough.

I had not reason to follow her there, and wished afterwards that I hadn't. I didn't particularly wish to, I knew, which is perhaps why I went. We were both dry enough by now, but for the elastic in the swimsuits, the hems, the seams in the wool; yet she fished out an enormous beach-towel and handed it silently to me.

'Don't need this, do you?' I objected feebly. The answer in her eyes was unequivocal. I kissed her again, this time in panic. Terrifying how naturally she slipped out of the costume and brought her damp nudity close. I leaned against the tree inside the house and thought to ask, What about that cigarette? I haven't yet had it. Which was absurd. So I said, 'We mustn't do anything silly, y'know.'

But she was so close I began to worry that surely she'd find out; touch me or something. Try as I might I couldn't conjure up the faintest flicker. In fact the whole lower region of my body felt not there. Not numb or anything like that; just not there!

I leaned against the tree in a manner that made it difficult for her to come too close, but I couldn't hold that too long: felt the strain. For something to do I made tepid fingering gestures in her hair, along her back, waiting.

And she too, obviously, waiting. No commotion, no frenzy, no intolerable access of passion; just simple surrender: innocence, trust. Ignorance, more accurately: all the more alarming.

It suddenly occurred to me to make her cry; that that might help. Yes, mess her and make her cry. So I began elaborately telling her about the day before, about Eve. Everything; the details. She loosened her clutch and slipped down on to the beach-towel. I watched her silence. Couldn't tell whether there were tears, but the whole thing made me feel better. Though there was still not the least trace of a flicker, I felt better: on top, somehow, of her challenging nudity, her alien womanhood. That was something.

The Arabs have a saying, Hit the bitch with another woman. All well and good, but in Islam the man willing to do the hitting is in a much more insulated position than I was. Catherine refused to be hit by Eve. What, then, to do! When, after a few explanatory blanks and pauses, I let myself down beside her, she was in fact so far from tears that she rose abruptly, went into a corner, and urinated. I should have suspected the exaggerated casualness. 'Lots of goats down over there,' she said, coming back.

I said, 'I meant that, you know!'

She began dressing. 'Love's energy, Lionel; just energy.'

'What's it that doesn't suit you, then?'

She was beginning to seem relieved, in the manner of a patient at last told the desperate truth. She said, 'I know you mean what you said, why repeat it?'

No, I didn't like something there: the way she was talking, her remote movements. Kind of nasty flavour coming up. 'Then what d'you expect?'

She said simply, 'I know!'

'Know what, Catherine?' Frightened, angry. Same steady containedness nude or clothed, same pallor.

'Don't shout,' she said.

'I mean, if you're satisfied I lack energy…'

'I knew you'd say that, it's not what I said; I said love's energy: quite different.'

'Yeh,' I jeered. 'Discriminating, Sunday-teacher, chapel-hound…'

'Lionel, why do you have to start a row now?'

'Well, why y'threatening me for; why can't a woman never do nothing but threaten?'

She began quietly putting things together: swimsuits, bathing-cap, beach-towel, pair of rubber slippers. 'Where's my hat, by the way?' Her privacy in the gloom, her incongruous propriety, her essential imperviousness. What the hell was the woman to, turned away, gathering things, returning to commonplace time, closing the door on something crucial without a word! Her familiar day-to-day movements, lightly brushing sand from the skirt, tucking the blouse with boyish deftness into the waistband, splitting hair-clips between the teeth, donning her public skin. Hell, no!

I grabbed her beneath the armpits and shoved her to the ground; abruptly.

Next day Hughie and I left Kutam for the Sudan.

14

Dear Catherine,

I don't know what woman you feel can shrink so far as to crawl through the small opening you left in the edge of my circle. I don't know, but I'm sure, like you said, that the gap's narrow. The hollow at the centre is at the moment occupied by a familiar that goes by the name of Lobo. Just a word you might as well forget at once – the person who invented it is dead – standing for a thing I do not know to exist, but which for me I feel must exist, somewhere outside, and before very long. I write this, really, to myself, hoping you'll perhaps never understand, but fearing that you will very well. No, I'm not content with you – how can I be with this gap rapidly closing whatever I do? As you know the state I'm in you see the question of love can't possibly arise. How could anyone be content with such a wretched compromise! I wish there was some more exact and honest word, but of course that too would be an unsatisfactory way out.

I'm pleased I came on this trek, after all. Maybe the old Queen of Meroë will have something to say to me. I'm dead serious, too. I feel like a supplicant off to consult an oracle. Hughie and I are in a Khartoum hotel, and will be leaving for the sites in a day or two.

You know, by the way, the story of Zagreus? Look it up, since now you know so much about me. He too was the son of an illicit union. Interesting, the many disguises he had to assume, the cunning. In the end, though, the rending of his flesh to pieces, somebody rescuing his heart and carrying it back to Zeus: union with the god and all that. I don't think much of that end part, but the point is, need Zagreus have perished!

Chew that over till I come back. 'Bye.

I felt like a supplicant off to consult an oracle. The next morning a feeling of flatness, self-disgust; because in some vague aware-ness of terror I had wept the night before while Hughie had carried on and on about Meroitic iron and the rest. I'd woken up with no wish to get out of bed, but Hughie had shouted, 'Hurry!'

and gone down to breakfast. I could think of no excuse for not accompanying him to the Institute of Meroitic Studies, so I put myself to it, though I had no business there, and, of course, no interest. In spite of a persistent constipation; a pain in my back like a jungle drum resting on my coccyx; a burning anxiety at the top of my stomach.

I thought of collapse; of the cause of my terror. I connected Hughie, somehow, with this idea of collapse; he was at the bottom of it somewhere. It was the terror of the boy going into the examination room with a bunch of dullards who would all pass, knowing beforehand that he himself was bound to fail. Because of being so much more clever; because he would read the questions differently; because he couldn't believe in the people who had set the papers: that they could mean merely what they asked. And because he would answer what he thought he ought to have been asked – taking into account the intelligence that was supposed to be under test – he would fail. It was that kind of terror. Hughie would pass every time; I couldn't but fail.

I got up from the bed depressed even further by the mahogany-coloured frugality of the hotel room; its deceptive sobriety disguising the meanness of a thousand anonymous transits. The shaving mirror bloomed leprously. My only suitcase – *L. Froad, Kutam–Khartoum* – reproached me like a maltreated dog from the washstand shelf.

I sat fruitlessly in the lavatory and wondered had I not better go back to bed. I couldn't face the thought of breakfast. And why should I go out simply to please Hughie? Why did I always seem to act in reflex: passively? Everything I did was the result of something someone had done or failed to do. Why? It was puerile. Just as I had created a false Catherine in order to oppose her and avoid belief, had I not done the same with Hughie? The Chief? Eve?

I told myself I should be positive; should initiate; should act. And this, in the circumstances, was the worst possible advice. Because how can a man act effectively who is *afraid* to believe! But I had to force myself to act if only to absolve the contempt I was sure Hughie now felt for me. I didn't want Hughie's contempt, I wanted his love. His contempt confirmed the impotence I feared to be the truth. He had forced me to come to Meroë out of contempt; I had to be bidden to do what was good for me; I was not responsible; I could not be appealed to; I had to be forced. It had come to that. He thought nothing of me. So long as the appeal had been made we were equals, professional men with differing viewpoints. I could play on the difference as a child provokes a mother in order to test the limits of her love. But he had sensed my inertia, and he had brought out his whip. That's what it amounted to. He would make me responsible, because he felt I *ought* to be.

Strange, instead of manly rebellion on realizing this, I felt now only fear. I was afraid of Hughie! Afraid of losing my job, yes; but worse, afraid of Hughie! Now I had to act; I had to prove myself. And this decision to act was calamitous in so far as I had to act without conviction. I couldn't believe; I was afraid to! I had to act simply because I couldn't bear Hughie's contempt. Catherine's, the Chief's, Eve's, they didn't matter. I could baffle and confound them: they couldn't deal with me. Not like Hughie. No, I would have to make myself, against my will, into a positive entity: a body with self-volition, a person defined by conviction; I would not be his reflex. I would stand firmly on my patch of pavement, flaunt my rags whatever the pain, and to hell with the holes. I desired fusion. More than anything I desired fusion. But my manner of operation must become opposition. Like his. Like he wanted: Western.

But before that I had to get this Meroë thing straight. I had been forced to Khartoum against my will. Now, how about turning that to account! There was all that Meroë had to offer a bastard with no past, no history, no memory. There I would recognize the shape of something long dead, but perhaps valuable still. I had to. I could supplant Catherine, and Mohammed, and put Hughie in his proper place, understand Eve, if only I could first come to dealing with this thing. It was, after all, mine: African. As he'd always said. I needed only to possess it in order to know what had gone wrong. It was the most rewarding thing that could now happen; and it was so simple!

I felt better straight away. It was like one of those miraculous biblical cures. Down at breakfast I met Hughie with an almost sprightly, 'Hi!' which he regarded with cynical interest. I had conditioned myself to the obligatory belief of a man who grins into the mirror to convince himself of a cheerful mood, or the dying patient who leaps out of bed shrieking, 'I am better!'

He offered, 'Here; there's a little something for you,' and handed over a Khartoum newspaper. I was fluttering in the top of my guts, eager to please; grateful. Humble. I practically put my teeth into the primitive-looking tabloid. Something about the pilgrim season; the plight of the West African faithful – the Fellata – in their thousands trekking the Southern Sahara, never to get to Mecca; to get, in fact, no farther than the cotton-fields of Johkara and the Sudan.

'No, not that, there…the pots.'

His morning freshness, as usual, irritated me; the pale blue after-shave chin, the little pink bruise or two on his neck, the smell of Imperial Leather, the professional-looking hairstyle (rather like that of a famous sculptor in my old art school). Even his bush-jacket – same material, same issue as my own – seemed more immaculate than mine; and I am a man careful with my clothes. But I sank my irritation beneath an interest in the article he wanted me to read. I wanted to read it because he wanted me to read it. I flogged my trembling interest to the last ungrammatical word.

'Umm-hmm!' I said. 'Exciting, that!' Studied the effect of this on him and added, 'Most exciting, Hughie,' trying to mean it.

He said, 'Isn't it!' matter-of-factly.

The Nile Frog motif! He was at it again: stuffing me, forcing my interest, measuring, challenging my betrayal. And he knew that I knew.

The article was not about the Nile Frog. It was on a find of Blemmye pots at Karanog, with two or three pictures. On one was a line drawing of the frog, and the Egyptian *ankh* symbol. I found the crude drawing, the clumsy bulbous creature, distasteful. How could anybody choose the frog as a symbol of life? Where's the connection!

He said, 'In these regions, of course, the frog means life itself.' I sometimes felt Hughie could read my thoughts. 'You know – water, the river, humidity…' In some things it was like we were married.

129

'River of life,' I joked lightly, but there was no humour in his gaze. So I added in a sober tone, ingratiatingly, 'This must've developed after they dropped the practice of mummifying…kind of religious transference, sort of…' Just a general swipe, hoping to humble myself, to be seen to humble myself, with one of his factual lacerations. For Hughie knew everything. Facts. Genetics, Moorish doorways, Aztec sculpture, the velocity of escape of nitrogen from the earth's atmosphere, Orphism, Morphism, Anthropomorphism, everything. You couldn't tell him anything. You had to be wrong. You had to be corrected. He needed to fish out a fact every time for want of being able to trot out a truth, and it was necessary therefore only to recognize this in order to know how to please him. Let him interrupt you with an 'Of course!' or a 'What you mean, actually, is…' and be silent.

His voice came rattling through the breakfast hum like a patient teacher's driven through the din of a restless class. 'Blemmye culture was third to sixth A.D., old man; you need to go back a bit for your frog. Besides, they were practising sati-burial in Nubia long before Meroë was ever thought of. There's the *Deffufas* at Kerma, remember? As well as Horse Burial – *ab antiquo* cultural connection between the Tuareg, the Napatan Kings, and cognate peoples of Southern Palestine. There's never been a question of mummification so far as Meroë is concerned.'

There was the depressingly splendid ex-British Administration dining-hall, no longer splendidly maintained; the incipient cracks in the plaster, the wispy grey cobwebs. There was the reluctant army of *farrashene* in white *gellabiyas*, white turbans; wrapped in coloured waistbands like fancy Christmas candles. There was the enthusiastic morning patter of commercial travellers – great big sitting-bulls machined to a hair's breadth (tractors, electrical equipment, fertilizers). 'If I sell these people half a million poundsworth of factory I've got to be sure they won't run it all to hell before the instalments are paid up, haven't I?'

These men travelled with portable typewriters and transistor radios and worked through the night: a European oasis in an African desert. There were the drawn venetian blinds, the irrepressible, fingering sunlight; the overwhelming odour of large quantities of food. I felt a small turning in my lower stomach as though I was going to be lucky after all; maybe it was the noxious food smell.

The loudspeaker cleared its throat and let out two blasts of metallic breath: 'Hhh! Hhh!' Everyone froze slightly. The loud-speaker said, 'Dr King, Room 205, wanted on the telephone; Dr King…'

Hughie rose and left without a word.

What the hell to do! I concentrated on a whorish-looking redhead across the room – aggressively dressed, that is to say, hardly at all – to test myself. Stripped her and worked up a fiery fantasy. Nothing doing. I mustn't get accustomed to this; it mustn't go on. I am a man well hung, like they used to say at school. Any woman. Whores! I kept my eyes glued on the spidery arms, the longish neck, the billows of glowing, advertisement hair. What a bloody waste!

Hughie came back. He said that we were leaving for the Meroitic sites after lunch. The redhead slithered past in a kind of satanic crimson cloud that settled gloomily around me. So per-sistently, in fact, that after breakfast, when we went to the Meroitic Institute, I looked at the gold figurine of Queen Amanishakete and sensed something of the same confusion and depth agitation that had first surprised me in the pages of the Lepsius. I knew that this image of Eve, this persistent female, would never leave me as long as I lived. And I resented this. She turned my stomach over and exploded into my torpor like a nasty great belch that leaves a confusion, an embarrassment. Gold necklaces, pendants, bracelets, rich stuffs of India and Arabia; Candace, Queen of Sheba, what have you! I ran my fingers greedily over the steatopygous body; felt a compulsive distaste.

Lobo spoke: This is your woman.

I am a man most profoundly attracted by light-coloured, Copt-coloured, mestizo, West Indian mulatto, women. Sun in the blood, copper in the skin; that's my thing. I don't give a damn about marrying white and improving the breed, or marrying black and preserving it. I lack a view of the future. Copper's my thing personally; sometimes gold, even occasionally silver, but copper mostly. This queen was bronze: close as the sweat on my skin. Too close; not my thing.

131

But she is your eternal woman, Lobo insisted.

Hughie said, casually, 'Pity she has no head.'

'Umm!' I agreed. 'Been knocked about a bit, hasn't she?' (One leg, head, and neck gone.) 'But she's there enough, all right.' In that moment of recognition she was so real she repelled me. Like one is repelled by the sexual appeal of one's mother or one's sister. There is a sense of racial as well as personal incest.

'I wonder,' he said.

'How come?' I asked quickly.

'The Meroitic racial type is yet to be established, you know, isn't it?'

'But these people were black, Hughie, Negro!'

'We can't set about the thing relying on feelings, can we now?'

'This queen, man, she's Negro, y'can't see?' I nearly screamed. 'My kind, Hughie; *me*! Y'don't have to prove that, I *know* it. Never mind she's got no head.'

'But you've got to prove it, my dear man; how could you talk like that! Do it, and you're well away to a solid start. It's the farthest you can get back into your history as things stand. Can't you see how crucial it is whether the thing's yours or someone else's? Simple pride, old man, if nothing else.'

So it was. A door opening into a room out of which another door opened into a darkness. Not enough to smell the thing out and sense it to be there; *know* it to be there. No, I had to prove it; prove Amanishakete and Eve and myself into existence. We had no being otherwise; not in Hughie's eyes. I had to do this, or resign myself to his contempt.

'I mean you could so easily establish the Meroitic type once and for all on an exact basis. You're trained for the type of thing: anatomical analysis, craniometry, skeletal proportion, pelvic angle, and so on. Why rely on hunches? You could take back rubbings and do your measurements in the studio. Needn't come to putting off your leave, if that's what's on your mind. Whole culture here, man, to be brought into being. Think what it'd mean to you personally.'

I laughed that down nervously; didn't dare cross him now. 'All right, Hughie, I'll make these people exist,' with trembling confidence. 'I'll try…I mean…well, I'll just try, Hughie.'

This was it. He'd pinned me all right. In his measured way he'd slowly channelled the whole show to this moment. He'd squared me up at last against my past. He would smash my tidy circle and plunge me, sink or swim, into external time, the time of human being, and watch. (Work, Froad, as I have; as a man must work to be!) He was watching me. 'You'll try?' he asked calmly.

'Sure, Hughie, sure,' like I was talking to God.

Well, it was a kind of that, anyway. I had to do it now, or condemn myself. Judgement had abruptly entered into the matter; Hughie had made me see that. And patiently watching he knew, oh, we both knew, of course. No triumph though, no encouraging grunts. Pipe between brown, assured teeth, he said, 'Fair enough, old man.'

Pity, I thought, about the 'Eunuch'.

PART TWO

Shadow sawn from substance
to shape a broad and luminous presence…

WILSON HARRIS: 'Sun'

15

Myself the judge, no doubt now. Lonely Froad on trial in a desert forest. Hughie, Harka, Hassan, the Chief – Christ, how could time and people come so messed and tangled! What is a man to do!

Catherine!

Catherine's gone now, Froad; gone since May, no crying out loud; time's nailing you sure. April, May, now June. Waiting in a forest darkness; withered acacia, leaves crackling, sand lifting, settling, wind burning. Dead Queen of Meroë, dead weight of Hughie's Burden, all that! Only left now the insistent guilt, the time all tangled, meshed, messed: the instants…

If only I had those two months back!

Well, time moves backwards too; backwards, forwards, either way. Your instant is a target, Froad, without contour. You must steady yourself; deal now with what was, separate it from what is, so that which is to come…

Right at this moment I am in a Johkara forest two months from Meroë, the fatal confrontation achieved, Hughie's Burden shed. I have rid myself of Hughie. I have stabbed the man. I have run. With the little I possess I am trying to think, dealing in my fashion with this cross of time and place, because Hughie…

No, not *that*, Froad; don't start on that again…

Well, at this moment I am at the end of our last trek, alone in a desert darkness. I have destroyed my judge, but I do not yet feel free. There are things I must still do, because Hughie…

Jesus Lord, why did I kill the man, why did I kill him? Hughie, O Lord Jesus, do not die!

The lights came slowly round the bend. They were looking for something.

Mean to say, Froad, you failed the man, what can you say…

I stood, steadying. From the tree trunk I moved shakily to find the Plough, stopped over the jerrican for a drink. I wrenched the flap-cap off and lifted it. Palms sliding down the groove along the side picked out the incised words: W.D. 1945, because I knew them well. Wartime stuff, donkeys' years old. And my left palm slithered into the heavy slime that had fouled the thing. Vomit.

I rose, wiped it clean on the smooth bark, and my mouth, then crept gingerly down the road, bearing the direction. If I could find the Pole Star and the Plough…

The sky was lighter than the darkness beneath the trees, but back down the road I noticed it light with this light reflected from a thick cloud of moving sand. Something coming: a truck, or maybe…was it Hughie, still searching?

No, Hughie would be long gone; gone on like I told him. All over between us. He would be gone; or dead.

I hurried back into the darkness beneath the trees; far in. I found the jerrican and dragged it farther from the road. Then the low prowl of the engine slowly coming; third gear or second. The road was bad, knifed and shredded by the last souk lorries going through before the rains. But this low-gear prowl was not on account of the roads. That truck was looking for something; someone. It must be Hughie. Maybe I hadn't slept for long, Hughie searching all the while.

He would never find me. No, not if I starved to death. How could he, even supposing he could get the beam of his headlamps into this gloom, khaki of my bush-clothes blending with the withered branches, the blackness of my skin, my stumpy height, night-crop of woolly hair; natural camouflage, native habitat: black intense, how could he hope to find me!

Grey matter toiling inside the shell of bone like hell. Quiet; only remain quiet.

Quiet. Steadying against a tree, standing on a jerrican, I reached out to touch the nearest thing, feel where I was. Few leaves in space crackling, a cobweb – aw, shit!

But this darkness is filled with bodies: trees red, embedded like people buried alive, Eastern style, in full regalia, in sudden caught-out attitudes, stretching from the black earth of Africa with claws aflame in the unconsuming heat towards the fretted dome, awaiting, half alive, the few inches of rainfall that would restore them between June and September to wait another thirsty year.

Northern fringe of the Equatorial belt, but all down this side of the river it is the same: arid. Down south the trees strike deeper, grow taller, denser; but each year they too buck their leaves waiting for the wind to turn, to cool the land, bring in the dampness from the eastern hills. All the way down this east side of the river.

All the way down this side of the river men, women, children rush out of the villages screaming with joy at the first rain, arms stretched to the dripping vault.

'Allah the Merciful, *el Hamdilela!*'

Men, women, children, noisily dancing, convulsed in the sunset, horns on their heads and things – things in their eyes; tinsel glittering, flashing, in the black flesh; flesh screaming through hungry rags like blood cast forth and clotted; sound shoved from joyous mouths:

'*Allahu Ahkbar! El Hamdilela!*'

It could have been yesterday, but it was today – a few hours ago. The village of Fellata Pilgrims Hughie and I passed through before sunset. Time meshed. The image refusing to settle forever into what has been; has been lived, formed, and is now finished.

I must be careful to fix what is finished, past. I must be careful to fix what is. So that which is to come will be simpler. So I will be king again.

Hughie is finished. Hassan, Eve, the Chief – finished. The dancing with the Fellata Pilgrims yesterday, today, that's finished. The neat dusty villages, sun touching sand and straw and earth; the patchwork prints joyously glowing, all the dancing goats' feet of the women, and the music and the wildness, not for me: finished. I am no savage; why pretend! That *is*! Sure.

Me, though, lingering with the…

'*Hughie!*'

The scream ripped out and there was no echo.

…me lingering with the nostalgia of those sweet rhythms, memories three hundred years; me back home now in Africa here called brother by savage women, perspiring breasts beating and dancing and calling, night coming.

And Hughie yesterday, today, waiting, not understanding. Hughie in a hurry to do the two-hundred-odd miles to the river before midnight so we could sleep; me reluctant to move on, enjoying it that he stood there aloof, angrily civilized. White people, they can't live in instants like we do.

Well, moving on, Hughie has his doubts. I am no savage, but in the speaking silence Hughie has his doubts, I know. Separation, he driving, me not caring; showing him the sketches I'd made, he coldly reminding me my business with him was purely scientific, he had no use much for this waywardness, saying the natural artists the black people are supposed to be never seems to amount to much, could I think of a reason, meaning, of course, mind discipline, that sort of thing. Me too content, I say, not caring…

Now the lights coming round the bend beneath the trees surely looking for something, someone.

To the left the trees took on a darker silhouette, began a slow retreat from the road as though to press closer round me, to protect. The lights swivelled their shadows round in sharp half-circles that kept falling backwards in continuous ripples, like water before the prow of a boat. And I could see the dark box-like shape of the Land Rover. Could be Hughie all right. I could imagine in the darkness the rigid toy-soldier profile, the slightly jutting chin, the nose always just about to overtake; eyes raking like scythes between the trees falling slowly back, looking for me.

The exhaust rolled a cloud from the sandy surface. It turned crimson in the rear lights, then was sucked away into the following darkness. Black closed back, shoved back by the dying growl of the engine. The jerrican rocked a little as I shifted my weight. It made a bulging sound that loomed large in the stillness; was drowned by another that cut like lightning through the dark:

'Froad!'

No echo, nothing; then:

'Lionel!'

Hughie all right. Hughie was all right! Must be badly wounded though. Could be dying.

I started to choke the answer, chest pumping with angry joy. It broke in a croak, broke off, fell out strangled, aborted; resounded with the accusation his voice threw through the air. I held on trembling; for a moment it wouldn't come. Cords stiffening beneath the palate pulled the lower jaw down; took the clenched teeth apart; pulled hot air hot down and anxious into a single shaft that burned the interior and sickened it and scoured it till it convulsed and pumped up its slime in spasms through the mouth-hole in the skull.

Bastard! Bastard! Bastard!'

Interior all spewed up and scattered all over the place in whimpers; me streaming foolish tears.

'*Lionel Froad!*'

Hughie calling hollow.

I sat on the jerrican, wishing the tears would stop. I drew myself close against the tree. When you have died with a chap, believe me...

16

I stood upright then to search out the Plough. Central pressure, giddiness, dark. I held the tree trunk; embraced it, chest high against the heave, forcing it back. No good, up it came – stomach contracting and spewing it; cement and gravel churning in a giddy mixer. Head spinning, out pitched the noisome spasms through the distended mouth-hole, thick acid ooze dragging from the crystal centre where I thought I had been king.

Turbulence; retching.

I slid down the smooth bark on to my knees. A cobweb pulled against my brow; guts contracted and pitched again. The mouth-hole stood open. Nothing. But it wouldn't stop, the retching.

Let go! Let yourself go! Don't hold on, let loose. Cry!

Sinking.

Then I was sitting, the sobs done. Felt for the jerrican to make sure I had not wandered. Dark earth; dried leaves. I rose, feeling round with my boots, and stumbled against it. Steadying on the tree. Steady. North Central Africa. Latitude…latitude…pumped-up bits of slime of one of the fifty-seven varieties. Guts-muscles like rope; pungent smell of my own interior coming up from the smelling body of earth mixed with the smell of sand and dry leaves underfoot. Insides spewed all over the darkness in the smelling earth of Africa North Central, waiting in the bitter heat for the rains to come.

Fire-winds sucking the world dry. Air dense with powder of hot sand slowly moving, settling slowly, suspended, clothing everywhere with active whiteness like death eating its way from the outside in.

This last time out together, last trek before leave; Hughie insisting we finish the Old Karo work, me past caring, working on those last columns before they perished in the rains. This last fatal trek. But who was to know!

Could be seen…

sky loaded down between dripping stars; webbed treetops black against the void.

Could be heard…

mind counting backwards; counting back to the zero condition beyond the fatal moment; trying to separate the traces, count out the guilt, take account of all those agents that play hell with the best intentions; clear the confusion. Forces of choice, ifs; time all tangles, meshed, tangles criss-crossing, tangled like the incised pattern lining the interior dome of the skull.

Dark.

Hughie says the reason Africans hate the dark is lack of the rationalizing habit. He's good at things like that; that's him.

'You lack the teleological faculty too, you people; never get yourselves anywhere till you realize that; never take over in the fullest sense.'

That was the time…the evening, how long ago…

The Chief entertaining the P.M. Me, content, not bothering with Hughie much. What the hell use wrangling over things like that, he set like one shrouded in the Union Jack about to be cast overboard. Stiffly superior and European, defensive. Old Colonial too: evening dress and cummerbund. All those loud black politicians grinning, back-slapping under the lit-up trees on the garden-party lawn, Hughie wasting never a thought on any of them, hardly noticing even the P.M. The situation really is what he sees, not the people.

'You owe so much of this African thing – whatever it is – to two European wars, don't you?'

Pipe between his teeth like it was a weapon; using it like a weapon against you.

'Every step you take out here it's been on the heels of some breakdown of power inside Europe, you realize that? some weakness. You tend to credit yourselves a trifle blindly, don't you!'

Never mind. You can still get on with a chap like that. So long as he feels you do not know; you must let him feel that. It is a thing with Hughie like among some primitive people, or children: his vision goes all one way – outwards. But a chap you can love just the same, work with, he doing most of the work because of his nature.

'Work, you know, is good. I love work if only to enjoy my rest.'

But a man like that, rest is only something in his mind; something to come, to look forward to, a promise to sustain the vacant present. Hughie can never really rest, because he cannot live in instants.

At Candace's Meroë, for instance, the nights we spent on site: the way he'd enter the tent, shoving back the flap, pausing to soften the intrusion; never entering before the pipe was finished, but never entering without it between his teeth. Watching him stare into the Tilley lamp same way each night, as though it embarrassed him to be so close. You could see that sometimes in his eyes; it embarrassed him. Then he'd make an excuse and climb the ridge between the tombs and dig himself a trench in the sand to sleep in. Like he'd done with the day and all the world, and wanted now only himself.

Hughie is a solitary sleeper; his rest is private. He respects it and treats it methodically. Gazing into the dead end of the day, the work running through his head, me propped on an elbow in bed thinking about little I could control, he says:

'Amanishakete's head, how did you manage?'

'Fine!'

'The amphora?'

'Finished.'

'The bronze lamp and the *kohl* pot?'

'Finished.'

'Think you getting anywhere, Froad, with all this?'

'No!'

Humbly, watching him put the whole day out of his head, item by item; the way for instance he clears the work table for lunch, then begins to relax. Methodically, limb by limb, lying on his back. Silence. You could see him set himself to it. You couldn't make him speak after that, never mind what you'd do. Not even if you talked about his deciphering. Hughie's big day will come when they find a bilingual script like he says they found on the Rosetta Stone. That's what he's working for, and the day will come. Stage by stage.

Stage by stage you could see him relax the mighty frame. You could see him go farther from you, some part of himself still in control where even sleep couldn't reach. Perfected the thing since Cambridge. Even after he'd gone he was still, in a way, there. Watch him, you see the eyeballs still making swift darting movements under the eyelids; you see the temples faintly throbbing, the little white crescents round his nostrils flush sharply pink then white again where the flesh twitches in some operation you feel even now he knows all about. Hughie's rest is like that: driving him towards tomorrow's effort. A white man's sleep is like midnight in a great city.

He has left me alone and the desert is suddenly silent, all of old Meroë flapping through the canvas like loose skin clinging only in places; wind coming under the bulges, lamp dying out.

If he comes smiling down from the hills between the tombs and I say, 'How could you, Hughie, sleep like that among those dead two thousand years!'

He answers, so gently you cannot argue, 'Age and death can never do you harm, Lionel; progress depends on your attitude to these things.'

Something like that, or, 'The desert is so gentle, old man; listen to the sound of space; the wind is quiet, never mind how strong: remote horizons, no resistance.'

And I know Hughie's fears are not mine.

How could they be!

How could the headless past frighten Hughie, he dangling a long leg out of the Land Rover, for instance, that first afternoon at Meroë, saying, 'There!' just 'There', meaning, This is it!

And Fadlalla the site-foreman adding, 'Three thousand years of it!' looking important.

'More or less!' Hughie, casually, focussing his field-glasses and looking absorbed. 'Mm-hmm,' he added. He meant: Now, let's see!

'More or less,' Fadlalla echoed, looking deflated; then, 'Coming up?' he asked me.

'Get me some water first.'

Hughie slid the glasses down his chest and said, 'Fine moment!' to Fadlalla. Fadlalla was patiently unlocking the jerrican round front.

Fine moment all right: perfect for raping somebody, or drawing one's last breath, or making some deathless utterance against the void, or arriving for the first time in the valley of the Kings of Meroë. I could see what Hughie meant. Once in a lifetime sort of thing; just that!

'Well, we can't stand here gaping, soon be dark.'

Fadlalla brought the water in an empty processed-peas tin. I drank, and splashed the remainder over my face. It dripped deliciously into my shirt. Fadlalla swept an important arm round in the direction of the South Cemetery pyramids. Their points were aflame in the last of the sun. They looked like bleeding teeth in a dead mouth. They circled the amphitheatre except for the mound of dry halfa grass where the hills petered out. That too was covered with bleeding sun. It looked poisoned. Hughie said, 'Who's got the camera?'

Fadlalla announced, 'Those go back to seventh B.C.; those are the earliest ones.'

Nobody answered. The creeping gloom was like a burden; you could feel it. I started walking towards the North Cemetery with its line of crumbling pyramids. Goodish walk up the slope; fields of corroded basalt, stretches of holiday-beach sand, patches of shoulder-high grass. In the middle of the grass Hughie fell into a hole and disappeared, opening the spot up like a small crater. Fadlalla laughed. Hughie looked at him. I didn't stop walking.

When the slope began to become real steep between the strew of broken columns, carvings, facing-slabs, the anonymous rubble of centuries, Fadlalla edged up and said, 'Mind how you go, Froad, all that stuff is loose underfoot.'

'Go lead your happy life,' I growled, and he fell back.

Hot evening wind, licking and fluttering. There was the howl of a hyena, like laughter. The silence was becoming green. I heard then, from slightly ahead:

'You'll notice the chapels all face east; they were all buried facing east' (Fadlalla).

No answer.

'Only aristocracy in the West Cemetery; royal relatives in the South Cemetery. As you know, they buried here ages before the Napatan Kingdom was transferred to the island of Meroë.'

'Indeed!' said Hughie. He meant, As I know!

Silence after that, by which time I was up the slope and examining the most easterly of the northern group. Very large, well preserved; but no chapel, no inscriptions, no reliefs. Where was number six? I counted from there, and my eyes rested on an unlikely pile of rubble. No, that couldn't be it. Hoskins had counted from the left, Caillaud from the right. Or the other way round. However, that couldn't be her pyramid. I began counting from the other end. A good way round and the sun going fast. A chilly subterranean green had settled in the bowl of the amphitheatre like an active distillation of some terrifyingly alien time. Crumbling sandstone, decaying massifs of black basalt, infinite stretches of sandy plain, a wild immense disintegration crushingly beyond scale. I felt excluded, apprehensive, and a bit defiant with, I suppose, the defiance of those Pharaohs who'd hoisted arms of stone against this corroding nothingness. Not with a defiance, true, that could produce the sentiment to pit against this thing. Simply I hadn't the mechanism to recognize it or fuse with it or anything, and I sure wasn't going to let it get me either; reverence, awe, grandeur, none of that.

I'd go round the tombs, have a look at the Lepsius images, try to see these people right; to put them, as Hughie wished, decently into history; find out what about them was sufficiently unique to thrust their image so stubbornly against this unyielding time; find out, above all, how African they were. That is, make my job significant, myself significant, Eve, my people, the whole show, significant. Like everybody else.

Irreproachable. Work, define, be responsible for your particular bit of the future by taking possession of the significant past: I'd heard it a million times. I'd come, against my feelings, to believe it. Which was the worst that could possibly have happened. Because by it and all unknowing, I now commenced this business of judging myself; Hughie, of course, witnessing for the prosecution.

I leaped and stumbled past the whole line of intervening pyramids, heart working like the inside of a combustion engine. Vague impressions of the reliefs and inscriptions, odd *grafitti* of long-dead travellers. Couldn't be bothered with any of those, they were all in the Lepsius; better! Lepsius had worked these things when there'd been something to work. He'd worked all those heads into anonymous blanks.

A deep gully had been cut by ancient rains before Amani-shakete's pyramid; part of the hillside had been washed down into the valley. I had to detour among the pyramids lower down the slope: wretched poverty-stricken erections little more than the height of a man, built of rubble from the earlier pyramids, of earth faced with burnt brick, anything. The last of Meroë: kings who couldn't even afford to bury themselves decently. Chapels pathetic; you needed to crouch to get into some of those still standing, crunching little dried-out pellets of goats' down to get a peep at the ghastly scratchings and approximations that'd taken the place of the earlier reliefs. After this Old Karo.

A minute from her pyramid, guts unaccountably failed. I came to a stop, stood gaping, a supplicant after all, before an inscrutable oracle, making excuses, telling myself what the hell, it didn't matter a damn, that I could turn on my heels and never see her and not care. But Hughie shouting, 'Froad!' pushed me on. Across the last gully, where a tumbled, washed-over, rusted signboard grinning in the sand warned that anyone found defacing ancient monuments… I thought that funny, after two thousand naked years.

The hyena laughed again. I gazed across the valley to the hills on the far side; at the green sky, the purple rock, the moonlight-coloured sand, the sheets of grass stiff and broken like the patina on old bronze.

The laughter of the hyena sank into the stillness. The South Cemetery pyramids stonily returned my gaze. I turned, made a resolute little run up the hill to number six, and came bang up against her chapel pylon, towering above me. This was it: the crucial, the reluctant confrontation.

They were loitering within earshot, Fadlalla saying, 'I mean, it's like everything else; people don't change all that easily.'

Hughie said, 'Hullo, what's this?'

'Like smoking; we've already adopted English tastes out here. That's another fragment of their cursive; late, as you know. These Americans, they sent us a black envoy; why do they send us a Negro? Ever been to the States, Dr King?'

'Well, no, never got around to that, actually.'

'What I mean. How is it. This colour bar. They not all Christians?'

'They developed this cursive before or after the transfer, would you say?'

'After; centuries after. Came late.'

'Something important happened, you know, once these people'd broken from the Napatan Kingdom. Somebody'll have to get to the bottom of that sooner or later, sort it all out. I mean, here we have the first real African culture worth the name and nothing coming of it. That palace yesterday, for instance…pure Negro, without a doubt.'

'Ask you something, Dr King. What do they mean, Negro? What do people mean by it?'

'Same as you, I suppose.'

'Not at all; our Southerners, they're not Muslims, it's different.'

'So there'll be no problem once they become Muslims?'

'These people are our slaves; until recently I mean. It's different – been going on a long time. Here, look at that; those are Negroes. See the way they're tied – necks, elbows, ankles, all – all in a line? That's two thousand years back. Been going on another two thousand before that; captives going into slavery. That's what Negro means. She's flogging them; see what I mean? It's different, Dr King.'

'Somebody's been defacing the thing; every one of the mouths and noses chipped or broken.'

'You'll find lots like that, all of them; shows people's attitude; makes you think, doesn't it?'

'But why?'

'Difficult to explain. Here we're Arabs, you see; makes a difference. You were a different colour from your slaves, but us…'

'Habit matures fast, ages slowly, doesn't it!'

'Why should we be Negroes, Dr King, tell me?'

'Never quite saw it as a matter of choice, actually, though I suppose it could be, who's to say? Pity about the monuments, though, isn't it?'

'Some people were slaves, some not; that's what makes the difference.'

'Not to worry, old chap, it'll sort itself out. What about these here, these cattle? Incredible drawing, isn't it!'

'Isn't it!'

After a stiff pause Hughie's voice came:

'Enough work here to last a couple of lifetimes.'

Fadlalla said, 'Yes, sure!' vacantly, then he repeated, awkwardly, 'Sure!'

It sounded after that as though they were moving on; I didn't look round. Stones slipping underfoot and rolling down the slope. After a while Hughie's voice again, reflective.

'Habit's a curious thing, y'know, isn't it! A mechanism you could call it, tyrannical – a tyrannical necessity. The slavery you've just been talking about is nothing to it, nothing.'

Fadlalla made an uncertain noise. Hughie took no notice. He continued, 'What I mean is, habit's really no more than lack of attitude to the past – any past whatever – lack of the critical attitude…' Then, in a more intimate voice: 'You know – girl I used to know, name of Virginia. Had a feeling for sort of thing. She used to come down to Rye to sit for my old man. She was going on the cover of *Gentlewoman*; smart thing to have happen and all that. Well, we got pretty deep as it happened – rather stupidly, actually, knowing how things stood. We started to plan. Then her people put an end to it. Couldn't have it. Couldn't have me, more accurately. They were the Church: generations. My old man was Art: nothing. That was that; you could call it an important thing. But you see…see what I mean, habit?'

Fadlalla said, embarrassedly, 'What d'you mean, sit?'

'Do your portrait, you know, for the Academy. Painting in oils. He was an Academician, my old man; Lombard King. Chaps at school used to claim he became better after he went blind. True too, I dare say. French painter I once read of did his best things with the brushes strapped to his wrist; paralysed!'

'How could you talk like that about your own father, Dr King! In our country –'

'I know; not in ours.'

'It must've shaken you a bit?'

'What?'

'The lady.'

'Some.'

'Was it she and no one else, as you people say?'

'Still is, matter of fact; except she's a string of children by now.'

'You won't go back?'

'I get my letters and the cricket scores; no reason, is there? Job to be done out here, after all – tyrannical necessity, see?' He laughed emptily. 'My dog wags her tail when I get home. What more can I ask?'

I stood agape, watching the carvings on Amanishakete's pylon. And nothing at all had happened. Coming up, Hughie landed me the usual thunderous shoulder-clap. 'You look like a consultant before an oracle. How's things, Froad, old man? Cheer up!'

Fadlalla added, 'It may never happen.'

'What d'you think might happen?' I looked him down sharp, sour.

They answered together. 'Anything!' (Hughie), and 'It's only slang, of course' (Fadlalla).

'Like you were expecting some sybilline prophecy from the old girl or something' (Hughie).

Fadlalla said, 'Only a joke.'

And Hughie: 'Never mind, we shan't hold it against you. Cheer up, you look positively wretched.'

And they drifted on to the next pyramid. Hughie shouted over his shoulder: 'Say, Froad! I found a smashing bit of cursive to take back, absolutely smashing. Perfect condition what's more. Fadlalla's cutting it off the face of the block.'

'What with, his teeth?'

'Oh, there're things in the Land Rover, not to worry; only sandstone, quite simple…'

He dropped his voice and continued to Fadlalla: 'Really incredible, you know, when I think of the stuff we have to go on over in Johkara. How meagre it all seems beside this…'

They drifted out of earshot.

She towered before me in the ancient blackened stone. There

151

were all manner of lines, incised and dreadfully alive. She was the lines. She had eaten into the stone the way the grey matter etches itself into the interior of a skull; the way a vine eats into stone and leaves itself behind long after it has died. She had died and gone two thousand years, and she was still there, two of her, one on each pylon.

There were the prisoners tied to her left hand, the royal sceptre in her right. She flogged a group of slaves, bunched like grapes on a branch, hanging, tied by the necks. She was cruel, gross, ugly. And awfully beautiful standing there, Egyptian-wise, profile style, body full-face, breasts bulging, pear-shaped buttocks; all the gold and all the jewellery of the museums around her neck and wrists, the *atef*-crown on her head. She was queen and destroyer. She knew hate and law. No trace of love and care. She was a spreading desert.

She was all but the skin and sweat of Eve, myself, the Chief; we were one in her, vessels dipping into time to be filled and emptied, filled and emptied; passive. She had died and gone, yet she was still there, filling and emptying vessels. But how could that be! How could real water exist at the heart of a mirage! How was I to believe *that*! I wished for the words to assault those stone ears with some claim of my very own, mine, me! But time passed, wind blew, sand settled, gloom deepened, and I could think of nothing; nothing at all.

And this was humiliating, this attitude – which was no attitude – to the Queen of Time, to my own past, to the past of my people. The vague guilt I'd all along been feeling began now to burn and throb inside like liquor.

But I wasn't drunk. I knew. I knew now, with the relief of a criminal accepting the process of law, that I had to condemn myself. That was that! What could Hughie's measurements and contrivings mean to me now; ever! There was no man, no brother, no Mother of Time, no people, nobody. There were only vessels; whole or broken, full or empty. At the heart of the mirage there was no water.

I firmed my jaws and walked down the slope towards the car; returned to my instants which had no contour, to the void of my perennial present, knowing.

In the established gloom Hughie and Fadlalla were gaily, boyishly, pegging the tents. A couple of Tilley lamps made a suitably mournful sound against the desert spaces. I joined eagerly, glad to be near them, glad to be engaged.

17

That time was deep and lonely. I daren't tell Hughie; daren't explain. How could he understand! How could the headless past worry a man like that! Now in this desert forest the darkness is padded thick. That noise…

What sort of noise was that; what was it?

Must've been a rabbit. There are things in this forest.

I crept down to the road, bearing the direction. After the retching, head clearing. Now I could see the Plough, tail up, right oblique, lying down to the Pole. Cold light of stars above the trees; smell of cooling earth. Arab counting you could make it anything between eight and ten; call it nine o'clock. Again I must have slept, Hughie therefore searching.

Head rock-steady now, reaching back. Like counting back on your drinks next morning to know when it was you'd passed out. Like trying to find your tracks in the desert when you know the sand has blown. Like what happened to us that other time…

In the circle of horizon sand like snow. Turning back to follow the tracks we'd made, and finding them blown. Hughie following the faintest whisper of a trace on hands and knees, me following him, taking the Land Rover gingerly like a baby's push-cart all the way back to where we struck the course we knew. Like that.

Turning now, counting trees back to the jerrican, lost in a Johkara forest, Hughie gone; no regrets.

If he doesn't die he'll send them searching. He'll tell the police; he'll send them searching. If he doesn't die he could wish to save me. He could tell the police that it got dark and I did not return, that he'd lost me. And send them searching. He could tell the truth too; the law is on his side; all the good, all the true.

Or, because he is a decent chap, he could tell the Chief. In spite of everything the Chief would believe in me. In spite of my never bothering to write the paper for him; in spite of Eve, the Chief would believe I am a man couldn't try to kill his friend. Like he refused to believe about Eve and me even after she'd told him the truth, the bitch. The Chief will go on chaining me in his certainties until the worst happens. Then he'll maybe slip out of his countryman cocoon – brother-blindness – and take a look at the world. A damn' good look and blind himself then, good and proper.

For instance, Hughie saying anything about me going for him with the screwdriver. The Chief would say: 'Let's get this whole thing straight. Lobo is no kind of violent man, you are his friend, both men of education; he couldn't've been trying to do you harm.'

All these thirty-odd years, all he's seen, all the underbelly of life in a place like this, and the Chief's got to come pinning his brother-goodness on to a chap like me. Pure bloody selfishness and ignorance!

But Hughie would simply stand up and tear the handkerchief off and show the raw gash. Was it a gash? A hole? Will Hughie live three hundred miles?

Hughie knows how to stay alive, a man like that. He wouldn't faint and smash the car and die a second time. He'll stay alive if only to get me. That's the man, that's him.

The Chief going silent behind his desk like the time they told him Eve had run away with Hassan; looking into the bleeding heart of the flamboyant tree, his hands pushing the corners of his mouth upwards with that thoughtful gesture, as though his fingers were sorry for him and trying to make his mouth therefore smile. It's when the Chief can frighten you most, that. Then, like I'd seen him do a thousand times, he'd lean right back in the old swivel-chair, and murmur with only the wind that happens to be in his mouth, not with his throat, 'Froad?'

Like the day Eve stood before us and told him everything; messing me.

He'd say Froad so you could scarcely hear, and his certainty would crack just a little, a little bit more, and you'd see the weakness in the strength. The Chief can't cry, but you'd see the puny shape quiver beneath the mass, looking hurt and terrible. Like that awful time, looking at his brother (pride and strength and the fine true purpose, y'duty to the race, m'boy), me saying, 'Right, well, it's true, Chief, she's pregnant!'

If that's what's in Hughie's mind, he ploughing now the darkness between here and the river.

Or he could come back. Go so far and then come back, taking it upon himself. Him exactly that: responsible. That was what, maybe, shouting Bastard in the darkness, I knew. That he could have heard. He could have heard and let himself not hear, wind blowing awaywards, the low-gear growl shutting him off.

Hughie has cunning. He could have done that: hear and not hear; leave the car some distance round the bend, then come footing it back to where he knew he'd heard. To find me. Man like Hughie has power, even in the dark. Man like that no obstacle can stop; no obstacle on this earth can stop him searching if that's what's in his mind. Mind of intelligence, Hughie. Not trusting that I knew, that I meant what I had said.

You could feel you have to save me from myself. Don't, Hughie, it would be bad. I should really have to kill you then; climb you up to the throat and sink the teeth into your windpipe like beast not caring, because where is a man to turn, another thinking that!

Do not find me, Hughie; let us live.

'*Hughie!*'

This forest does not echo.

If I scream it's not because I'm feeling. I wish your name was God, Hughie. After we've been together in the chariot, man, why leave me free to kill you now!

But the tears sprang burning, just the same.

'*Hughie! O my God, Hughie!*'

The forest echoing not at all.

18

Sitting on this jerrican, thinking about little I could control, I feel the sediment settle; watching in the darkness like Catherine at the riverside, the gold-dust separate from the clay and sink into the depths. But with Catherine now gone, where's the point! That last night at Meroë, for instance; easy to see now it wasn't a lot of hot talk and rubbish, the story about Catherine. Easy! How though was I to know that the man wasn't hot-talking me for my own good; hot-talking me as usual into responsibility. Last night on site, him talking…

'Inner type, you know; Celtic: romance, dream; country girl besides, natural. You know, you shouldn't think she's out here just for a career.'

(Well, how could he know that; it's me she talks to, not him.) Me, though, shoving the matter off, curling warm on the roof of the Land Rover.

'Don't tell me about women, Hughie; lotta worries, I don't want to hear.'

'After Amanishakete you shouldn't think so; you should have lain those phantoms by now? Or perhaps it's a bit early?'

'What phantoms?'

'African woman and all that, Eve; should be sorting itself out by now, shouldn't it? Simplest thing, after all, to get into perspective, a woman.'

'You can talk!'

'Catherine ever told you, by the way, about the Congo boys?'

'What Congo boys?'

'Thought so; you should ask her some time.'

And sitting on the canvas stool outside the tent, he started spouting; me dangling a leg from the roof of the car, the Tilley moaning between us. He said Catherine had said…

But before that, 'You know, of course, her old man's a Baptist minister?'

Well, hear the man talk!

'Something about preachers' daughters, isn't there!' I said lightly, carelessly.

'She would hardly have told you, actually, not without some reason; it only came out because of something I said to her the day before we left Kutam.'

'If it's some kinda secret why should I ask her?'

'No secret at all; only it'll make more sense coming from her. You weren't around that last morning, for some reason.'

'Weighing in the baggage, y'know that.'

'She came into my room looking absolutely rotten: pale, tired. Been swimming the day before, she told me, in the river of all places! I asked her was anything the matter, but she wouldn't speak, merely kept gazing through the window in that manner she has, not trusting herself, apparently, to open her mouth. So I offered to run her home. But she'd have none of it. It's nothing; bit of a headache, she kept saying. Not much sleep…that sort of thing.

'Well, what was I to do! She took a bundle of files from my desk and turned to go, but suddenly, as she touched the doorknob, she started crying. The files slipped to the floor, and she stooped to pick them up, pathetic. I got up and took the files and made her sit down. Couldn't think what to do that didn't seem ridiculous. She sat stifling her tears for ages.

'I told her that out in the colonies nowadays we lead odd emotional lives, and that I understood that she could be fundamentally upset about things she feels no one else knows anything about, but it's no use bottling such feelings up; not the climate for that sort of thing. Expatriate life nowadays is really for fools or freaks, and we're all in the same boat really – quite unnatural – but there's no point in fussing. There isn't, actually, is there?'

'Wouldn't know, it's not one of my problems.'

'Anyway,' he continued, 'I couldn't make sense of anything she seemed to be mumbling until she mentioned you!'

'Hell, me! What for?' I nearly fell off the roof. She couldn't've been talking to him; no, not *him*! It was a trick. I couldn't see much of his face for the glow of the Tilley between us, and it was anyway distorted by dark upstriking shadows.

'Yes, she started talking about you, Froad. Actually, old chap,' he said in a kind of friendly tone, 'it's quite clear, even to me, that you're not exactly strangers to each other…'

I began crawling down from the roof, ostentatiously stretching, fingering a prolonged yawn.

'Who said we were strangers?' Expelling air rudely through the mouth.

'I never thought your little antics could upset her so much, believe me, but of course –'

'Antics like what, Hughie, didn't believe what; what y'talking about?'

'Look, Froad, come straight; none of my business, but man to man there're things one just doesn't do, y'know.'

'Hughie, if I got to listen to any pious crap about Catherine all the way out here, y'can save your breath; there's nothing between us.'

'Then where's the point in frightening the woman, boasting about your political tangles and pamphleteering and the rest? Why should she care so much if there's nothing between you? I told her you're the least political chap I know, but that didn't explain anything. She's got an idea you're up to your eyes with Southerners, Communists, general elections, the lot; where'd she get it; tell me?'

'I'll ask her next time we meet, Hughie. Actually, if she was that worried why leave it till the very last minute before we went on trek?'

'You should know, old chap. My guess is she could be worried that this is just the moment you need for writing your articles and the rest. What's it all about, Froad; what're you up to?'

'Hot talk!'

'I've a feeling, y'know, I haven't heard the whole of it.'

'How should I know!'

Yawned aggressively once more; went into the tent, pulled the flap, and began undressing.

'Hughie!' An idea had just come clear.

'Umm-hmm?'

'Hughie, listen! The day we get back to Johkara, soon's this trek is over, I'll write you my resignation.'

No answer. Then after ages, 'Suppose you know what you're doing?'

'Been thinking, Hughie. This job, y'know, I'll never do it. Quite meaningless to me, no use pretending.'

'Bit late, isn't it, to start playing the conscientious failure? Doesn't suit you one bit, either.'

Why should I answer that! The shadow of his clear profile fell on the translucent ochre of the tent-cloth, pipe and all. The boy who'd pass the exam I couldn't but fail. No, we'd been too long together.

He said, wearily, 'Well, that gives you till June to think out what you really want.'

'I'll work your three months out all right, Hughie, don't you worry.'

'I'm talking about what it is you want, Froad.'

'I'll go back to Kutam and marry Catherine; that's what I want for a start.'

And of course he said nothing.

19

Dear Lionel,

It will be weeks before you get this, I know, but I must say what I want to right away. I'm glad you think the trek to Meroë could be fruitful after all. I hope it will be. I've made a decision which I think, too, will help. I've resigned this job – I can't think clearly why at the moment, but it's what I wish to do. I shall have lots of time to unwind at home. Inside me everything is in a whirl, and of course going on merely makes this worse. I had thought being in Africa would have been so very different. I suppose the same goes for you, but you are a man, and can manage.

You mustn't think that I'm blaming you or that I regret anything if I say I feel utterly useless and defeated. I can't help that at the moment, but it won't last, I'm sure. I understand everything about your letter; it's so naturally the kind of letter that gets written to people like myself. However!

I know, Lionel, how much you are in love with your Burden and how necessary it is to you, but I really don't think you profit one bit by the comparison with Zagreus. Zagreus knew no protest; to be hounded to death by his father's enemies was the only fate he knew; he accepted flight and disguise without question, passively. But you! What am I to say to your egotism, your ruthlessness, your defensive dishonesty. Are these disguises to last? It would be odd, surely, if I didn't feel hurt and defeated.

I understood very well your motives in telling me the dreadful stories about Eve, but none of that matters now. Be careful with those desert creatures, and don't work too long hours. Remind Dr King to eat.

Catherine

The trek to Meroë ended and we returned to Kutam. I went at once to see the Chief.

'And the people, Chief, what do they think?'

'People! In this country there's only Muslims and Negroes, son, no people. And both with rings in their noses.'

Bearing round on me in the old swivel-chair; bringing me up to date, talking about the scavenger crisis: the buckets overflowing, the stench rising. Three weeks away, and more ferment in Johkara than I could understand.

'There's a force behind it, son; somebody's poisoning these Southerners. I know my boys; it's not their kind of thinking.'

'But something must happen soon, Chief; there'll be typhoid or something when they come awake after Ramadhan.'

'There's some already burying the stuff, waiting on the City Corporation; y'ever heard anything more fantastic?'

'And if the Corporation keeps holding out?'

'Their funeral! The boys got nothing to lose, the power's all in their hands. What I can't get the Corporation people to understand is that nobody but the Bungoba will do the work, none of the other tribes. But they don't think it's serious; they think they can talk the boys back, or frighten them, or sack them wholesale and get new ones, or something. They won't be blackmailed, they say; the camels'll be striking next for daylight, they say. Politics, they say; Communists.'

So the buckets continued to overflow. The sanitary situation became impossible; the 'Colony' had to close, because of which Eve sourly returned to her room under the old man's roof. No one, not even the scavengers themselves, realized as yet the full civic force of this threat.

The Chief said that Zagreus had to perish because as a bastard he lacked the moral force to pit against the Titans, i.e. titanic nature, i.e. evil. Because the link with his people had been broken. He said: 'What's the use quibbling, no man can live without this link, this moral certainty. A man must live in time; it is his nature.'

Ha!

In this forest I am dozing minutes at a time, braced against a tree; braced against Hughie. Minute or less I know. From the position of that last cricket chirping in the darkness behind, left, not yet moving. Minute at a time, but I must not sleep. I must separate what was, what is; what's finished, what's to come. Catherine wouldn't marry me: that's finished. Yes, well it's finished. No regrets, she said, withdrawing. Marriage would hurt too much; us both. You know that, Lionel, surely now…

What is a man to say!

'You know, by the way, my father's a Baptist minister?'

Hear the girl talk!

But before that…

'Europeans in the tropics these days lead odd emotional lives, you know – Dr King and I were talking – distorted, somehow; lack of role…'

'What about the Congo boys?'

She in her usual place on the old settee, me on the high stool by the drawing-table.

'I don't mean to be annoyed because you're rude, Lionel, but really you're worse since you've come back. Why? What's the matter now?'

Well, what y'mean what's the matter? Y'don't think anything's the matter?'

'See what I mean? Bullying and…and abrupt, and evasive; and when you try to be funny…'

'O.K., we know your heart, Chicken; where's the story?'

'And of course the self-righteousness that makes you talk like that to me.'

'Well, what does it matter now, Kate?…'

Us both realizing, but saying nothing: first time I'd called her that.

She then telling me…

She was young then: fat and fifteen (fat! it's what I'd always suspected); pink, shy as a young mouse, pigtails and gingham. Summer and home for the holidays.

She talked about the African student coming up from Bangor. An event. Controlled confusion; down the road, about the house. All very muffled and polite. (Well,' she said, 'North Wales is still in the nineteenth century, you know; place like Old Colwyn.')

'Is your father at home, please?' the black man asked.

The man was uncomfortable; her father too was uncomfortable. Each in his own way.

'African, you see; West African. Bangor University.'

From behind her father's chair she watched the darkness in the dark suit merge with the black mass of the Welsh dresser and disappear at the edges against the oak-coloured dado lining the walls. She listened to the deep-river voice.

'African, you see; West African. The university at Bangor. People told me you could help, you a Baptist minister. The Reverend William Hughes…the Congo Institute…that you'd know something about this Congo Institute. They said you could tell me about the man.'

It had been like a ghost come knocking.

'Reverend William Hughes! Well, surely now, young man…'

Her father had seen a ghost. This young man with the polished-football face, hands lying like punching-bags on his thick thighs, knocking up the past of eighty years ago.

'But that's – now, let's see – a long time now. You won't find anyone still alive today. The Reverend William Hughes!'

He leaned tensely forward.

'Yes, sir, please; the Congo Institute of North Wales.'

The fellow was alert, literate, gently persistent.

'Many people I've spoken to; they tell me you might know. Papers, too, in the college library. The Congo boys, you know.'

'Well, I don't. I mean, young man, they've told you wrongly. I was only a boy, of course, when the whole thing failed. People spoke, naturally; but I was only a child. I was a young boy then. Long time back, you see.'

The disreputable past. African youths; Welsh maidens. Welsh, well, I mean, shocking! For the times, anyway. Colwyn Bay was a small place – is a small place. Defend? Condemn? People have closed the issue, why rake it up? William Hughes now forty years dead. The shame of the thing; the disgrace! How, with dignity, even discuss the matter with this man, Catherine present. Defend? Condemn?

'Catherine, will you hurry the tea along, darling?'

And she listened then outside the door.

'Well, now, between us, young man, how much do you know? What're you after? What have you found out?'

And the deep-water, sweet-water, African voice:

'I knew he brought our people here…a good man; a great man. We see today that he was right. Of course, the native African trained like that in a Christian environment in a place like the Congo Institute here in Colwyn Bay, well, the idea was revolutionary. We take it nowadays for granted: this is the normal thing. What I'm here to know, sir, they ruined the man: people ruined him to the grave, sir; why?'

'You realize, you'd better realize, the Baptist people didn't sponsor him in any way. Founding this Institute was all his own doing, his own money. Who is to say whether he was wrong or right. It certainly upset everybody, and that must be taken into account.'

'But why, sir, why? He brought them here to learn useful trades; help their people when they got back. Where was the evil?'

'I can see you don't know it all. We live in a different age now, it's not easy to get it into its proper light. You're young, you don't know. Colwyn Bay's a small place.'

And her mother brought the tea. Which gave them time to think. It became late, sun rolling down among the clouds, among the leaves, behind the hills. Summer time: still quite light.

Nothing happened during tea to alter her father's attitude (polite non-cooperation), but when the things had been cleared he suggested, in an off-hand manner, 'Something, by the way, I can show you.' To break the atmosphere.

And they walked down to the cemetery at Llaneilian. Damp little overgrown place, filled up, whispering in just-recognizable tones of the nineteenth century: of a past that still lay in attics, in cloistered sitting-rooms, in people's reluctant memories. To the cemetery among the hills which Catherine had watched, uncomprehending, unheeding, before she went away to school – creep down to the road, back to the chapel, round along the brushing stream, down to the line of cypresses where the fields began; fill all that with the final silence.

She watched her father unveil from beneath the creeping bush, like a painter returning to a picture that has failed and faded, the first African gravestone. She watched her father's goodness, his comprehension, contained where the polished shoe-tips printed the damp earth. She heard his voice say, as it would, any day, Good morning, Mrs Jones: 'Five of them in all. These are the ones that died here, see? We live in different times, young man. Well, people have forgotten, now…'

An oblique experience. Like the sound of violence across a river at night.

'Now these Council flats are coming up Gwynedd Road; shame!'

She watched a tear or two come into the young man's face. Somebody had made a gesture and no one had answered. She wondered.

I sprawled on my desk, amused. Said to her: 'Really, you're adorable, Chicken; y'only came out here, then, chasing your sun? What's the moral: Christian love is blind, or something? Don't get y'meaning.'

And she, rising with her meaningful voice:

'We all do that, don't we? You never found your Meroë, did you!'

Standing taut, the curve of the nape of her neck drawing a pure Florentine line against the map of Johkara behind her. I pleaded hastily: 'Catherine, don't go, listen! Don't answer, listen to me. I want you to change your mind now.'

Holding her by the wrist, desperate.

'Please marry me, Kate; change your mind, please. I love you.' Sort of choking.

But no; her head goes the other way, her eyes go through the window and find the mirage and dwell in it as in a familiar element; and I hear the answer I do not wish to hear.

'Lionel, I'm too different from your Eve; and you're so different from…from anyone. How can it be!'

I didn't understand.

I couldn't let go of her wrist; she had to see I needed her. I had to make her see that, anyway. But Hughie came in.

They began to talk; I don't remember what, work or something, I didn't care. I'd been hung up. I dropped down on to the settee, waiting. I looked at them. They were talking so easily: saying what they meant. How? I tried to think of what I'd just said to her. Couldn't get there; my mind wouldn't go! Someone was making promises on my behalf that couldn't bear inspection. Why couldn't I, too, say what I *meant*? I tried to think of anything I could call unconditionally true in what I said or thought, began to think of words I was in the habit of using, things I meant to make people believe, not caring. Where to start! My mind went into its usual fog each time; like a familiar stretch of road that disappears into the gloom.

Catherine left. We talked, Hughie and I. I tried to be careful; to mean exactly what I said. I told him the Zagreus story, trembling in the fingers. But he answered only with the old intelligence, fingering his wet pipe-stem. He said the story was significant only in so far as Zagreus took account of historic circumstance and opposed it; that Zagreus was a figure of circumstance; that opposition is the fundamental attitude of being for *homo sapiens*; that self is, after all, only sensation; that paradoxically there is no liberty except in spurning circumstance with self; that, therefore, to encounter all experience in struggle is really the tragic state – the state of human being.

Balls! Why can't a man – equipped *as he is* – be happy? that's what I wanted to know!

On an impulse I left him and dashed down the corridor to Catherine's window. How could she leave me feeling so empty!

She was returning from one of the bookshelves to her desk. She stopped dead in her tracks when she saw me, because my voice was louder than I meant. It was screaming.

'Catherine, y'might as well know I gave Mohammed the article. For the money to marry you. Because I've given up this job.'

She stood like a patient wife, straight. She said, straight into my eye, 'Is that the worst you think you've done, then?'

I didn't understand.

20

I must not sleep. I must listen to the cricket chirping. If it stops …but perhaps I am already asleep. I must think against this darkness, Hughie searching. I must think. I must not sleep.

In this forest there are *Sabara* and *Grt-grt* and *Far el wadi* and *marfayyib* and *arnib*, and…

I must not be afraid.

'*Hughie!*'

If Hughie should die!

He won't! Hughie won't let himself.

I crept down to the road, bearing the direction. Plough now tail up, left oblique, lying down to the Pole. Arab counting you could make it anything between ten and midnight. Call it the eleventh hour.

Smell of cooling earth. Fingers up the bosom of the bush-jacket found the vomit sticking. Cloth clotted hung in places only, flapping as though the skin had come loose, wind blowing under; cool. I flung the stinking rags away, torn down from the armpit where he'd wrenched the screwdriver from my grasp. Flung the pants aside. Stood naked.

Smelling sweat; smelling my sweat. Passed an arm along the nose: warm. Fingers walked up the belly, beneath the scrotum. My shame dangling like a tail. Like my anatomy lecturer had said; like Eve always said. Like the girl in the Hammersmith Palais saying, 'Is it true that black men all have tails?'

I say to Eve, 'Look at the way you're made, you'll know why,' and she gets annoyed, preferring the white man's way, the embracing. I say to her, 'We're different, Eve,' and she raises her voice, and I'm worried about Jawlenski and the other bachelors in the other flats. 'So it doesn't matter,' I say. 'It doesn't matter, not important; only means we'd better know what's ours and what's theirs.' And she thinks that primitive, undignified, no proper style for a civilized African girl. Like an animal, she says.

So I tell her that's just where it came from. 'Real Africa, I mean, like in the South; not those who been in contact with foreigners.'

And she draws off and sulks as though I'd been most improper. Then after a long time saying: 'That's how you really think. I know you're not joking; but one day it won't matter any more, you'll see.'

Threatening blindly, as usual, in her manner. Because she knows I've got her. But she's not ashamed the way girls are who feel they've given something, given much. Which means she's no idea how African she really is. No guilt, girl like that; she's free, no shame about the flesh. You can't take anything off Eve.

'And you, one day you'll find out what's good for you, Eve girl. You think you're modern and all that, but it doesn't amount; it can't change what's real.'

Her eyes slanting up from the pillow, it could be poison or hate; like a witch-doctor's acolyte doing things with smouldering bones. She throws those eyes at you; they hit and spatter all over like blood-drops spattering sacrificial skin.

'What's the use of words!' Snarling like a terrier, top lip curling. 'What's the use talking!'

And she goes over on her belly, flesh like the night sky laid out in delicate shapes between sheets of cloud.

No, you are beautiful, Eve; the light from the venetian blind going over your shoulders like bloody fingermarks after some bloody sacrifice. How, too, the light strikes your back in stripes and falls dead in the dark pit down the spine and in your armpits…

I think to pull the sheet over her nakedness, it is so active, but she goes over again on to her back, and with those eyes on me I change my mind. She mustn't see my shame, so I get busy dressing.

'You're so abominably young,' I say, and she doesn't answer, looking me bolt-straight in the eye, but inturned, as though she's talking to someone inside herself.

And when I'd got dressed she said: 'You become terribly important afterwards, don't you? Y'know what that means?'

Which being nothing a girl should even think, let alone say face to face, I go out on to the veranda without answering. (There isn't

169

one damn' thing you can do about me, Eve.) I walk right up against the mesh to watch the day die, the garden already darkening, the last dusty odours of the neem, sun coming through the tops of the trees like the leaves were made of splintered glass; the swallows in small thousands breaking the splinters to pieces, making the light to dance along a million shifting beams, arguing, flying off, settling again, so you see in the end only drowning blue and purple shot with active stars.

'*Allahu Ahkbar!*' The chant of the muezzin; faith of the faithful.

A scream from the railway yard. Exhaust sounds of taxis never stopping along the river road. So many trees around this garden it feels subterranean: green subterranean light; the verandas of these apartments no longer echoing to the accustomed footsteps; deserted of the life for which they were built. Garden gone all to hell since the British.

I break off a twig of poinsettia, too much for her, but I take it in to Eve. I'll say nothing to make her laugh or angry. A gesture; it's so very much like her.

She's dressing and becoming less lovely with each garment. The room is full of her; like the smell of dead damp wood alive on a forest floor; a virgin smell. I toss the poinsettia among the sheets. She looks up into my smile, and I say:

'You should never've been taught to wear clothes.'

A woman making up is like a cannibal sharpening his teeth. She answers:

'You think of nothing else, do you?'

Nor, of course, does she. But I don't want a fight; it's not what I meant. She's beginning to look like something in one of those French magazines that use black girls to advertise lingerie. Someone should think of a way to advertise black girls. But not like this; show them what they really are.

'I didn't mean anything like that at all, you know that, Eve; why y'jump so! You seen the people in the South, naked and so beautiful; what's wrong with that? It's what our colour means…and this climate. I mean I was only joking, not that I expect you to walk around naked; just you'd be so beautiful in these flowers.'

All the while she's training a violent curl over each temple. Her head begins to look like a waxed black rose. She's put on her public skin and her public scent, and now she's like the Chief has made her: a father's daughter: formidable. Like a glossy page; touch her now, something's sure to crack.

Crack! bellowed the jerrican, and I started violently.

'Don't know how you don't bore yourself being such a good African. Y'don't have to make up to me for being born misplaced; what's the matter with you, making such a fool of yourself the whole time?'

A woman half dressed after the act of love is like an arrow poised to plunge back to earth; poised to return with mass many times its weight. I could feel her force gathering.

'All this fuss about being African only because you're really white. You're white inside and you can't man me because the whiteskin woman's on y'mind. You come to me with the whiteskin woman on y'mind, s'how can you be any good to me! You come to me half man and thinking I don't know. There's nothing wrong with you, Lobo; I'll get the whiteskin woman outa your mind; I won't stand for this, I tell you.'

Always threatening.

Threatening like the time I found her dancing at the Tigrinya wedding. I'll mess you, Lobo, so your whiteskin woman won't ever look at you again.'

(Eve, if you only *knew!*)

The guests were shouting; they were weaving themselves, men and women, round the marriage palm, and shouting. They were dancing, and the crowd shouting on the edge of the moving oval clapped, double-clapped; hand-clapping. Those inside the oval were gliding; singing in the ancient Tigre language of Ethiopia, me watching in the shadow of a mud wall near the doorway.

Eve weaving and going round with them could not see me; she couldn't see anything, while the man with the *tirah* bowed and followed round. The marriage palm standing in the centre of the circle was a person, a symbol, so the bride and groom sitting on their thrones down the bottom of the yard could be left alone. (Y'have to leave them alone. I mean, y'see. That's what it means!)

The dancers paused around the marriage palm like people stand to attention all over the world to a flag. A flag or a tree can be more real than a person, more awesome than a king or a god.

The bride and groom on their throne were so much like a queen and a king I wanted to laugh. At the king, strangled and unhappy in deep formal suit; at the bride in frothy white, hung with glittering savage things; all the guests sweating in violent rags and prints, shirt-sleeves rolled to the armpits. The king and queen numb and innocent in their labourer's gaiety, speechless, maybe frightened, hands clasped in the for ever promise just laid on them by the ritual in the Coptic church, gazing at the marriage palm, the tinsel, the coloured lights, the festoons and ribbons and bits of rainbow straw hanging from the trash roofs.

Eve – I could see the sweat trickle down her neck and across her back as she glided with the women, the women dancing like doves, like feathers floating, like women, their little goats' feet tripping lightly over the beaten earth. Like they were wafted by the music; like palms in the wind, so still as they moved inside their *tobes*, standing sometimes couples together, swaying almost imperceptibly on the same spot, gently weaving. Swaying some-times, they seemed to be sinking into the earth, gradually sinking and melting into the folds of the *tobes* until they were metamor-phosed into small birds, things with simple shapes: earth things, rudimentary like shells or eggs, or the swaying buds of flowers, which at a turn bloom marvellously again to full size. A twist of the neck, a shrug of the shoulders, and they were women once more, meeting and parting with the haphazard inevitability of ducks on a pond.

Easy to push through bodies packed like this. You could uproot a man and push him down bodily somewhere, he would just sprout again: gone. Walking along the inside of the circle outside the dancing oval, I hear, 'Lobo!' and she was beside me. Breathless, sweating, barefoot; like all the others, but in a pretty dress. Very sophisticated, breasts heaving bright with sweat like ebony subtly polished. I'd've liked the feel of her skin on my tongue, putting an arm round her waist, but, 'Don't!' she snapped. 'The Chief's here!'

I went down like boiling fat hastily removed from the flame.

'Chief?'

And I looked quickly round, sober. Hundreds of black faces bobbing and shining with their own lights.

'He came to the Coptic church,' sweat trickling down between her breasts.

'Y'ought to be careful, y' know, perspiring like that.'

And the flames, still dancing inside her, shot up.

'Why y'went away, Lobo? Y'don't have to come places like this, y'know, if it's not good enough. Y'went to your woman; y'didn't have to come. These are my friends and I don't give a damn.'

'Where's the Chief?'

'Over by the bridegroom, sitting with Mother.'

The Chief said, 'Watch for the men; y'haven't seen the men dance.'

But the women were still shuddering on their haunches, one knee each touching the earth, arms akimbo. Chief sitting next to the bridegroom, me next the Chief. I must've stuck out like a solitary dead fruit on a green tree, because first thing the man playing the *tirah* did was to assault me direct with his strange one-eyed music. Curious the sense Africans have of the stranger, the *non-sympathique*. Or he may simply have seen me gazing incredibly at the instrument: the curious square box covered with hide and up-ended so it made a diamond shape. A shaft through it, a head, and it seemed the archetype of all stringed instruments. From the single string the fellow drew – you can only say drew, because the music came out uncoiling and moaning like the black guts of some jungle mammal – yes, he drew out the sound as though it were already there in the darkness waiting to be uncoiled at the touch of his leaping fingers, he standing before me shoving the music down my face, singing in his hoary Tigre tongue, me confronting him with face marked by store of senseless knowledge, stamped all over by three hundred years of error. It must have been this he recognized, the mark of the slave, the expatriate African, the distorted blue-copy, the misplaced person, the sham. He could have been trying to exorcize it, so sure was his effect, with a cunning greater than love. He was coiling all round me like a man-eating snake; uncoiling his beast noises and tightening them like an anaconda dealing with a man alive;

dealing with the alien in me, the fake intelligence, the off-colour finesse, the slave-brand.

The Ethiopian next to me, a man from the Embassy, said to him, 'He doesn't understand you; he doesn't understand.' Which hurt the way a woman is hurt who loves too much. To make which worse, the bridegroom at once sent the music-man packing.

It seemed a known thing that the music must not die out. It died down to small pebbly sounds from the drums, fingertip noises that meant the welcome was still there, the thing still on; that nobody was tired, nobody was tired of anybody. You could hear the breathing of the continuing welcome, through the hush the potency in suspension; you could see the people all over the ground cross-legged and happy. Faces; all the bodies rippling to the sound of pebbles dragged by tide retreating, beating into one another: the heart to heart: the one-thing convulsed, quiescent now. You could tell the drummer was a heart pumping sound into willing, waiting vessels, they all rolling, gently beating, and resting, answering in the flesh. Nobody was tired of anybody, that was a seen thing, all grinning and happy, waiting.

Eve came by carrying her shoes; disappeared into a little bedroom opening on to the veranda where the crowd danced; lots of blowzy dresses hanging from mud walls, an unmade bed covered with more clothes; three four old women gazing with the blind sight of ages, a baby asleep.

Watching the tone, carefully picking the words: 'Y'know, Chief,' I said, 'good for her she feels some sense of community here like this; good these Ethiopians being in Johkara, she could feel one with somebody.'

And he not at once answering, I added: 'Give her some kind of outlet among people like herself, y'don't think? Christians, Africans like herself. If she can't really mix with the Muslims...'

'It's not what she was trained for; I didn't raise her up for that.' Silence.

'I've been careful with the child, son; very careful. I raised her up to be the pride of my days. Y'understand my position here among these Arabs. When she did what she did I had no choice. My people in the South, they were waiting for me to act: waiting

174

to see what I'd do. I loved my girl, son, my only child; but it was a test. Thirty-seven years of my life on trial: everything I'd built up. The Church in the South is a weak growth; it needs strong examples. I couldn't act otherwise, whatever it cost. Y'understand that, son? She had to be sacrificed. No one but God knows what my feelings were, son, but as long as I continue to believe in what's good for my people I'd do it again.'

Now the men going round; the men shuddering down, faces facing: coupled. You could hear the *tirah* bull-roaring like a beetle in the heart of a hibiscus; but the men, each shuddering into himself with the agonies of ague, you couldn't take your eyes off them. Shuddering like penitents in the grips of unknowing wrath; shivering from the guts with the nerve-taut orgasmic shivering of drowning men or men in fits, spontaneous shivering of life let free from will pulsing on its own; the last life-spasms of decapitated bodies. Sinking into the ground, slowly, down on knee and ankle, hissing into one another, spitting all over one another. They were metamorphosed into rocks, symbols of life eternal, spewed up from the firebelly of volcanoes, into shapes black and square and jolting, coiled round and tightened by the vaporous sound of the *tirah* buzzing like a wasp at the heart of a sunflower.

The *tirah* drew them up again full height, uncoiling them. And with a furious stamp, a leap, a backward half-fall, they touched, backbone to backbone, and moved again in circles.

'I see y'meaning, Chief.'

'I've done my best, and I'm not finished. Now she's under my roof again there is my duty. I've got to be close with her; deal with the passion in the girl. I can't let her ruin herself and everything I've tried to do. The husband won't divorce her; she's got to be protected. Y'understand, son, if ever there's another man in her life what that would mean? I am old, son, I can't abide another disgrace.'

One wearing a sugar-sack, the crotch of his cotton drawers sagging to his knees. On the sack printed an enormous shamrock, red, in one petal C, another S, another E; around it: COMHLUCHT SIUICRE EIREANN. 2 cwt, net. Tare 25 oz.

Silence.

'Y'see that, son, don't you!'

His voice came like from the inside of my bowels.

Talk, Froad, he's watching. Say if thy right hand offend thee; tell him it's only thy right hand can offend thee, none other. Say if you cut you cannot also keep. Say you should have left the girl alone, Chief, when you sacrificed her; not take her back, father or no father, without compassion. You should have let her grow in the pit: the only chance she had to get the air. Take her back without compassion, only corruption could issue. Say it, don't be afraid, man, be a man; don't stammer, don't say you don't know.

'Don't rightly know, Chief. She…girl like Eve, she's maybe… maybe you could say she went out to meet this Moslem thing same way like you yourself had to deal with it all these years; that it's the same thing; kind of…of some kinda curiosity or searching. She is a woman, Chief…like some sorta temptation.'

Chief's eyes are old and red, and in the black you could see a milky film creeping so the black looks grey, already dying. But the Chief is strong; his ox-body is thick and strong.

'Son of my country.'

'Chief?'

'Brother of my blood, your learning has perverted you, son. How can you say that! Daughter of my own flesh so she cannot think a thought I do not know; how could she be so tempted! How hate this evil less than I who taught it her!'

Whispering so low I could hear the mouth eating of one behind, sound of food going down a hungry passage.

'See, Chief, I mean she's African, girl like Eve; she's all these things; she's not like us.'

'Lust, son,' he said. 'Evils of the flesh. You don't understand these things, son; don't know 'bout women. Day coming you got to learn, of course, 'bout the powers of lust.'

'Could be that, Chief; could become like a temptation eating inside her; like something born inside when you were born, not your fault. Things happen to people like that. Could eat you so you got to act; because only by acting you could deal with it: see how you got to deal with it.'

'What; see what, son?'

176

'Call it sin, Chief.'

And he stayed silent, resisting. Elbows on knees, hands clasped, head bowed as in prayer or anger; resisting, I could tell, with all his soul.

'Y'don't understand, then, 'bout baptism, son? Original sin?'

'Beast to be purified by Grace, Chief, I know. But maybe a man needs only believe in forgiveness of sin, that he needs first to recognize sin, by act, in himself. Chief, there is no other way a man can be forgiven, is there? If thy right hand offend thee, means you, *only you*, can cut it off. Not so, Chief?'

There was a silence at the heart of the flying bodies; there was a soundless sound; there was a motion meaningless as the awful collision of particles beyond sight; there was an energy purposeful of intention but beyond understanding. A man must lose his life to find it.

'Son!'

'Chief?'

'If thy right hand offend thee, cut it off; it says so.'

'Yes, Chief, sure!'

'It didn't cost me easy, son. How y'say she must've been tempted, I can't afford to think that, son; a man's got a purpose to stick to; the word of the Lord is clear. The fellow was a Muslim; never mind my feelings. There was no other course; she had to be cut off.'

And he fumbled for his stick, and found it; and then he put it between his knees, and held it. Awfully; serene. Like a Sistine patriarch. And he said:

'Don't tell me action is the only child of temptation, son; don't tell me 'bout things happening to a man through no fault of his own. Remember the Lord Jesus: why He came. Your duty to this continent, remember. A leader must have clear thinking, son.'

'We're not all leaders, Chief.'

Then in dark tones he said: 'Remember the Jews, m'boy, the days of their bondage. Remember Joseph. These things is human truth, m'son. We were not sold for *nothing*!'

And he rose up, towering up, holding the black wood. And he said, so I was frightened to the guts:

'You were sold for *that*, son; to be a leaven. It was the only hope.

Work, m'boy, as I have done. Weakness and temptation, they must be crushed.'

And he ground his wood into the dust.

And in all that happy clamour fear sat next to me shouting, Tell him, tell him!

And then he said: 'Fear nothing, son, remembering the Lord. Act for the Lord, forgetting self. A man must lose his life to find it.'

Tell him! Make him break! Don't let him power you, Froad; pull him down. Breach his power. Tell him the way she clung to you in the hotel room, nowhere to turn; not Muslim nor Christian caring after he'd cast her off. Tell him you bought his guilt not knowing, with *all you had*, Froad, that you're still paying. If you betrayed him let him point the wood.

'Chief!'

Tell him you love him, Froad.

'Son?'

'Eve needed love then, Chief, way I see it…'

Don't stammer that way, look him straight. Say it into his eyes like nothing's on your mind; keep your face facing him. Stand up, don't be afraid, man; speak! Scour the power-smile outa his mouth.

'You have a good heart, son. Brother of my blood, your heart is full of love, singing. Do not let it weaken you, son; leaders must be strong.'

Me going down, head bowed, not caring. How confess away this brother-blindness.

'Son!'

'Chief?'

'I am old…'

'Sure, Chief, sure.'

'You young. There isn't much left to me, son, African and man. The world is waiting for you. Fear nothing, as I do. Leaders of the men must be strong; blame yourself for nothing, remembering the Lord Jesus…'

He crossed himself.

'My slate is clean, son, God knows. I sent her food, money, things for the child in the times of her distress; it can never be said she went without, me serving the Lord. I have not failed in my duty, son, but standing before the Lord I will not fail the millions needing me.'

Faces facing, eyes four, he smiling.

'Now I'll take them home.'

The Fast ending with a whimper, buckets overflowing; people, along the river walk, in hedges, in deserted alleyways, among the flowers and creepers, defecating everywhere; stench rising high, air mighty with flies and the first of the typhoids. Some dutifully burying the faeces, but most too broken by the rigours of Ramadhan.

And after the Fast a frugal Feast. Where, though, the Festivals!

The Americans bringing in white lime gratis; tons of it, tons.

21

Things in this forest, they are treacherous. This forest is full of
poison; I must not take the boots off. Even so, naked, I must stand
on the jerrican, bracing the tree. I must brace cautiously, for
desert spiders fleet as light in the bark; deadly. I must be careful
to tap the bark all around before I brace, making no sound. I must
make no sound. I must not leave the jerrican to pass water; I must
do that here, away from the small snakes that burrow in the sand,
fangs outpointing. This earth is full of menace.

I must be careful, too, of scorpions: many varieties. They come
silently, seeking warmth. And of poisonous ants, and minute
creatures, bugs and fleas that burrow into the skin. Most of all I
must mind the touch of the blister-beetle that sears the skin
aflame and raw. I must lick the spot with spittle if it touches,
remembering to spit the poison out, making no sound. There are
insects can smell a man in this darkness: by the sweat. And, of
course, animals. No large beasts here…yes, large beasts. *Tigil!*
Image of a man, cunning of a man, strength of ten. *Tigil*: could
strap a man to a tree and flog him silly, then rape his woman.
Marfayyib! Attacks in the guts, man and beast. I must not sleep. I
must keep the sound of the cricket in my ears. I must be watchful;
who knows…

There are precautions I must observe; little things, it's all I can
do, but I must organize. First, I must not smell. To clear the
perspiration, wash. This is important.

I counted five trees down to the road, feeling from each to
each. First right oblique, the others in a line. I'd beaten some kind
of pathway in the sand; couldn't be sure. Some patches the
ground felt firm, but that could've been anything. Could've been
places the grass had held after the last rains and dried, no footsteps
passing there; spots which had been more exposed, between the

trees. You couldn't say where had been foliage and where not. Only thorns remained, and branches webbed and tangled. Withered acacias. If the wind blows you could tell there are few leaves. From the scraping, the crackling, the sudden echoless snapping.

There are no echoes here. If you scream it would ribbon out and die, like the beam of Hughie's headlamps dying in the dust-clouds. Where there are no echoes space has no end. Moreover, because of the dryness in the air, sound carries far. An alarming thing. The snapping of a twig, the scurrying of an *arnib*'s feet, they could be anywhere; could be anything. Like being under water, or in the air; dimensionless. You establish dimension with your body. Senses cannot exist, or do not help.

Black on black I counted five trees down to the road. Nineteen paces; first right oblique, the others in a line.

Pole Star and the Plough. Round back the Southern Cross tilted right as on the grave of one long dead. Arab counting, you could therefore make it anything between eleven and one: call it midnight. I must plan in case I sleep. Sleep may come; I must plan. Tomorrow…

Turning. Four paces to the first, I followed the line to the fourth, then right oblique. Foolproof. I came to the jerrican. I knew so exactly where it was I no longer stumbled. I snapped the flap-cap off, making no noise; lifted it. Heavy, nearly full. Enough water, a man not setting up for a siege or anything. I could wash.

Legs apart, knees bent, I washed. The water did not trickle into my boots. It was warm, still holding the sun from its place in the cage at the front of the Land Rover. I rubbed carefully all over, under the armpits, round the neck; careful. There must be no smell of sweat on the wind in case I slept. A man in a darkness in a desert forest cannot guarantee against sleep.

My hair needed much water. Wool and sand and sweat and petrol: manly smells. Good! Could feel the salty taste in my mouth as it came dribbling down; the particles of sand, grit clearing from the eye-sockets. I rubbed the shuttered balls of the eyes inside their sockets, swivelled the eyes in the darkness to freshen them. Up the nostrils; behind the ears and in: grit. Patted and massaged the cheeks and exercised the neck for keeping awake.

The water from my body dampened the earth all around. The damp earth I stamped hard, all round the tree, round and round under the jerrican, pouring more water into the dry sandy places. You could hear it sucking into the parched earth, a sharp, unfriendly smell coming up. Some kinda salts in this soil. Stamped and stamped again until the ground was solid; that way to prevent the small snakes burrowing. I replaced the jerrican beneath the tree and stood on it, bracing.

I am exhausted, but I feel freshened; my head is clear. I can think. The cricket chirping…I am not asleep.

The clothes!

How stupid! Must find those clothes; bury them. They smell of my insides in addition to the sweat. I must do that now. Not wait.

Finding them, the smell of the vomit came up. What a bloody fool! Anybody could've smelled them. An animal. Hughie.

The clothes were caked on the outside, caked and stiff. Inside, covered, the slime was fresh, pungent; clots of Heinz food sticking: vegetable salad, tuna fish, cocktail sausage – thick, clinging ooze, still warm.

How carelessly I eat! Almost like an animal; as with everything else. I am careless; that wouldn't do. I must acquire method. This is essential. Hughie, knowing my carelessness, could be searching even now, banking on it. I must take that into account. He could find me in this darkness because he has method; his mind is trained.

I dug a pit; very carefully, with boot-heel and fingers, using a twig to clear the ground, feeling; mindful of snakes. Listening, making no noise. I put the clothes in and covered the pit, stamped it softly down. Felt the darkness back to the tree, and stood on the jerrican, thinking.

What have I left undone? Tomorrow…

I must deal now with tomorrow. Tomorrow will be too late to deal with itself: they will be coming. I must think of many things; what was, what is.

Hughie is finished, count him out. Harka, Hassan…

Oh, my God, what if Hughie's *dead!*

Hughie!

And I wanted to run screaming down the darkness.

If Hughie's dead; Jesus Christ, what if the man's dead! *Hughie! Hughie!*

'*Do not die, Hughie, y'hear me say?*'

How could I live then!

No, steady, Froad; don't panic, no profit in panic. Keep your head clear. *Think!* Think of particular things. For instance, where are you now?…

'Johkara north: semi-scrub desert: Moslem country.'

'What's Arabic for Eve?'

'*Hawa*: the first woman.'

'English for *Tigil*?'

'Chimpanzee!'

'*Marfayyib*?'

'Wolf!'

'Why is your heart pounding so?'

'Because I am alone in a darkness.'

'This darkness is full of life, Froad; think! Why did you kill him? Last trip back from Old Karo, your columns complete, your three months up, why did you have to kill the man? Suppose you have to answer that? That's what they'll ask.'

'How could anyone know what the man's done to me; this thing's not for judgement; what judge can ever know?'

'Well, what sort of answer's that, Froad? No one will understand.'

'This man's made me condemn myself, but who'd believe? What was I to do! That crime's got no name, who ever heard of it? who'll understand!'

Not the Chief. The Chief had said, 'Arrogance and selfishness.' (On the way to hear the Constitution Debate.) He'd said: 'Cowardly, if y'ask me, blaming forces outside y'self for your own inertia. A man's duty is clear. The white man has left a vacuum out here after his withdrawal. We need new spiritual direction, or what's to become of Africa? Communism? Islam?

Constitution Debate a fiasco. Just as the Chief had said: a vacuum. In the House Government and Opposition, and down the bottom, on the Opposition benches, the Southern bloc opposed to both Opposition and the Government, which was all Arabs: all black. Wouldn't agree for the agenda to be adopted so the debate could commence. Confusion, angry exits, which, added to the continuing ravages of the scavenger crisis, was as far as bad management could go.

Few days later came the *coup d'état* – the military all over the place; the scavengers suppressed; flamboyant promises on behalf of freedom; easy jubilation. End of the private joke of democracy, first try; no crying: no regrets.

'Paralysis, you see!' The Chief had said: 'This Noba visit made them all fanatic, both sides. Tell you, son, something the whiteskin people never taught us. Africa will bleed.'

Then the 'Eunuch' appeared.

Catherine, when she came to see me, her silence more and more difficult to bear, her smile more and more thoughtful and in-turned; her calm more and more difficult to breach.

'Your spirit's already back in Old Colwyn, Kate, that's what it is.'

'And yours? What will you do?'

'Well, as you see' – showing her the *Southern Cross* – I've found a new trade: selling niggers; by the million. Easy; a few thousand words a time. I'll go into business with the money when you've gone; buy a jeep and continue the old trade all over Africa.'

'There isn't anything more we can say about that, is there? It's not what I'm talking about, anyway.'

'What then?'

'I meant, will you marry Eve now?'

'Now?'

'Now she's pregnant. She rang me, you know.'

Brave quivering in the lower lip, round the corners of the mouth, gaze on the distant hills; then the flood of hot tears on my shoulder, hard sobs against my chest. I put my arms round her, holding her chin up to my face, soothing.

'Lionel, well…you've won; what shall I do!'

How could anybody weep so bitterly!

'Catherine, it's not true; I'm sure it's not true, she would've told me first thing; why hasn't she told me? Couldn't be true or

I'd've known. Besides, y'know yourself, Kate, how I'm not strong that way. Don't you believe it, she's trying to mess me; I mean she's only trying to hurt us, Catherine!

'Catherine, I love you only; why won't you speak!'

22

So I went to find Eve. Had to find her: the same night.

Darkness and heat like the devil had raked all the embers out of hellfire and tumbled them wholesale into the receptive atmosphere. The ochre mud houses looked as though they'd expired in the sand and shrivelled. I left the car behind the Pepsi-cola factory as her mother had directed. The road was really a drain with a narrow depression down the centre, into which trickled dribbles of urine and filth escaped from the house latrines. It was so narrow I could touch the walls on either side as I went, spread-legged, picking my way in the gloom. The stench was permanent but mild, mixed with the acrid smell of hot sand: familiar.

At the crossroads a huge cart drawn by a pair of camels jammed the way. From two or three directions scavengers, invisible in the darkness, piled the cart with buckets of nightsoil, singing, talking in their habitual loud voices, savagely isolated.

I passed through the stench round the cart, crossed over, and continued straight along, following the directions. Faint sound, somewhere, of drumming, like the black heart of the night itself broken and beating in some obscure place beyond any finding. That's where she would be.

The mud walls dampened sound so effectively that a scream a few doors away would've sounded like friendly laughter. Turned right at the crossroads, following the scavengers. Down the long main road where the latrine-holes pierced the mud walls like port-holes in the side of a gigantic, rusty liner. The scavengers, now back on the job, sang wild songs of their south-eastern homeland: songs like that coming from the mouths of blacks, you're surprised: real feminine. On account of the fresh stench they raised they held tacit control of the night. That was their power. They ruled the city when they operated. They sang. If you happened to be about, this singing put a screen between you and

186

what they were doing; your mind stopped at the singing. They sang, moreover, with the passionless freedom of deaf people, because no one understood their singing. Or the reasons for it.

They sang. Sometimes they laughed. And when this laughter ribboned out into the night with its piercing melancholy, people would wonder. If the laughter burst suddenly beneath your window and tramped through the garden, you'd fall silent; furious maybe, maybe embarrassed, maybe even pitying. Nightly the scavengers brushed by unseen, vanished unseen.

I could not see them, but I could guess at their position in the darkness. By the creak of the hinges as the latrine-flaps went up, the sound of metal scraping concrete as they dragged the buckets free, then the clang of the flaps dropping shut. They moved in the overwhelming stench that hung on the air like a quality of the darkness. I was glad I was as black as they. They couldn't see me, either. Barefoot in the sand, they made no more noise than I did.

I kept well behind them; well back of the stench. From the Yemeni shop on the corner an oblong of acid-yellow neon reached across the road and propped itself up against a mud wall opposite. A man praying in the sand, knees and forehead in the dust. Three others crouching on their haunches round a bowl of crushed beans smothered in goats' fat. Past the neon strip I could sense the space open out to the right: by the feel of the hot wind carried across the open space, by the quality of sound borne across the sand, by the greater density of the darkness. The drumming came from back of this open space.

I crossed the road, found the space closed by a low mud wall; leaped, and landed surprised in a pile of rubble: broken bricks, old tins, bits of paper; nameless rubble. It was a kind of square, a light glimmering from a doorway in the far corner, dim, almost on the visual threshold. I started following a line across to this light, through the rubble, crunching over piles of broken bricks. Stumbled, went flying headlong, and fell. My outstretched arm touched another stone. Then another. I felt around, exploring unrecognizable bits and shapes. There was a foot of slab sticking out of the ground. More. Many. Blunt slabs shoving up into the darkness, thrusting up at crazy angles, all facing east. The place was a Muslim graveyard!

The drumming came, like dry, sapless sound, across the graves. Low chanting; like wind in old hollows. A few feet more than half across the line, someone came out of the lit-up doorway. A man. The darkness sliced him off and buried him. The footsteps, too, died and were buried in the night. So, then, there was an exit! Houses, a village where the drumming played. That's where Eve would be, her mother had said.

The sound of the scavengers began coming back. Couldn't hear them singing, but there was the faint regular clang of the latrine-lids dropping shut. They were doing two sides of a triangle while I did the third. We'd meet at the apex, somewhere in the heart of the village.

Through more rubble and slabs and shallow pits to a small gateway, or free disintegration of the earth wall, then out again on to the sand road. At once it became hotter. The village lay down like a sediment in the darkness, thicker than the darkness. The air, laden with human settle – along the streets, behind archways, doorways, behind windows 'glazed' with mud brick, beneath trash roofs, beneath trees parsimoniously shrivelled – seemed choking and poisonous. No soul in sight.

A shriek!

Well, what the hell.

The drumming rose harsher, raised its voice. And beneath it, again, a shriek. Everything stopped. Like someone had been killed. Like lots of people had gathered round a death, making a dry silence.

I came to the crossroads. Gave me a bit of a turn when the sounds of the scavengers started coming.

Now, which was the doorway? No nonsense, no beating about the bush and shilly-shallying. Go straight to the door, knock, and say you've come for Eve. You prowl around a place like this with your life in other people's hands.

But I knew I'd do nothing like that. I had to have a peep: see what she was up to. Do what no man anywhere in the country would dare think of: pry into the inner *hoshes* of the Muslim women. No illusions about what would happen if I were discovered, but I had to see for myself. Whatever had brought her here I had a right to know; I'd risk my skin to know.

The cart was still some distance away, but the men were coming on ahead of it dragging the buckets out. The usual arrangement: each man working four five houses at a time, emptying one bucket into the next until the last was too heavy to carry, then waiting until the others had finished and had caught up with him; load the bucket on to the cart, replace it with a clean one, and start off on another five or so houses.

I couldn't see them, they couldn't see me. Not far off I could hear one of them deposit his load with a careful grunting release of breath. The bucket was full. He was going easy, getting it down from his head without spilling the stuff. He would stand there and await the cart. I heard him stretch, then go down on to his haunches, knees cracking loudly.

A narrow passage opened to the left, and down the bottom of this the drumming played. Chanting, low wailing, women's voices cantillating. A triangle of mud wall, high up, dimly caught the light like ochre velvet in a darkened room, vanished and reappeared again from top to bottom as someone shifted a lamp. The drumming did not stop; the wailing.

I slipped noiselessly past the crouching scavenger, who seemed a lifeless coagulation of the darkness, down the passage. I smelled the mud wall – the passage only two three foot wide. It came to a dead end down the bottom, widening out to a rectangle the size of a carpet, closed by three towering mud walls, each punctuated by a latrine-hole. Nearby, behind the wall to the right, across a mere few inches of earth partitioning, there was the drumming rattle, the whining wail, the singing.

The cart took up its position at the mouth of the passage. I heard the clatter of the buckets – the dry ones – dragged free; the feminine voice of the driver steadying the camels. I heard the clean bucket replaced next door. When the scavenger started coming down the passage I didn't hear, but that he had I could sense. From the time elapsed since the last operation, from a heightening awareness in the darkness. Soon he would be entering the little space where I stood, but pressed up against the darkness in a corner, or, better, crouching into a ball away from the nearest latrine-hole, I could remain undetected.

Then I heard the man breathing: smelled him – stench and

sweat; heard an empty bucket scrape against the mud wall, a few dry bits of earth falling dully on to the sand floor.

Quickly I dragged a bucket free from its aperture in the right-hand wall, let the latrine-lid rest over it, and on this hoisted myself on to the lavatory roof. Easy! The scavenger, the occup-ants of the house, each would think the other had made the noise.

I daren't move. The man fumbled. I heard him breathing. He pulled the bucket free and emptied it into one he'd brought; replaced it, emptied the other two into the first, each time grunting faintly. He must have been holding his breath. The stench shot upwards with the force of fumes escaping a fire just quenched: fresh, pungent. I breathed against it; useless to do otherwise. It ate like a nasty stain into the membranes of the nose and down the passages; like the fire of liquor fingering the vitals. Sickened me, so I felt the sick pulse acidly somewhere, but terror kept it down. One move, I knew, and I wouldn't live to make another. I swallowed the nausea back into the stomach, head beating with the effort.

A gasping release of breath, and the scavenger heaved the full bucket on to his shoulder, exhaled a fresh bit of stench through the teeth with a whistling sound, and padded thickly down the passage.

I turned over to face the stars, waiting for the air to clear.

The drumming came with the startling intimacy of a secret laid bare.

Waiting for the courage to look!

Shifted round, gingerly, so my head faced in the direction of the *hosh*; so I could look any time I liked. It wasn't right to look, but what was the bitch up to? I had to know.

Fear said, They'll mash you to pieces.

I looked.

A square of sandy yard; a rhomb of bilious lamplight; a pile of shoes outside the door where the drumming played. They were inside the hut.

I let myself down from the roof. The corrugated sheeting bucked and cracked once or twice. I froze each time, breathless. Landed in a darkness beside the lavatory, I edged round past the open lavatory door, and began inching along the farthest earth wall. I could just see them sitting in a circle inside the room when the light began to move.

Someone coming.

I slipped hastily through the lavatory door, and stood in a dark corner, quaking. Through the open door I could see the light shoot up the house wall, collide with a darkness under the eaves, dance unsteadily for a moment, then make way for a gigantic bulbous shadow that stretched across the yard in the shape of a lazy yawn, and began heading for the lavatory. Two giant shadow feet, a patch of lit-up skirt; two giant bare feet bearing shadow…

Have to clap ma hand over her mouth and bash her…

The feet thudded mustily across the earth floor.

Have to skin off ma shirt and stuff the bitch; mustn't make a sound!

From across the yard, in the room where the drumming played, came the first word I'd heard:

'Drink!'

Sounding terrible. It was Eve's voice.

And low moaning.

Then the woman put down the lamp just outside the lavatory door; deepening the shadows around me. Good. I watched her hitch her skirt up to the navel and drag her massive drawers down, then pause. She took incredible ages growing into me, into the skin and sight of me, following my form up from the dusty field boots. When our eyes made four I was as rigid as a guardsman.

We stared each other so long, unmoving, I thought she'd give me a chance: hide me, go back and not say a word. Like I'm sure it's in the nature of some women to do.

But suddenly she let out such an ear-splitting yowl the image of the back of her throat registered before I was through the door. Up the mud wall, but so frantically, it simply kept coming down in small avalanches. The sandy, cow-dungy stuff flaked and crumbled and scraped down my shirt-front, into my eyes, covered my hair, while I clawed and uselessly bruised my palms.

The drumming raised its head and looked around, shook itself briefly, and expired in alarm.

When the women started tearing crazily at each separate square inch of my flesh I thought it so absurd I couldn't resist.

You're not supposed to see a Muslim woman, let alone touch her. I went down beneath the tons of breasts and sweating back-sides. Then there was Eve's voice sweetly screaming, '*Lobo!*'

Then there were the angry voices of the men. Sticks. Spears (now they'll mash you to hell). I tried to shout mercy, but the *zaghareet* rose up. As at a dying.

The bitch had saved my life. There she sat...

Well, hand it to her she'd done it; she'd wrapped herself round me and screamed them off.

Now there she sat by the bed head, beaming; me huddled down the bottom near the fan.

Bit of a temperature, few bites here and there, lips like powder-puffs, a bandage over a wild throb somewhere on my forehead, numb ache in one shoulder, and, of course, palms like raw meat. Nothing much, but the Chief had said rest. In his house; in his room, where I could be seen to.

Madonna and Child sweetness all over her. Well, fair play, she'd...

'And to think y'always trying not to be a foreigner, and that's just what saved your life!'

It was she who'd hidden me there, she'd told them; I was her father, Ethiopian; didn't speak much Arabic; meant no harm. I was worried; I wanted to see her work her devil out at a *zaar*, that was all. I wished to see for myself; I wasn't after the women. Anyone could see I was a good man: Christian type.

'But why y'been to a *zaar* for, Eve?'

'Wasn't a *zaar*, really, was a funeral.'

Well, what did the woman take me for? She'd just said...

'It was a *zaar*, Eve, y'just said so. I know it was a *zaar*; I saw everything. What y'went there for? I saw the *daluka* and the *tambura* and the big *noba*, and the Mother of the *Zaar* with the fresh blood; and the *bokhoor* smoking in the crucible, and the woman chanting under the veil. I saw. I don't understand what a girl like you been doing there, Eve. *Zaar* is for women sick with things on their minds. What y'got on y'mind, then, so?'

'Never mind now, eh? When you better we can talk.'

'We can talk now; nothing's wrong with me. What y'worrying

about so that y'went to a *zaar*? Y'father know that y'went to a *zaar*? What kinda Christian daughter y'call y'self?'

''Course he doesn't know. I told him you had a fight with the scavengers bringing me back from the dressmaker. You'd defend me, wouldn't you, Lobo, if anything was wrong? Tell me.'

With subtle movements of shoulders and breasts.

'Same way like I defended you? Say you love me; just once!'

'Look, Eve, I'm in your old man's bed; behave y'self.'

But she stretched out on top of me. She whispered: 'He's busy downstairs; y'think he's bothering his mind with you?'

I began to get restless; palpitate.

'Lobo,' she said.

'Um-hmm?'

'You would defend me if I was in trouble? I want to know.' Fingering the bite on my neck.

'Eve, why y'told Catherine that you're pregnant if y'know it's not true?'

'Y'better get a good rest now, eh, if y'staying here tonight?'

Rising, half sitting, rubbing my bare belly with the back of her hand.

'Not joking, Eve.'

'Well, but it's true!'

'Look, Eve; why y'trying to mess things for? Y'didn't believe the woman's going away?'

'Is true I tell you, Lobo; what y'making trouble for?'

'Like how y'mean true, Eve?'

'I tell you I'm pregnant. I'm worried because I'm pregnant. Y'so blind with the whiteskin woman y'can't see? I'm nearly outa my mind thinking about it all day and nobody to talk to: that's why I had to ring her up. She is a woman, she'd understand. If Hassan hears about this he'd take the child, by law; he's got the right. What would I do then? and you going away too! Y'still want to know why I went to a *zaar*? I'm nearly outa my mind, I tell you.'

'Y'lying, Eve!'

Believing; angry. And again she bent over me, rubbing close, promising. I shot up.

'Y'bloody lying, I tell you; I don't believe.'

And she flared up.

193

'Shout louder! Tell the world! Mamma's outside, she'd love to know. Go on, shout!'

'Y'messing me, that's what! I'm no sort of a man for breeding anybody, y'know that all right, don't you!'

'Only because the whiteskin woman's on y'mind; there's nothing wrong with you, y'can't fool me.'

'That's why y'trying to mess her for?'

'Lobo, why y'can't be decent to me like y'are to her? Why y'don't want me to have your baby? Y'see how angry y'get soon's I talk about it. If Hassan hears he'll divorce me and take the child. Then…and then we'll…you and me, Lobo…'

No, I couldn't stand that. I leaped up from the bed and told her to shut up, hell with anybody hearing. I couldn't father anybody's child, what she thought it was all at? But she crawled up, snaking and breathing hard. I could see the beads of perspiration on her upper lip. She put her arms round my shoulder, tight, as though she'd never let me move another step; ever.

So I yelled: 'Leave me alone I tell you! Y'couldn't make me believe y'bloody lies, not the way how I know I am. We'll see!'

And she screamed, 'What y'mean, we'll see?'

Grabbing the pyjama jacket and pulling at it to make me listen. Hell, what sort of thing was that! I shoved her and she rocked the dressing-table so that one or two things fell and the mirror went askew.

She came back clawing, angry, tearing. Part of the pyjama jacket shredded out like a bandage. Her voice came in bawling blasts.

'Y'going away with the whiteskin woman, y'think I don't know that? Y'think I don't know y'going back to marry with her in England and leave me here? Y'think I'd let you after what y'done to me? I'll kill the two of you, y'hear, y'hear?'

Shaking, screaming, tugging like a maniac. Had to grip her wrists with all my strength. She was straining forward like a dog on a leash.

'Y'think I'd let any whiteskin whore take you from me? All whores; whores! Y'think a woman like that wants your child, Lobo, like I do? Only because you young and strong, take it from me; the bitch won't want you later. You'll be her slave, that's what she wants: make her feel like somebody. All you chaps running after the whiteskin women minute y'get an education. Y'think is right leaving y'own women who y'belong to?'

Silver tears running into the spittle dribbling down her mouth-corners, fanning out into the sweat round her neck. She was breathing as though it hurt: small whistling noises in the chest. Sure she'd collapse. I daren't let her wrists go.

'You made me so now you know I've got you child. You won't…I won't…y'hear? She won't…'

She was talking nonsense. She tried to place a bite somewhere on my chest. Tangle; pushed her off, face behind my palms. She shrieked louder each time.

'Leave me alone; leave me, I tell you. Go way and leave me be.'

The noise frightened me so, I pressed her down on to the bed and stood over her. Her face was wet. It came down into my belly, and she went limp, sobbing jerkily.

'Don't upset y'self so, Eve.'

She was gripping the sides of the pyjama pants for support.

'Look, ease off and lie down a bit; settle y'self. We'll talk about this later; we can solve the problem; don't upset y'self.'

But she showed no sign of hearing; she was dead, clinging to the pyjama pants – his pyjama pants – like dead weed against rock, when the Chief came in.

I didn't like his eyes. One look – she still clinging, face in my stomach, sobbing – and he knew everything, and I didn't like his eyes at all. They looked like parking lights on a mammoth machine in a deserted night: something massive behind them.

One look he knew. Of course! But he said quietly, voice rolling out on ball-bearings, 'What's this, Eve?'

Looking at her, speaking to her; showing me he knew I'd given him no cause for assault. Saving me up. He said, 'Eve!' like an earth-mover shoving its maws into the guts of the earth.

And she answered from my belly:

'Yes, Papa?' frightened; not moving. Like a child cowering under her mother's skirt from her father's hiding. She said, 'Yes, Papa,' in the sense of, All right, Papa; I'm sorry, Papa!

Submissive.

But he whispered again, 'What's this, Eve?' groping with his maw.

Then she looked up; not at him, but at me; straight, questioning. As though we were together in something: as though I was the big brother and should – say – introduce, set the ball rolling again. That didn't help. I did nothing.

'Nothing, Papa,' she said.

'Nothing, Eve?'

Then his earth-jaws gripped. She was inside; caught, compressed. I could feel her begin to tremble; I felt sorry for her; on her side. Then he swivelled his parking lights round and rolled out his ball-bearings:

'What's all this, son?'

(Son?) I felt Eve's tear-maps freeze on the skin of my belly. A few scratches above my navel began itching evilly. She shifted humbly away. The electric fan groaned. He said again:

'What's all this for, son?'

'Nothing, Chief. She's a bit disturbed about last night.'

'How disturbed, son? What happened last night?'

Beginning to levitate. Two-three clods of soft earth dropping from a height.

'She didn't tell you, Chief? The scavengers?'

Couldn't go on. I'd already told him it was a lie, that it was all a lie; everything; all along. An old cold lie. My voice said so: the emptiness in it, I knew. But he was pressing me with his silence to declare. In a minute he'd pick my soft head up in his steel jaws and leap for the sky and justice.

Then, in cold dictionary tones, Eve said, head bowed, 'I went to a *zaar* last night, Papa; I'm very worried about my baby.'

My head was splitting. She spoke like a patient sister doing her level best. It could have been enough for the Chief, but the word drove the last wedge into my brain. Her baby! Well, she had a baby, true, that she could talk about, prevaricate with and mystify ham-fisted old men. But the wedge in my brain forced reason out; forced my mouth open:

'Right, well, it's true, Chief, she's pregnant!'

Then Hassan sent for me. A public flogging – maximum fifty lashes – was threatened, did I know, for the affair with the Muslim women. Now the military were in power they meant to deal very sternly, I would understand, with matters affecting Islamic tradition in Johkara: the African threat had to be faced. The offence was serious, of course, but he'd managed to use his good offices with his minister – I knew, he supposed, that he was now private secretary to the Permanent Under Secretary of the Ministry of the Interior – to guarantee that I'd be out of the country very shortly. He'd stood me bail, in a manner of speaking, and had kept the matter quiet.

'Now, under my own roof, of course [still Harka's mud hut], I'm bound by our traditions to show you every hospitality, and naturally, as this is such a personal matter, it couldn't very well be discussed elsewhere. Why I've really asked you here, Froad, what's all this about Eve being pregnant? She rang me, you know.'

'It's a bloody lie.'

'You're talking about my wife?'

'Sorry, Hassan, but, man to man, I don't mind telling you I couldn't breed a virgin in a month of Sundays in my present shape. Out of form or something, climate or something, I don't know, and that's the truth, s'help me.'

'You'd like to marry her?'

'Never thought of it.'

'The only condition on which I'd divorce her.'

'Can't see much point in marrying anybody as things stand, anyway.'

'Think of it.'

'Why in hell?'

'Because her father's down on our programme for the Christian missionaries. You see, after the trouble we had with the scavengers the missionaries must now go. Somebody was behind that strike; and it did no one any good. Remember our little talk some time ago, by the way? Cultural unity, that sort of thing? Johkara is an Islamic state. The missionaries have always been too powerful in the South. They will all now go; slowly, of course, as we tighten our grip. We're expelling her father.'

'Not wasting much time, are you?'

'None to waste; Christian Africa's not waiting, y'know. As you know.'

'And Eve?'

197

'I automatically get the child; the moment her father's residence is withdrawn.'

'So what's it matter to you, then, whether I marry her, pregnant or not pregnant?'

'I've a future to think of; no woman is left uncared-for in our country. Besides, my wife: a Christian bastard? They'll be deciding on you in a few days. It's entirely up to you, Froad.' Smiling acidly.

So Catherine returned to North Wales not dreaming it wasn't true. Goodbye at the airport to Hughie and me for the last time. Deathly pale; eyes full, but not a tear; not a flutter in the voice. Her head stayed down, though, all the way across the tarmac to the aircraft, maybe only because she was struggling against the wind. The pink-and-white stripes of her sack bellied out at the foot of the aircraft steps, so she looked for a moment pregnant. God, how I remembered that joke on the river road about having a wife pregnant that Saturday morning she'd given me a lift! She paused to gather the dress about her, and I hoped she'd turn. Just once. Just to see her face once more. But no, she went straight up the steps, hair streaming against the polished aluminium, and into the door, stooping slightly.

'Well, that's that!' I said, and shot a side-glance at Hughie. Blazer, grey serge, suedes, pipe. No answer.

'Three weeks more for me, and that's that!'

He turned on his heel and walked to his car without a word. The aircraft screaming before me, the Land Rover revving behind – well, it was like these two people were working the ends of a saw whose blade tore hot through my vitals. I went back to Eve and nearly beat the last breath out of her (God strike us, why should I take the Muslim lash!) till she admitted it wasn't true.

23

There was a cross bearing a mass of yellow straw in front of my eyes. There was a cracked mud wall and a gloom inside. There was nothing in the room beside the *angarib* on which I lay like an Egyptian corpse. (How the hell had I got into such a fitting posture – palms across the breast!) There was a mud-hole high up, like a Cyclopean eye. I could see the sky and God, infinity and all that; a triangle of thorn bushes raising itself up like a forsaken crucifixion. Tree for hire! Who'll have this rotting cross? Vicious white fangs trespassing into eternity.

> 'Stars nail our blood to this,
> this cross of time and place.
> Stars nail our blood to this.'

Depends how you say the last 'this'. Means – could mean – you're down to bone. Always bone beneath blood, thank heavens! Good that, though. Bone; can always get down to bone where all is, come to think of it, white!

Hughie said: 'Right! Now you've had your nap…'

'Haven't slept a wink, actually, too tired. Besides, the noise, the singing and dancing! Did you sleep?'

'Not on your life,' he boasted. 'We must find our route before it gets dark, so we'll hit the river before midnight; get some sleep.'

'Oh, but it's lovely here, Hughie; these people so happy. Our last trek together, man, the columns complete; we'll never see Old Karo together again, where's the hurry!'

Whole village of pilgrims dancing against the sunset; whole heap of them. Yesterday? Today? Steady! I must fix what was.

That was yesterday; finished. I am no savage. Three hundred-odd miles to the river, and Hughie impatiently waiting. But those men and women dancing, noisily chanting, convulsed in the sunset, horns on their heads and things – things in their eyes; tinsel glittering, flashing in the black flesh…

'*Allahu Ahkbar!*'

That was yesterday.

If he should bring the police…

Well, let him. Maybe I'll not even try to escape. How escape in this desert, anyway? Back to the Fellata village? Without food? In this devilish heat? Besides, they wouldn't take me in; they wouldn't understand. They loved me yesterday because I wasn't one of them; they were flattered. But live with them? Settle among them and live; take wife? They would never understand that; count it out.

Now I no longer smell I must plan. I will plan.

But you cannot plan, Froad; you don't know how. You have never devised a system for anything in your life. You have used systems as you've worn clothes, not thinking, not even needing to. Systems come from minds in contact with problems. You've never had a problem in your life, Froad, worth the name. You are passive; you must become active.

Hughie has system; he knows my habits. He has all the equipment in the Land Rover. He could be tracking back on a dead-sure course even now, seeking me. What is to stop him? He is responsible; he has a sense of duty; I am his friend lost in a darkness. He could have set some kind of trap, knowing the land. Hughie knows the land better than I do: it's his business. This immense plain between the river and the hills is crossed at intervals by the great *khors* running to the water; you're always on a back of land between two *khors*. What kind of *khors*; how deep; deep and hollow, or deep and filled with powdered sand? How close together? These things Hughie would know. Somewhere about here is the great Khor Abu Shama; right, left, where? He'd know; from the maps and instruments in the Land Rover. I could see him poring with his prismatic compass over them, calmly plotting around the arc of his protractor, foreseeing my intentions, working out times, distances, coordinates, probabilities. I could not get back to the hills, he'd know that: too far. If I should make for open country to left or right, he'd know how far in each direction I could go; before I start. He'd know how much of the land I know; what plan would most appeal to me; he'd plan to head it off. He knows my mind; he'll come stalking. It would be his ultimate triumph, the last shedding of his Burden, to save me from myself. I should be for ever indebted for that.

Do not do it, Hughie; do not find me; let us live.

I must plan outside the limits of Hughie's intelligence. I must think of that.

But suppose he should find me now; before I've planned anything!

Calm, Froad, no panic. Think!

Sinking down on to the jerrican; crouching.

Your mind is clear now, but sleep can take you. You've covered more than two hundred miles since yesterday early, more than five hundred from Old Karo. Lay your plan so you can sleep.

One of the limits of Hughie's intelligence is that he thinks I think like him. Plan on that.

In a given situation he'd think I would act like him, making allowances for carelessness, laziness – all the things he knows about me. He'd think, for instance, me shouting Bastard in the darkness was a blind, that I'd be five six miles away by now. He'd never credit it anybody's mind working naturally so slow; that I could still be in the same spot thinking. He'd be working out a location on a radius five six miles from this centre, through 180°, since even me wouldn't be so stupid as to start walking in any direction towards him, towards the river. He'd be planning like that. Hughie comes from a race where system is all. You can't look into anything of Hughie's mind and not find system; he can do anything; find anything; in any darkness.

What if he finds you!

You're not even sure he's looking. How can you know for sure he's looking?

Because Hughie is responsible; most of all he's that: responsible for other people. Won't let a man alone. Him saying, for instance, yesterday, today…no, yesterday…

'Pity about that Eunuch article, wasn't it!'

Suddenly, out of the blue; driving along, profile like stone.

'Like how y'mean, Hughie?'

'Could've had you on the carpet for it, too, you realize; except you resigned. Poor taste, just the same.'

After all this silence?

'What's biting you now, Hughie; f'Chrissake, man; poor taste what, the money?'

'That, yes!'

Wouldn't leave a man alone!

'Look! It's all finished and done with now; f'get it.'

'There're very many people who won't, you know. Don't you think that a rather irresponsible thing to say?'

Why should I answer that! The desert was talking to me. It flowed through the car like racing river entering a gorge. Through windows and eyes and hair. Ringing in ears, it mumbled and sighed and clapped through the canvas. It said, I am long dead.

It pounded and rapped the floor, assailed the growling machine with grit and pebbles. It said: I am bigger than big oceans. I devour endlessly. I cannot be filled. I am wide. I am empty.

It searched like knife beneath the skin. It scorched the tongue and roofs of mouths. It shoved dry breath hot back into bodies, like into corpses choked and stiff and strangled. It said: I am parched. I exhaust the lusts of sun and earth, child of neither. I know no love, no pity. I weep and have no release. Neither like forest nor like ocean; I do not proliferate. I am barren.

Between Europe and Africa there is this desert. How fitting! Between the white and the black this mulatto divide. You cannot cross it, whoever you are, and remain the same. You change. You become, in a way, yourself mulatto – looking both ways. Looking back to the vertical, sideways to the horizontal. Backwards to the old mastery, sideways to the timeless mystery. Back to will and back to willing – ai – and sideways to the calling, the crucifying, the unspeakable-of, the reed shaken by the wind.

What the hell was the man to?

The desert said, I consume.

After ages, 'Money!' he said. Just that. Money! Bitterly. And I should have learnt something. Because I knew then it was coming. Controlled myself. Wouldn't take; wouldn't answer. I had given this desert all my soul.

But then we stopped in the last light to wash; cool down for the night, my turn next to drive.

He said, 'What's rattling like that the whole time; damn nuisance, isn't it!' Irritably. As though it were my fault, whatever it was. Because I'm going, I told myself; only because I'm going away. Never mind; for something to do I inspected the car while he got out the jerrican and the wash-basin. Thought it might be the offside door-lock come loose from the vibration. I got out the screwdriver and began tightening the screw-heads; peaceful. Few days more and not to worry. Not to worry about his duty and his vision and his damned contempt. Few days more I'd be free, *hamdilela*, content with my naked instants.

'Basic dishonesty in your attitude, actually, that's what it is, isn't it?'

Couldn't believe my ears! I'd been whistling 'Grey Sand and White Sand', thinking about nothing; well, just thinking about that, that I'd be going. Now I stopped; I watched him. He was covered with soap, bent over the wash-basin, bare to the waist.

I said, 'Hughie, f'Chrissake, man, let's not start all that again, eh?'

'Pardon?' he spluttered. The soap.

'I couldn't've done the work, y'don't understand; I've told you before I couldn't do it. Y'expect bread out of bone or something, Hughie? Why y'don't leave me alone? You could never understand, so leave it, eh?'

'What y'mean, actually, is there was no profit that you could immediately see, no money in the thing, don't you, old man? I understand now what your instants mean. Ideas are simply wasted on people like you: responsibility, sacredness of time, that sort of thing. You won't ever cease to be driven.'

What was I to say!

I started humming 'Where the Bee Sucks', but I couldn't sing; he was stopping me from singing. How I was humming that song my voice sounded like a moan. He said:

'Aren't they, Froad?'

Sharp. A high tone. A boss tone.

I raised myself upright and looked at him again. The nacreous yellowy-white back curving down to the khaki waistband, the toughened sunburned neck lathered with soap, one large improbable ear sticking through the foam. All these things…they were ordinary, like everybody else. Where was the steel?

'Answer me, Froad!'

And I started to say something; tried to say something I meant and felt; something he would feel I meant from deep. But only a soundless sadness would come: a kind of tears.

He rattled impatiently, 'What was that?'

I felt my arm begin swinging heavily towards him. I could feel the weight of the Phillips screwdriver: light as a pencil, but I could feel its weight.

'You been putting this thing into my hands from the start, Hughie, from the very start.'

Speaking soft; kind of humble moan, kind of pleading hum. Like I was hearing someone else inside a tent talking.

'What on earth are you talking about; what thing?'

Turning; soap in his eyes. I didn't answer; couldn't. He straightened up. He couldn't see me, but he turned too fast. So fast it was as though he was greedy for the screwdriver; he came hungrily into it, like we were lovers understanding this inevitable moment. He'd groaned, 'Oh!' and then, 'Oh, God!' before I heard the tent-voice say:

'This!'

Trapezius, sterno-mastoid, and into the neck. In.

Before he began to totter I'd grabbed the jerrican. Before he fell I'd run.

24

So now! His blood has run; he'll come to find out why.

Or he might come in anger, violently. But no; Hughie's too proud for that; his knowledge and his mind are too big for violence; he won't do that. He could never old man me again if he did, he knows that well. Hughie will not come in anger. He has a different purpose. I must look to myself.

I stooped on the jerrican.

I must use my brains, conscious of Hughie alive or dead.

I scratched a slight sore itch on the shoulder-blade.

In this darkness I have the advantage. Black intense, native habitat, night-crop of woolly hair: I cannot easily be seen. Not by one afraid of giving his position away by using a torch. There is a torch in the Land Rover; he would not use it for the same reason as he's taken the car round the bend and put off the lights.

If that's what he's done…

It's what he's done, I know him; tactics are instinctive to Hughie.

I scratched again; side of the belly: a sore bump, hard.

Suppose, though, the man's alive!

They'd come to find us both, like that other time – the time at Shaggerat. My plan must be to remain undiscovered even if I sleep.

But how, Froad; how?

Better not sleep at all; watch through the night, watch till daybreak.

But sleep may come, you have no guarantee. You are exhausted. Your head is clear but you are very tired; inertia is creeping through your body. You are aching all over; in the joints and muscles, aching in the bones of your skull. Your insides are tight and sore, and your throat. You are forcing your head to think, but how guarantee against this creeping inertia; how guarantee that sleep will not come?

Prepare, Froad, so you will not be found even by daylight; even if you sleep.

What is this itching; why am I scratching?

Sweat!

I leaped from the jerrican, bruised my back against the tree in panic, dizzy with the fearful promise of this new trouble. Jesuschrize, sweating again!

A buzzing in the darkness; something drew a razor-hot line along the inside of my left thigh.

Blister-beetle!

Wash! Quick, Froad, wash it before the blisters rise. Stoop down and lick, quick; lick and spit!

Spittle and tongue I licked my leg like a cautious cat; but I could get only half along the line, the rest too near the scrotum. Suppose it should get you on the balls, Froad, quick!

I snapped the flap-cap off the jerrican and began furiously washing, splashing precious water heedlessly, rubbing hard. But on the upper part of the bruise the flesh had begun to grow warm, to sting where the poison had already bitten. Soon the blister would blossom and spread, and the pus from that form new blisters.

Dragging the jerrican back under the tree, I sat down to work the thing out.

Now you are perspiring again what do you do! You can be smelled. You are alive; you can't stop yourself perspiring, and panic only makes more sweat. That was poor thinking, Froad; you must do better than that. You can be smelled. There are things all around can smell you now. Poisonous insects, animals; Hughie!

Wash, then, again? Can't keep washing through the night; I need the water. I am in a desert. Besides, suppose I wash and then fall off to sleep; suppose that!

Calm, Froad; *think*!

I listened for the beetle. It could strike again. It could strike over and over again; could attract others. I'd be a fine mess then; couldn't touch myself or hardly move. Fine state for a man alone in a darkness. It was buzzing somewhere on the ground, maybe tangled, maybe upturned and helpless. I leaped down from the jerrican and started stamping all over the earth, mindless of noise, stamping in a frenzy.

I've got to kill the thing; got to find that spot in the darkness and kill the bloody thing before it strikes again.

Leaping and stamping like a naked savage; sweating.

Then it stopped. Dead.

What, though, of the others! You smell. Anything can smell you now. Anyone. You're sweating with a Negro's sweat, Froad, white as you are.

I couldn't brace any more, stooping against the tree, because of the bruise along the spine. I raised myself, stood limply, dreading the desire to give up.

A man can't stop sweating in this heat. You can't stop living; so long as you are alive you must perspire. Simple. You cannot choose not to perspire; not by will or anything. A man may not choose that; hasn't the power; you cannot choose not to smell, whoever you are; and smelling means others can get you. You cannot cut yourself off, however you try.

But I must. For a while, anyway.

Sweat is time itself, Froad; you cannot withdraw from time.

But this night is valuable to me; I must keep myself from poison and from further assault. I must not be smelled by anything; anyone. It is crucial.

Helpless under the smell of this body, I could see myself already found by all the insects in this forest; see them swarming and buzzing and raising the blisters, laughing, Hughie at last standing over me with the balms and cures and all his knowledge; whispering, soothing, saving me. Don't you worry, old man, all will be well; I have come…

No!

I leaped off the jerrican once more, frantic. I began digging up the sand, thoughtless of things burrowing. I mustn't be smelled, I mustn't!

Scraping and digging, heedless of noise, down to earth: down to clay: alluvial deposits of centuries a few inches down; dry, hard as rock.

I cleared the sand into a large hole and fetched the jerrican. Careful with the water, you don't have much to spare; you are in a desert, remember.

Paying no mind at all, pouring the water and scraping the clay into a soft mess, warm, squelching it through the fingers, rubbing it smooth between the palms, making a paste. Then I began to plaster. First the scrotum. You are a man and you mean to live. Scrotum and penis plaster well. Plaster well around the anus, not blocking it. Be careful of that. Plaster round the eyes; thin on the eyelids, but plaster those well. All the face, minding the earholes, for you must listen!

Now your vital points are protected. Take your time with the other parts; not too thick, or the clay will flake. Cover your hair. Remove unnecessary thickness from between the legs so you can move freely. Armpits treat with caution for the same reason. Do not be in a hurry, work calmly. See the distribution is even over the body: thin, to minimize the need for subsequent patching. Have a thought for the amount of water remaining.

Do not exult. You have done well, but do not allow yourself to crow; this is weakness, and it can betray you. Take thought, rather, of what remains to be done; you are certain to find hitches.

All covered, there remained only the portion of back between the shoulder-blades. I plastered a thick mess of clay over the dry patch and rubbed this gently against the trunk of the tree. It soothed the bruises. Then I waited for the clay to dry.

Later I will refill the hole.

I took a walk down to the road to bed the clay in, let it take the air. Nineteen steps. First right oblique, the others in a line. Five trees, a look at the stars, and back again. Touch the jerrican and back down to the road. Slowly backwards, forwards, the movement of the muscles bedding the clay in. I felt so sure now of my position I thought I could even risk a walk along the road. Would've been quite simple: leave the jerrican as a marker in the wheel ruts, and go as far as I wished in either direction. Returning, I needed only feel for the pathway and follow the line of five trees back home. But it was not worth it. I should have had to think of a way of obliterating footsteps as I went along my little path and returned.

These footsteps are enough worry as it is; I shall have to deal with them before placing myself open to sleep. If I do that in good time, the lightest wind through the night will obliterate all trace of my work.

The clay dried in patches; in exposed portions where I'd laid it thin. On the chest and back and calves it contracted and caked and bit the skin. I could feel the small hairs stretching from their roots, over the sartorious muscle of the thigh, along the lumbar region of the back. In these spots, and at the joints, the movement of the body and the extra heat generated by the action of the muscles dried the skin so quickly that the clay peeled and fell, leaving a chalky residue which nevertheless provided maximum insulation with the least restriction of movement.

Now I must be careful as to friction. Heavy caking round the neck and under the scrotum, for instance. These are uncomfortable, but they must be lived with. The armpits, too, are a nuisance, and the joints behind the knees. I must not think, though, of these; I must not think negatively; I must think positively. Sacrifices must, after all, be made for total security, total isolation; this at least I have learnt. I am uncomfortable, but I am insulated. I cannot be smelled.

I have laboured. I have found at last a belief. Like everybody believes. Like Hughie, Harka, Hassan, the Chief. Like Mojo Kua in his *mare clausam*. Like all these happy people, I am insulated.

Down the nineteen paces once more and back again, carefully obliterating my path with a trailing bundle of twigs. Backwards, going backwards into a darkness. Sleep can come now if it likes; I have taken every precaution. Now only remains to dispose of my body in such a manner that even by daylight, blending with the earth, it will not be visible more than a few paces away. I must not be contoured against anything. I must find a position such that should I oversleep the dawn, the broken sunlight filtering through the branches would camouflage my mass with everything around it. For this reason I must be mindful of the shadow likely to be cast by this tree trunk. Such a shadow crossing my body would give it bulk, reality. This, of course, will not do. From the Pole Star, the time of year, latitude – latitude…say 17° North – I can guess, more or less, the direction of sunrise and the course of the sun. I can calculate the arc which the shadow of this tree trunk is likely to make over the ground as I sleep.

But this is a forest, Froad; you do not solve the problem by thinking of only one tree trunk; there are all these trees to be taken into consideration; what of them!

Also, whatever position you may take up, you still have to think of the menace from the earth: snakes and things. You're not all that insulated. You have to think, too, of chance; stray footsteps, stray animals, dogs. They may bring dogs searching; Hughie has your smell in the Land Rover. If he does not come searching, if he's dead, there will be the police with their dogs; they would need dogs in a vast emptiness like this. Do the Johkara police use dogs? You're not sure; you're never sure of anything like that, Froad. You are very careless; do not observe; do not note particular things. You live from day to day as you feel. This is bad. You must train yourself to take note of your surroundings; of particular things. You get nowhere without determining your environment.

If the Johkara police use dogs they could yet be beaten. Is your insulation sufficient? Are the clothes buried deeply enough? Committed now to this new sense of care have you done all of which you are capable; thought of everything? Are you insured entirely against discovery; against defeat?

Because, Froad, care is love: a view of time: an argument – do you realize – with the future: a necessity that is not tyrannical. You have separated what was from what is. Good. But Hughie now circling, searching, through this night, could find you – because he too might care – with *love*! What do you do then? how deal with that!

I must not doubt now. I must move from this spot; get off the earth, go up a tree. I must use the wisdom of a savage, the cunning of an animal, acting in a manner that would baffle the most intelligent search; confound the mind of man, the instinct of beast. I must labour further. The water remaining in the jerrican is not much, but it must do this last little job. Those clothes must go deeper, go down into the clay proper.

I felt for the pit, hands and knees, where I'd buried the clothes; found it and tore them up with ease. Getting the feel of working in the darkness, I poured more water into the clay and dug it deeper; deeply enough to bury them beyond the scent of man or beast.

The socks! the shoes! Bury those too; leave every last touch and trace of the world behind; nothing to be smelled.

No, but this is ridiculous. A fanatic extremity in anything is ridiculous. I'm a straight, ordinary chap, after all; I'd need my shoes in case I strike back for the Fellata village. Shoes and sufficient water for four-five days.

But if the water goes!

Well, there are snails in this earth; snails' fluid that can keep a man alive, not to worry, in any desert. In the shell of the *Ehrenbergi Roth*, for instance, half a teaspoonful of fluid per snail, three hundred to the pint. A man could stand up.

I filled both holes, carefully smoothing them flat, then moved deeper into the forest, obliterating my footsteps all the way with the bunch of twigs, bearing the direction straight line more or less – so I would not lose the Pole Star and the Plough. Feeling the trees; counting. Feeling for the one that began forking highest over my head. Then coming to a smoothish bark – *Hashab*: flaming red underskin beneath the peeling cover. There are *Kursahn* with incongruously festive yellow blossoms in this darkness, but this was *Hashab*. Number nineteen: seventy-one paces from the road.

Not such a hospitable spot as the last, where I'd, after all, learnt my paces, established dimension, stamped the ground free of snakes, bedded in, insulated myself, made the place home. Now this new place…well, life is effort.

Should Hughie come with love…

And I began to laugh: a helpless nigger-laugh, ripping out like a banner in the wind. Should Hughie, in spite of all, come with love! What then? I thought of all the really funny things: Compassion, God, and all that. They didn't seem funny any more. Future of Power, African vacuums, human vacuums: no, not any more. Still I laughed. So helpless I couldn't move, tears streaming, forest echoing not at all.

Tears streaming long after the laughter.

I thought of the Chief: Original Sin: the New Baptism: the

Cleansing from Menace. There was this Cleansing from Menace before us all; I had to tell him that. Tried to laugh again; couldn't. I stood in the darkness, light filtering faintly through from the stars, and felt the anger rising again. But I didn't want this anger: it didn't comfort: it was no longer mine. I'd done with it. I was free of even that.

I moved.

If ever I should see those mountain eyes again, Catherine...

I went up the *Hashab* tree.

Seventy-one paces, though, that was nothing. Nothing! They wouldn't even need to leave the road to find me. This forest has no mass: cannot conceal. Even naked, effected in clay, bare only in the eyes, I could be *sensed*! By any man, any beast, life calling, as it does, to life. Day cleaning early, my time is short. I must escape the life-pull of those searching because, who knows, hearing them in broad daylight, seeing them in such an emptiness come seeking, I might well fail to resist this pull: call out to them with all my heart like a man irresistibly drawn to leap from a height, 'Here, brothers, oh, hear!'

That wouldn't do. If I am not to imperil myself through my residual humanity I must not *see* these men. As long as you can see a man, believe me...

I must move on; go deeper: some place I would not see when they come searching, would not hear them calling.

This jerrican, too, it can bring me no good; not natural for a man naked in a desert darkness; I must rid myself of it. No water, and in a thirsty place hounded by man and beast, but it is a chance I must take. Snails' fluid: I must rely on that; sleeping days, hunting by night; hunting and running: a condition I must now learn to accept. I must be found as a savage, if at all, living without shadows – without any shadow whatsoever. Shoes, socks, water: they must go.

I used the water, then, to bury itself, the shoes, the socks; covered them with dry earth and brushed the spot with twigs. Then moved on, feeling from tree to tree.

Hundred and ninety-three paces, I found another *Hashab*; sturdy trunk, high-sprung fork, good smooth branches. Too close.

Three hundred and seven paces, in an inviting cluster, another, not so good: workable. Too close.

Four hundred and forty-six another; excellent, but growing in the bed of a *wadi*; crown not much higher than ground-level. Too close, anyway.

Five hundred and eighteen, too close.

What is this unclear feeling in my head. I must not sleep…

What does it matter, Froad? lay yourself down for just a moment. You have reached the heart of the mirage: there is no water here but you are insulated; what does it matter now?

I move on, nevertheless, feeling from each to the other, sure in the darkness, but fighting confusion.

How beautifully these crickets chirp; millions, never ceasing, how tumultuous the scurrying of the *arnibs'* feet; the roar of dry pods dropping endlessly from the *Kursahn* trees… If I could sleep for just one moment, even standing braced. Standing braced I'd promise myself once more to work. If I could sleep, trusting these treacherous limbs…

If you sleep you die!

How close these singing stars, how dazzlingly bright; how cold their beauty in this burning air. These noises whirring in great arcs…

Catherine, it will have to be, if ever I see those mountain eyes again. I'd tell you then what you asked and I never answered; I'd tell you who I am, since now I know. I am a man hunting and running; neither infra nor supra, not Equatorial black, not Mediterranean white. Mulatto, you could say, Sudanic mulatto, looking both ways. Ochre. Semi. Not desert, but not yet sown. Faecal, so far; shadowless. Never mind, though, Kate, there are whole heaps of things. Like you've always said…like everybody else…

I must not pause.

These multitudes of tongues…these crisp leaves withered between the thorns…these noises inside. I must work. If I could trust these treacherous limbs…

Seven hundred and eighteen paces.

'*Hughie!*'

Oh God, why did I do that!

No echo.

Nine hundred and five.

Thousand and…

Can't see anybody now…anything.

Now, having removed my body and the last traces of it, I am without context, clear. Going up this new tree, picking the thorns bare, one by one, I am in a darkness nowhere at all. I am nothing, nowhere. This is something gained. Shuttered against even the dry bitter wind which I can feel now only on the lips and in the nostrils, I can look to tomorrow, which is already here. Two, three o'clock at least, maybe later, working on the outside from the Pole Star and the Plough. This time of year day will clean early. I've gone beyond sleep, I think, but not with anxiety. I am feeling, in a way, the faint beginning of perhaps triumph. Hughie has not found me; I have outwitted him. I have achieved a valuable state: a condition outside his method. It would make small difference now even if he appeared beneath this tree or found me in the broadest daylight sleeping here, since I have cast off all by which he is accustomed to recognize me.

Same goes, too, for the law. No one can now expect me to make the faintest gesture towards a civilized language. I am a savage, shadowless. In my own time I can make my way back to the Fellata village. Only remains now to remove my consciousness. This I can do whenever I wish. I am free of the earth. I do not need to go down there for anything.

Now I can think of what is to come: Catherine and all that. Because, hell, why shouldn't a man, equipped as he is, be happy?

The lights then slowly coming round the bend beneath the trees, still looking for something, someone…

But here, now, surely that's only…

Only, no…

The first hot grin of yet another desert day?

ABOUT THE AUTHOR

Denis Williams was born in Georgetown, Guyana, in 1923. As well as authoring two novels and writing important books on art (*Icon and Image: A Study of Sacred and Secular Forms of African Classical Art*, 1974) and anthropological archaeology (*Prehistoric Guyana*, 2003) Williams was a highly accomplished artist and teacher. From 1974, was Director of Art and Archaeology with the Guyana's Ministry of Education and Culture. In addition to numerous prizes for his paintings, Williams was awarded the Golden Arrow of Achievement Award from the Government of Guyana in 1973. He died in 1998.

CARIBBEAN MODERN CLASSICS
Spring 2009 titles

Jan R. Carew
Black Midas
Introduction: Kwame Dawes
ISBN: 9781845230951; pp. 272; 23 May 2009; £8.99

This is the bawdy, Eldoradean epic of the legendary 'Ocean Shark' who makes and loses fortunes as a pork-knocker in the gold and diamond fields of Guyana, discovering that there are sharks with far sharper teeth in the city. *Black Midas* was first published in 1958.

Jan R. Carew
The Wild Coast
Introduction: Jeremy Poynting
ISBN: 9781845231101; pp. 240; 23 May 2009; £8.99

First published in 1958, this is the coming-of-age story of a sickly city child, sent away to the remote Berbice village of Tarlogie. Here he must find himself, make sense of Guyana's diverse cultural inheritances and come to terms with a wild nature disturbingly red in tooth and claw.

Neville Dawes
The Last Enchantment
Introduction: Kwame Dawes
ISBN: 9781845231170; pp. 332; 27 April 2009; £9.99

This penetrating and often satirical exploration of the search for self in a world divided by colour and class is set in the context of the radical hopes of Jamaican nationalist politics in the early 1950s. First published in 1960, the novel asks many pertinent questions about the Jamaica of today.

Wilson Harris
Heartland
Introduction: Michael Mitchell
ISBN: 9781845230968; pp. 104; 23 May 2009; £7.99

First published in 1964, this visionary narrative tracks one man's psychic disintegration in the aloneness of the forests of the Guyanese interior, making a powerful ecological statement about man's place in the 'invisible chain of being', in which nature is a no less active presence.

Edgar Mittelholzer
Corentyne Thunder
Introduction: Juanita Cox
ISBN: 9781845231118; pp. 242; 27 April 2009; £8.99

This pioneering work of West Indian fiction, first published in 1941, is not merely an acute portrayal of the rural Indo-Guyanese world, but a work of literary ambition that creates a symphonic relationship between its characters and the vast openness of the Corentyne coast.

Andrew Salkey
Escape to an Autumn Pavement
Introduction: Thomas Glave
ISBN: 9781845230982; pp. 220; 23 May 2009; £8.99

This brave and remarkable novel, set in London at the end of the 1950s, and published in 1960, catches its 'brown' Jamaican narrator on the cusp between black and white, between exiled Jamaican and an incipent black Londoner, and between heterosexual and homosexual desires.

Denis Williams
Other Leopards
Introduction: Victor Ramraj
ISBN: 9781845230678; pp. 216; 23 May 2009; £8.99

Lionel Froad is a Guyanese working on an archeological survey in the mythical Jokhara in the horn of Africa. There he hopes to rediscover the self he calls 'Lobo', his alter ego from 'ancestral times', which he thinks slumbers behind his cultivated mask. First published in 1963, this is one of the most important Caribbean novels of the past fifty years.

Denis Williams
The Third Temptation
Introduction: Victor Ramraj
ISBN: 9781845231163; pp. 108; 23 May 2009; £7.99

A young man is killed in a traffic accident at a Welsh seaside resort. Around this incident, Williams, drawing inspiration from the *Nouveau Roman*, creates a reality that is both rich and problematic. Whilst he brings to the novel a Caribbean eye, Williams makes an important statement about refusing any restrictive boundaries for Caribbean fiction. The novel was first published in 1968.

Roger Mais
The Hills Were Joyful Together
Introduction: tba
ISBN: 9781845231002; pp. 272; October 2009; £8.99

Unflinchingly realistic in its portrayal of the wretched lives of Kingston's urban poor, this is a novel of prophetic rage. First published in 1953, it is both a work of tragic vision and a major contribution to the evolution of an autonomous Caribbean literary aesthetic.

Edgar Mittelholzer
A Morning at the Office
Introduction: Raymond Ramcharitar
ISBN: 978184523; pp. 208; October 2009; £8.99

First published in 1950, this is one of the Caribbean's foundational novels in its bold attempt to portray a whole society in miniature. A genial satire on human follies and the pretensions of colour and class, this novel brings several ingenious touches to its mode of narration.

Edgar Mittelholzer
Shadows Move Among Them
Introduction: tba
ISBN: 9781845230913; pp. 320; December 2009; £9.99

In part a satire on the Eldoradean dream, in part an exploration of the possibilities of escape from the discontents of civilisation, Mittelholzer's 1951 novel of the Reverend Harmston's attempt to set up a utopian commune dedicated to 'Hard work, frank love and wholesome play' has some eerie 'pre-echoes' of the fate of Jonestown in 1979.

Edgar Mittelholzer
The Life and Death of Sylvia
Introduction: Juanita Cox
ISBN: 9781845231200; pp. 318; December 2009, £9.99

In 1930s' Georgetown, a young woman on her own is vulnerable prey, and when Sylvia Russell finds she cannot square her struggle for economic survival and her integrity, she hurtles towards a wilfully early death. Mittelholzer's novel of 1953 is a richly inward portrayal of a woman who finds inner salvation through the act of writing.

Elma Napier
A Flying Fish Whispered
Introduction: Evelyn O'Callaghan
ISBN: 9781845231026; pp. 248; February 2010; £8.99

With one of the most delightfully feisty women characters in Caribbean fiction and prose that sings, Elma Napier's 1938 Dominican novel is a major rediscovery, not least for its imaginative exploration of different kinds of Caribbeans, in particular the polarity between plot and plantation that Napier sees in a distinctly gendered way.

Orlando Patterson
The Children of Sisyphus
Introduction: Geoffrey Philp
ISBN: 9781845230944; pp. 288; November 2009; £9.99

This is a brutally poetic book that brings to the characters who live on Kingston's 'dungle' an intensity that invests them with tragic depth. In Patterson's existentialist novel, first published in 1964, dignity comes with a stoic awareness of the absurdity of life and the shedding of false illusions, whether of salvation or of a mythical African return.

V.S. Reid
New Day
Introduction: tba
ISBN: 9781845230906, pp. 360; November 2009, £9.99

First published in 1949, this historical novel focuses on defining moments of Jamaica's nationhood, from the Morant Bay rebellion of 1865, to the dawn of self-government in 1944. *New Day* pioneers the creation of a distinctively Jamaican literary language of narration.

Garth St. Omer
A Room on the Hill
Introduction: John Robert Lee
ISBN: 9781845230937; pp. 210; September 2009; £8.99

A friend's suicide and his profound alienation in a St Lucia still slumbering in colonial mimicry and the straitjacket of a reactionary Catholic church drive John Lestrade into a state of internal exile. First published in 1968, St. Omer's meticulously crafted novel is a pioneering exploration of the inner Caribbean man.

Austin C. Clarke, *The Survivors of the Crossing*
Austin C. Clarke, *Amongst Thistles and Thorns*
O.R. Dathorne, *The Scholar Man*
O.R. Dathorne, *Dumplings in the Soup*
Neville Dawes, *Interim*
Wilson Harris, *The Eye of the Scarecrow*
Wilson Harris, *The Sleepers of Roraima*
Wilson Harris, *Tumatumari*
Wilson Harris, *Ascent to Omai*
Wilson Harris, *The Age of the Rainmakers*
Marion Patrick Jones, *Panbeat*
Marion Patrick Jones, *Jouvert Morning*
Earl Lovelace, *Whilst Gods Are Falling*
Roger Mais, *Black Lightning*
Edgar Mittelholzer, *Children of Kaywana*
Edgar Mittelholzer, *The Harrowing of Hubertus*
Edgar Mittelholzer, *Kaywana Blood*
Edgar Mittelholzer, *My Bones and My Flute*
Edgar Mittelholzer, *A Swarthy Boy*
Orlando Patterson, *An Absence of Ruins*
V.S. Reid, *The Leopard* (North America only)
Garth St. Omer, *Shades of Grey*
Andrew Salkey, *The Late Emancipation of Jerry Stover*
and more…

All Peepal Tree titles are available from the website
www.peepaltreepress.com
with a money back guarantee, secure credit card ordering
and fast delivery throughout the world at cost or less.

Peepal Tree Press is the home of challenging and inspiring literature
from the Caribbean and Black Britain. Visit www.peepaltreepress.com
to read sample poems and reviews, discover new authors, established
names and access a wealth of information.

Contact us at:
Peepal Tree Press, 17 King's Avenue, Leeds LS6 1QS, UK
Tel: +44 (0) 113 2451703 E-mail: contact@peepaltreepress.com